FALLEN SINS
BOOK ONE

HEIR OF SIN

C. L. QVAM

HEIR OF SIN

FALLEN SINS
BOOK ONE

C. L. QVAM

QVAMINGTON

This is a work of fiction. Names, characters, historical figures, places, events, and incidents are either the product of the author's imagination or used fictitiously. Any resemblance to actual persons, living or dead, is entirely coincidental.

Copyright © C. L. Qvam, 2024

All rights reserved. No portion of this book may be reproduced, distributed, or transmitted in any form or by any means, including photocopying, recording or other electronic or mechanical methods, without the prior permission of the author, except in the case of brief quotations embodied in reviews and certain other non-commercial uses permitted by copyright law. Furthermore, without in any way limiting the author's and publisher's exclusive rights under copyright, any use of this publication to "train" generative artificial intelligence (AI) technologies to generate text is expressly prohibited. The Author reserves all rights to license uses of this work for generative AI training and development of machine learning language models. For press & permission requests, contact the publisher at contact@qvamington.com

Published by Qvamington Press, 2024
Qvamington Press is an imprint of Qvams Forlag

ISBN 978-82-94035-09-0 (eBook/ePub)
ISBN 978-82-94035-10-6 (Hardcover)
ISBN 978-82-94035-11-3 (Paperback)

Dust jacket by Maria Spada, www.mariaspada.com
Naked cover created with Canva by the author
Chapter background and ornamental break created with Canva by the author
Map and illustrations illustrated by the author

Publisher website: www.qvamington.com
Author website: www.chaselouiseqvam.com

First Edition
10 9 8 7 6 5 4 3 2 1

AUTHOR'S NOTE

Dear reader,
if you're happening upon this book after reading my former works, you might find this slightly different than what you've come to expect. For one, it has open door spice *insert mischievous smirk here*. For another, it is less plot-heavy than the *Spindle of Life* trilogy, and the world-building is much simpler.

While my debut fantasy trilogy was written to hit on emotional and difficult themes close to my heart, this romantasy was written as a break from those heavier topics. Not that there won't be some hurt and valuable take-aways in this book as well, but because we all need some escapism from time to time. Including this writer.

Mostly written to enthral and make your toes curl, I hope you'll enjoy this book nevertheless!

FAQ

Is this series connected to your other series?

Yes. Although it takes place in an entirely new realm, this realm does exist within the same universe as my previous books and, chronologically, *Heir of Sin* takes place *after* my debut trilogy.

Do I need to read your debut trilogy before this book?

That depends! It's recommended if you're a YA fantasy fan who loves to build theories, hunt for Easter eggs, etc., in which case chronological or published order will make this easier. *BUT...*

I'd definitely start here if you're a romantasy reader with a preference for romance and explicit spice. Worst case scenario, *Heir of Sin* is a quick read that may easily be reread after you've read my debut trilogy.

Finally, above all, if you're a fellow mood reader – hi! – then you picked this book for a reason. Kick your feet back, cuddle up under a blanket, and enjoy.

Any content I need to be aware of?

This book contains a few scenes featuring bullying, a drugged drink, and a scene with sexual coercion that happens pretty early in the book. My choices for including them are personal, but also to offer representation for those of us who have gone through similar things. For a full list of content warnings and where to expect them in the book, please visit www.chase.qvamington.com/contentwarnings

There are also Easter eggs and teaser crumbs dropped throughout the book to past and future titles, particularly towards the end.

At last, an apology to a friend who coincidentally and unfortunately shares the same first name as a rather unsavoury character in this story. The resemblance ends there.

This book uses British style and spelling and is written in the author's second language.

CONTENTS

Prologue	1
1. The Hunt	5
2. Caught	13
3. Obsession	21
4. Engagement	27
5. The Djinn	34
6. Spoiled Fruit	38
7. A Deal	46
8. Promenade	55
9. Checkmate	63
10. Hunter	71
11. Touched	81
12. Predators	88
13. Prey	97
14. Devoured	100
15. Peaches	111
16. Lies Served	120
17. Lady Indulgence	130
18. Into Faerie	136
19. The Inn	149
20. Betrayal	168
21. Possession	183
22. August	192
23. A Witch's Ritual	196
24. Puppet Masters	200
25. Divine Fire	211
26. Aftermath	220
27. Regret	224
28. Release	230
Epilogue	236

Afterword	241
Dear Reader	243
Bonus Scene: Honeymoon	247
Acknowledgement	251
About the Author	253
Also By	254

The Realm of Equinox
"Illnora"

The Winter Court
"Up North"

The Spring Court
"Faerie"

The Autumn Court
"Oryastes"

ETrion

The Woodland Woods

The Summer Court
"Theveserin"

N
W E
S

To the women who were made to feel small so that the men would feel big,

I give you Elijah.

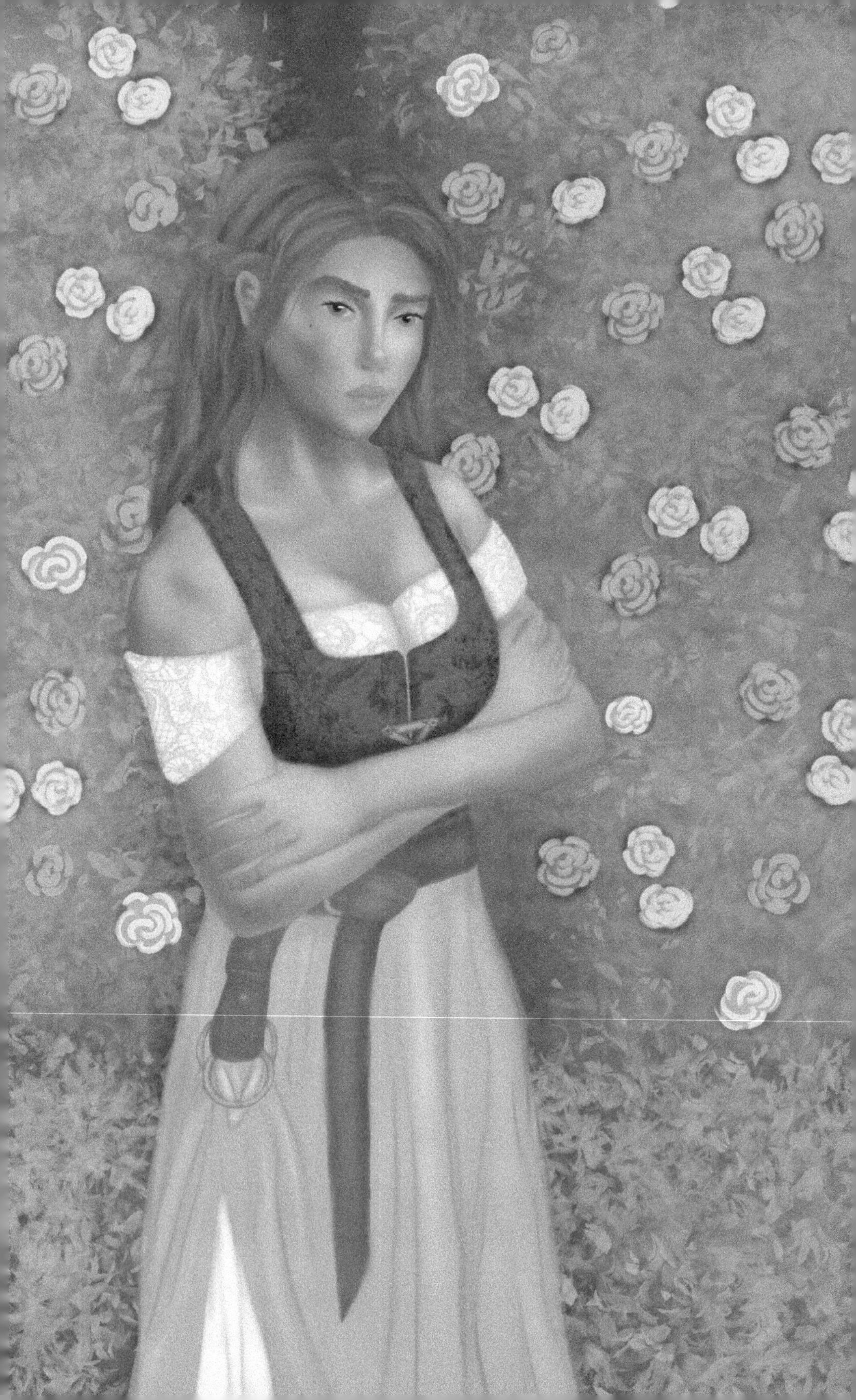

PROLOGUE

Djinns will take your whole hand if you give them a finger.

At least, that's what my nan used to say.

'What if you give them *the* finger?' I once asked.

'Then they'll take your hand, and body with, and take you—'

But wherever they would take me, I never learned, as my parents interrupted with, 'Home! *They'll take you home, Keira. To be scolded by your always-loving-but-horrified parents. Isn't that right,* Mama?'

My nan would shrug and go about her cooking, passing me a wry little wink with a slice of whatever ingredient was at the mercy of her cutting knife. In that wink was a promise that she would tell me the rest later – later that day, later when I was older – but later never came. Not when I became a teen. Not as I made my first steps into adulthood. At first because my parents would always intervene, but now – now they can't even do that.

I wonder, what they would have said in this moment, if they could see my soon-to-be-nineteen-year-old, should-know-better-self, holding a vintage oil lamp, prepared not only to give any djinn within it my fingers, but whatever else was in my possession as well. My late mother's jewels. Thornfield Cottage. My firstborn – I'd give it all to have my wish fulfilled.

Everything and anything besides my body, really.

That, surely, would defeat the purpose of the wish.

When I was younger, I always assumed nan meant the djinn would take me to the shadowlands or other realms where demons and monsters still existed. That's where they were rumoured to come from, before spilling into Illnora and the realms beyond.

Once a bit older, smarter, and slightly less immature, I'd begun to wonder if my old Grandmama's warnings held a more nefarious meaning. That the djinns would simply *take me*, as I am, and have their way with me in the same way the town's pastor would describe as sin.

The same thought occurs to me now, leaving me hot and cold all over, but I shake it from my mind.

Djinns were said to have been godlike creatures: powerful in their magic, angelic in their appearance, of which they could change at will. Shapeshifters. I can't imagine what they'd want with someone as ordinary as me.

Of course, they could confound my mind like the folks of Faerie and *make* me want them. Or...they might not even need to go that far. All who swore they had seen a djinn would declare them to be easy on the eye. Or so I've heard. I don't actually know anyone who's claimed to have seen one, except my nan. And she never said more about her encounter except that she recognised the djinn for what it was and chased it off her porch with a rolling pin.

I believed her back then, my toes always curling as we laughed together. Now, I'm more inclined to believe it must have been a poor, possibly charming, salesman at her door. Still, a smile at the memory tugs at my lips and I'm held back, yet again, from turning the lamp's wick adjuster, wondering what she would say if she were here.

But she isn't.

None of them are or will ever be again. There is only one person left in this world that I love, and if I don't do this, he will be gone too.

I won't let that happen.

The twist of the pin is so swift, so impossibly fast that I half-wonder if I touched it at all. Nothing happens, so perhaps I did it wrong or not at all. I'm about to give it another go, when the copper base grows hot and I drop the lamp, startled.

Thick, soft, violet smoke drifts out of its pipe mouth while I back away, gathering into a thick cloud in the middle of the room. And, as I squint my eyes, my heart pounding in my ears, I can just about make out the silhouette of a man, coming towards me, his smile feral.

Earlier that day...

1

THE HUNT

The Nightladies whistled, raising their glasses and bottles of sparkling wine at the people passing them by. Some fluttered their eyelashes at the onlookers, while others angled their bodies so that their full bosoms threatened to topple over their white corsets – much like their baskets brimming with fruit, bread, and cheese.

Sat on a larger-than-life picnic blanket, dressed in their signature white, the ladies chortled amongst themselves as their startled bystanders reddened and rushed away on urgent legs when addressed. The rest of the villagers did their best to ignore them, focusing instead on their sons appearing from the Thornfell stables, horses in tow, ready and dressed in their scarlet riding coats.

Perched upon her own horse, Keira's eyes roamed for one familiar face without luck, when a girl's voice filled her ears, and the child in question pointed towards Keira. 'Mummy, that girl is a hunter!'

'That girl is a *servant,* dear,' answered the mother, and pulled at the girl's hand while she eyed the colour of Keira's jacket – brown like dried blood – as if it were a sign of the plague. Still pointing, the girl scrunched up her nose and turned away from her, the impressed light in her eyes dimming to a dull gleam of disappointment.

Her smile long gone; Keira longed to call after them that she *was* a hunter. She was in fact a finer one than many of the young men that would be riding out today. But, for her to ride, she needed to be dressed as a servant.

Of course, calling out such a thing would only draw unwanted attention to herself and cause her to be refused from participating in the hunt, so she held her tongue and bit back her words instead. There were far more important things at play today.

It was the first of August, the first day of the annual hunt, and as such the one day a year where all the villagers left the idyllic streets of E'Frion to venture into the first plains of the Woodland Woods where the stables stood.

E'Frion was a small village not much larger or wider than as far as the eye could see from its clocktower, complete with quaint cottages built in honey-coloured stone, steeply pitched roofs, lilac-framed windows, and flower-filled gardens. It perpetually smelled of wildflowers and the fruitiest delights, except for during the colder seasons of the year when the autumn breeze came in from Oryastes, and the winter wind howled from the north. It would have been a haven – if it wasn't for its people.

A Nightlady hollered and blew a kiss towards one of the young riders, drawing Keira's attention. His mother turned around with a scowl of disdain at the temptress, then faced her husband – perhaps expecting to see the same emotion on his face – and elbowed him in the ribs as he, poor soul, was caught staring a little too amusedly at the young beauties. Then he, too, carefully moulded his expression to mirror that of his wife.

Keira bit back a smile and looked down so that the riding helmet would hide her amusement. Prudishness and prejudice ran rampant within the town that had retreated into a more conventional life after the age of the Tyrant Emperor.

Once, Illnora had gone by the name of Equinox; a realm brimming with magic and creatures of all kinds. Split into four courts governed by faeries and elves, there'd been the Summer Court (Theveserin), of which E'Frion belonged, to the south, the Autumn Court (Oryastes) to the east, the Spring Court (Faerie) to the west, and the Winter Court up north. Then came the Tyrant Emperor – the conqueror – and changed it all. Casting the realm into a costly war that changed it forever, setting back progress and modernisation by decades as if it was somehow afraid to move on. Now, all that remained of the old Equinox was restricted to Faerie bordering the moors of E'Frion, but no one from the village really talked about or went there. Except the Nightladies.

The Nightladies were said to descend from the Tyrant Emperor's harem itself. A rumour Keira suspected was spread by themselves, although it did them little favours. If their lifestyle wasn't enough to bring the village's scorn upon them, such history surely would. But, at least, it permitted them to fetch a prettier coin when the men stole into the night and went to see them. Who wouldn't pay up for a royal muff?

One of the Nightladies caught her observing them and ran a finger along the rim of her glass, licking the taste of wine off her finger in a slow, sensual manner.

Keira's cheeks went aflame, and she instinctively moulded her face into reflecting the disdain that one was expected to have whilst observing the Nightladies. Just in case anyone caught her looking.

Once she thought no one was, Keira instantly slipped back

into observing them with the same curiosity as before. As if she couldn't help it.

It was something about them that caught her attention and curiosity – and always had – in much the same way she felt when she spent time with Isolde of the Woodland Witches; the freest soul Keira had ever known.

More of a guardian than a friend, but the closest thing Keira had to a friend nevertheless, Isolde made indulgence look like a sport as she enjoyed her partners and wine, with or without witnesses. By the social conventions of E'Frion, Keira knew she was supposed to be appalled – knew she was supposed to judge – and yet she could not help but feel the surge of a thrill upon imagining taking such liberties herself. To share such intimacy with the one she held dearest.

August.

As if conjured by her thoughts, a young man, lean and square-shouldered, came riding from the stables, before steadying his mare next to a tall man and woman with the same shiny white hair as his. His parents, her masters. The Thornfells, owners of E'Frion's largest estate, spanning one quarter of the village.

Even though his mother was speaking to him, August's golden gaze met Keira's while he gently stroked the mare, drawing Keira in like a moth to a flame. All other sounds and impressions subsided in his presence. There was only him, and the curve of his bottom lip as his tongue moved across it ever so tangibly.

'You need not worry, Mother,' August said, turning back to his parents. 'Keira will be right behind me. If anything happens, you can trust her to seek help immediately.'

Lady Thornfell turned towards Keira and narrowed her gaze, forcing Keira to cast her own to the mane of her horse, to the way the rough hairs split in different directions, and mould her face into perfect obliviousness.

Whether the Lady of Thornfell Manor knew their secret, Keira did not know, but she could feel her hawk eyes scrutinising every expression on her face.

Soft-spoken, polite, and dashingly handsome, August Thornfell was the darling of the village and every maiden's first choice for a husband, be they single or not. But most of those hoping to gain his favour would find themselves disappointed, the vacancy closely guarded by his mother. No one was good enough for her son, especially not those she deemed of lower station than them.

'Looking sharp on that horse, Keira,' a voice bellowed out of the blue. 'One would think you've ridden before.' A group of young men passed her by, one of them with a wicked grin and spite in his eyes. His friends chortled just a moment before the insinuation dawned upon Keira, and she felt certain her face coloured the same shade as their riding jackets.

Miles, the caller, had been in love with August for as long as she had, and thus they had been rivals just as long. Every day she longed to toss the truth in his face, but she bit her teeth together instead, knowing it would risk everything. At least today she knew something Miles did not.

Butterflies fluttered alive at the thought, and she dared a glance from the corner of her eye back to the Thornfells. August remained tall and proud upon his horse, still offering assuring smiles to his mother while exchanging words of confidence with his father. The Meronis had joined them as well, with their daughter Gianna, a petite pretty little thing, by their side, staring doe-eyed up at August.

A sting of envy tore through Keira's chest. Not just because of Gianna's close proximity to August, but because of the parents standing by her side, proudly introducing her to the village's most eligible bachelor.

Keira should have had that. She should have had her mother

already making wedding arrangements and her father giving her some last pointers for the hunt. Instead, she had neither. She *did* have Isolde, but she had told her not to come. She did not want to expose her to E'frion's prejudiced murmurs and glances that occurred whenever the Woodland Witches were nearby. Especially when Keira wouldn't be around to keep her company through it.

The first blast of a horn sounded, alerting every rider to gather by the lake, close to the spot where the Nightladies had settled to wave them off on their way.

With calming sounds, Keira soothed her stirring horse, eyes trained on August as he said his final goodbyes to the Meronis and his parents. His father patted the backside of his mare and his mother bit her lip nervously as August went to join his friends.

Clicking her tongue, Keira manoeuvred her horse to follow and mingled with the other servants on horseback, keeping as close to August as she could without seeming conspicuous and drawing attention to them. Her stomach did a somersault at the thought.

They were *so* close, and he'd worked so hard to get her into the hunt. It would not do to do anything to confirm his mother's suspicion now, nor trigger Miles', who cast long glances after August when he thought no one was looking.

Holding her breath, Keira eyed the Hunt Masters, counting the beats of her heart until the second horn sounded.

Then they were off.

Multiple pairs of hooves thundered through the woods, the ground shaking as they flew over it and passed the lake.

Ahead, August and his friends hollered with excitement, their lips cracked into wide grins as they challenged one another, betting on who would catch the stag – the ultimate prize of the annual hunt. Then, group by group, they began to disconnect from the others to go their own ways.

Her heart twinged ever so slightly as she saw August's group shoot off to her right while hers continued onwards. But it was the plan, and she had to stick to it.

She had to keep her eyes on the others, judging and calculating the right time to disappear, when the hunt had swallowed them entirely and they no longer cared for anyone but securing the stag – any stag – for themselves.

The moment came with a 'Whoop!' and a gesture in the air, and her group kicked off after the spotted prey, leaving her behind. A cloud of dust was the only thing that remained after them as Keira brought her own horse to a slower pace, smiling smugly to herself.

Amateurs, the whole lot of them.

They would be scaring off every animal, extending the hunt by hours upon hours.

Perfect. It would take them ages to return.

Clicking her tongue, she steered her horse onto a different path, trudged up by animals only, and kicked her heels. The horse took off into a trot, each step pumping excitement into her body.

It did not take long before she reached a secluded section of the lake.

Partly hidden by low-hanging willows was a small fisherman's hut that had been out of use for years. She paused her horse beside it, listening for sounds, yet heard nothing but the rustle of leaves in the wind and gentle ripples of water lapping against the side of a tired-looking rowboat resting on the bank.

Impatiently, she kicked her leg over the saddle and slid down gracefully. The moment her foot hit the ground there came a sound of rustling foliage, and her chest fluttered alive.

Unable to suppress her excitement any longer, she turned around and beamed at the figure who had stepped out from behind the bushes, his smile mirroring her own.

'Finally,' August said. 'Some time alone.'

2
CAUGHT

'Did anyone see you sneak away?' August asked and closed the door to the hut behind them.

'I don't think so.' Keira turned to face him, nervously fumbling with her riding gloves. He stepped closer and took her hand, holding her gaze while he carefully manoeuvred her fingers free, one by one, from their leathery prison.

'Good.'

The rapid beating of her heart seemed impossible with the stillness of the moment.

His voice lowered to a whisper. 'I've missed you.'

There. Her heart skipped a beat. Staggered and collapsed in confusion and feverish delight. They'd been meeting in secret for a while now, basking in stolen moments lived in the shadows here and there. Still, she could not believe such words to come from his lips. That this was real. That he was here, with her, looking at her like he had only done in her dreams before.

'Come.' He led her by the hand to the small bed pushed into the corner and sat down. She lowered herself with him, half by his guidance, half because she did not trust her legs to be able to stand. He cupped her face in his hand, and she leaned into it, taking in how the warm morning light lit up the auburn-coloured streaks in his pale hair. Shining in the colour of the season to which belonged his name.

'It has been torture, these days apart,' August murmured. 'Every time I see you, I just want to kiss you. Grab you and hold you in my arms forever.'

She closed her eyes. She knew the feeling well. For years now, she had watched him, hiding behind house corners, seeking him out. By the vines, heavy with clusters of grapes, in the cornfield working away with his father. Sometimes with his shirt on and sometimes without.

How she had watched him, longing to be the sweat rolling down his back. Longing for him to see her as more than just a servant girl.

She opened her eyes, finding his own still upon her. She had nearly not believed it when he sought her out at the beginning of summer. When he began to gaze at her a little longer as she handed him water. When he settled on the concrete next to her outside the stables, not saying a word, his pinkie inching closer to hers. Even less had she believed it the first time he asked her to meet in secret. And here he was, telling her he wanted to hold her like there was no tomorrow.

'You could, you know,' Keira murmured. 'If you told your parents.'

He pulled back, and she regretted her words instantly. Regretted the chill that filled in the space between them as a result.

'I thought we'd been over this.'

'I'm simply trying to understand why.'

'You know why. We can't make our relationship known until

I've inherited Thornfell. You know my mother. She will not see you the mistress of it.'

'But if you only told her how you felt... If you only...'

'You rebuff me,' August said. 'You blame me, as if you can't see how much it pains me to be away from you.'

She reached for him, gripping the soft material of his velvet jacket. The rich fabric gleamed scarlet between her fingers. 'Oh, but I do. Please, forgive me. I'm just as equally anxious to be with *you*.'

At this, he turned his gaze back at her. 'Do you really mean that?'

She nodded vigorously, her mind scrambling for the right words to say. 'I do. I'm so sorry. I'm being insensitive.' She leaned into him and pressed her cheek to his chest, holding him close.

Soon after, he wrapped his arms around her and held her tight. 'It's okay. I probably overreacted. It's the stress of it all...the hunt...my parents...'

Keira looked up. 'Is there something I can do to help?'

August hesitated for a moment, and a shade of pink crept up his throat and over the bridge of his nose. 'There's one thing I've desired for a long time now...one thing that I can't get out of my head. One thing that would help me take the edge off.'

She took his hands. 'Tell me.'

He leaned closer and caught her bottom lip between two fingers. 'I'd really love you to...take me in your mouth.'

She blinked, the words registering without their meaning, her mind struggling to comprehend – to believe – what he was saying. To kiss him, was that what he meant? Because surely, he wouldn't ask her to...

Perhaps reading the questions in her eyes, his own wandered downward and beckoned to his crotch.

This time, the blush on her cheeks surely surpassed his. 'But we are not married!'

'But we will be. It's only a matter of when.'

She creased her brows and bit her lip, thinking it through. Aside from the scandal it would cause if anyone found out, she did not even know how to do...*that*. Unease swelled and crept through her like mud, making her insides squirm.

She'd wanted to be with August for years, that was true. She'd even taken notes from Isolde's escapades, as well as enjoying some fantasies of her own once or twice. But the thought of this act, of all the things there were to do, filled her with discomfort. Made her feel vulnerable. Less...confident.

He must have seen, must have read in her eyes what she thought, as he pulled back from her. 'I see,' he said, and brushed off some lint from his breeches. 'The thought disgusts you. You're disgusted with me.' He rose, and a pressing confusion rose in her chest along with him. 'Well, I'm glad to know of it now, before the union between us would have been complete.'

'Wait!' she gasped and grabbed his hand. He stilled and half-turned to meet her pleading eyes. Panic coursed through her, racing almost as fast as her thoughts. He had shared something with her, and she had not responded the way he wanted. If she did this wrong, if she made the wrong choices, she could end up losing him. She could not stand the thought. It was one thing to have loved him from afar and never know what it meant to feel his lips against hers. Another entirely to have loved him and lose him. The ache of that thought alone...

But could she do what he asked? If someone saw...if someone saw, then they would treat her no better than the Nightladies. But if they didn't, and she and August married, then what would it matter if they did it before or after the wedding? Who would care that they explored each other's bodies, if only a little?

But to do it in such a way, on her knees as if she were somehow beneath him... And the act... She did not even know how to—

Discomfort and awkwardness squirmed within her, and once again it must have shown on her face, because August's hand tugged away from hers.

'I–I'll do it!'

He paused and turned fully. Studying her. She swallowed her unease and held his gaze, afraid he might not believe her and turn to leave again if he caught the slightest whiff of her uncertainty.

His hands moved to the front of his breeches, carefully starting to unbuckle the buttons. 'Are you sure?'

She did not trust her voice not to wobble and jutted out her chin in stubborn determination instead. If this would prove her love to him, she would do it... She wouldn't—

His breeches fell and *it* stood up before her. She did not know how she had expected it to look, or if she had ever considered how it would look at all. She had heard the tavern-maids gossip with the Nightladies about the different kinds they had seen. Small ones. Big ones. Ugly ones. Pretty ones. But looking at it, she could not tell whether it was one or the other. She understood, however, by the look in August's eye that he was expecting some kind of reaction. She swallowed again. It seemed to do the trick. His mouth curved slightly, and he reached out a hand for her. She took it, letting him pull her from the bed to her feet.

Once she stood before him, he dipped his chin and somehow, her legs obeyed and lowered her to the floor so that she was face-to-face with it. It remained in high attention, like a king before its kneeling subject. She half expected it to tap her shoulders.

August led her hand to wrap around it. Skin against skin. The muscle was solid and hard, yet the skin was soft against her palm at the same time. Her eyes darted back up to August, who raised his brows expectantly. *In your mouth*, his expression seemed to say. Tilting her head towards his length, Keira parted her lips ever so slightly but hesitated by the tip, her insides squirming so terribly that she feared her jaw might clamp together and bite it if she brought it any closer.

A musky scent filled her nose, one that smelled partly of August, partly of buckskin and sweat.

His hand came to rest at the back of her head. It startled her, like the gun that would signal the start of the hunt, and her mouth opened and closed around him.

A gasp escaped his lips, and his fingers dug at her skull.

She stilled, uncertain what to do next, the edges of her mouth already pinching at the unfamiliarity of the shape within. Her tongue buckled, trying to find space to move, and August sighed and trembled against her lips. She tried to move her tongue again, with the same result.

'Suckle on it,' he whispered, and she frowned in concentration, attempting to do as he wished. Yet somehow, she could not make her lips and tongue work in the way she wanted them to with the length obstructing them. She could barely breathe.

Perhaps, she thought, she should stop and try it another time. But one glance up at August and she caught something akin to impatience in his countenance. His other hand came down to rest on her shoulder and she tried again, feeling a scorching flame of embarrassment and frustration creep up her throat, her cheeks, around the edges of her mouth.

Finally, she attempted to pull away, but before her jaws could fully relax, August's grip on her head and shoulder tightened and pressed her towards him at the same time he thrust his hip forward, his member poking against the back of her throat.

She gagged, the muscular reaction causing her to clamp her

lips tighter around him. He moaned and pulled back again before driving it in once more. Her whole jaw ached with the force of it, and tears rose into the corners of her eyes at the strain: the strain of housing his manhood, the strain of breathing, the strain of her panic at how utterly miserable and awful she felt about what they were doing.

Seemingly unaware of her struggles, August kept on thrusting into her mouth, his gasps coming in rapid breaths and grunts. She grabbed his thighs, nails boring into his skin in an attempt to hold him back, but he must have misunderstood her. Like a whip to a horse's flank, he spurred on instead. Faster, harder, until she thought her lungs would burst and her head with it if he didn't—

Something rapped on glass.

Instantly, August pulled out, his face turning to the window while Keira grasped her throat, soothing her heated cheeks and bloated lips, drying the tears out of her eyes.

She froze.

Peering through the glass were three wicked faces, Miles being one of them, their mouths open in raucous laughter and their fingers pointing in her direction before they disappeared. August turned serious and buckled up his breeches, hiding himself from view.

'I'll talk with them,' he said curtly, heading for the door. 'Make sure they don't tell.'

'August,' Keira croaked, her mind a chaos of fractured thoughts. He turned, his face collected and calm as if what had just transpired had been nothing special.

It occurred to her then that perhaps, to him, it hadn't been. She was pretty certain she had been terrible at it. Perhaps so terrible that she had disappointed him.

Her chest quivered at the thought. That after all that, not even something good had come out of it. 'Was it…was it how you wanted it?'

He pursed his lips. 'It was fine, Keira,' he said matter-of-factly, and left the cottage.

3
OBSESSION

'Well, hello love, didn't expect to see you here,' Isolde said, pouring deep berry-red wine into a couple glasses as Keira entered her hut. She was dressed in a white camisole of sorts, laced tightly over her luscious shape. It complemented the glow of her brown skin, making her look ethereal. 'Aren't you supposed to be joining the hunt?' She looked up, perhaps about to offer Keira a glass, when she caught sight of her face and stilled.

'One moment,' she said, then carried the two glasses she had poured into her bedroom to serve the two women sprawled over her bedcovers. Echo and Makenna both waved their fingers at Keira in greeting, Echo wearing a panelled corset and undergarments, Makenna wearing nothing at all – all three clearly being in the middle of an afternoon of indulgence – before their expressions shifted and changed into concern, just like Isolde's had done.

Returning, Isolde picked up another bottle and tilted it towards Keira, looking questioningly upon her through her curtain of fiery red hair. 'Wine?'

Still trembling, Keira bit back her rejection and nodded. She needed it after what had gone down between her and August.

It had taken her some time to scramble off the floor, most of it spent chastising herself for having been so completely unprepared for what to do with his *thing* in her mouth, the other part spent worrying what people would say if they heard, if Miles and his friends spread the gossip before August could stop them. There was a part of her mind that thought darker thoughts too, a part where she felt used and humiliated and something else, but she had not allowed herself to linger on those for long enough to put words to the emotions.

'I'm sorry for interrupting,' Keira said, taking the glass of wine, and glanced around the familiar space of Isolde's hut to avoid her gaze.

The wooden walls and roof were filled with dried bundles of nettles and corn, flowers and straws. All were hung up to dry around the cottage like meat at the butchers. Either they were plants that smelled good, leaving a fresh, earthy scent, or herbs that could be used in a potion or two. It was the mark of a good Woodland Witch to know how to utilise them for every purpose – from healing a tummy ache to stopping the heart of a man – and Isolde was the best at both, the leader of her clan.

'Tell me *why* you're interrupting, and I'll let you know if an apology is warranted or not,' Isolde crooned and took a sip of her wine, raising a brow.

'Can't I simply call upon my closest friend without a reason?' Keira asked, picking up a dry rose petal from Isolde's worktop table and crushing it between her fingers, avoiding her piercing gaze.

'You can. But it is the first day of the hunt and the sun is still up, so I repeat myself for the last time, Keira, what are you doing here?' Isolde clicked her tongue against her teeth. 'Surely, you're not tired of hunting August already?'

Keira felt her smile stiffen. Once she had come *off* the floor, she had decided to act like nothing. To act like what had happened had been a perfectly natural thing to occur between two young adults who loved one another, that she was confident it had been the right choice, and that she had done it right. But as Isolde turned her eyes upon her, she felt her bravado falter, her inner turmoil brewing, and the mood in the cottage darkened as the witch saw through her.

'*What* did he do?'

Keira stared into her glass, the liquid rolling from side to side in her trembling hands, shivering like her insides.

'Did he stand idly by while his friends mocked you again?'

'No...'

'Have you seen him with someone else?'

Keira clamped her mouth shut and shook her head, looking away.

'Kiki...' Isolde started, her harsh tone blending into a soft hush. 'I know you think yourself in love with August, but...' She paused as if weighing her words while tears pressed behind Keira's eyelids. 'Sometimes we think ourselves so much in love with a person that we mistake who they really are for our idea of them.'

'I know August,' Keira forced out, like she had so many times before when they'd had this conversation. But before, he had not... She struggled for breath, and her mind spun.

'I'm not saying I don't understand. It is far easier to love an idea. It hasn't hurt you, yet. But—Keira!' Isolde rushed over as Keira sank to the floor, sobbing.

A door creaked wider, and she could hear Echo and Makenna stepping into the room, the swish of silk robes, and one of the women asking if everything was alright.

'It's not him who has done anything,' Keira cried. 'It is me. I failed. I took him in my mouth, and I was terrible at it!'

The cottage was struck with silence, save for Keira's heaving sobs.

'You...what?' Isolde stared.

'He said...he said it would help him take the edge off.'

'I bet he did,' Echo murmured, while Makenna scoffed beside her. Isolde ignored them both and helped steer Keira to a chair, ordering one of her lovers to bring her the cheese platter they'd been enjoying in the bedroom.

'Tell me everything, love. From the beginning, please, so I might have a chance to catch up.'

'We've been seeing each other this past summer,' Keira murmured, bowing her head at the intensity in Isolde's glare. When they had kept it a secret, they had kept it from everyone. Even Isolde, although Keira could not quite remember whose idea it was, hers or August's. She remembered wanting to tell Isolde, but that August had told her not to and that she had agreed with his reasons.

Tears trickled into the corners of her mouth as she thought of him again, the images flashing by drudging bile into her chest. She told Isolde everything, and even before she finished speaking, Isolde had risen to her feet and was pacing the small space, dark blotches upon her brown face. Makenna wrapped a blanket around Keira's shoulders while Echo attempted to offer her some more wine or cheese.

'And then he left,' Keira finished and looked up at her friend, ignoring the bit of white cheddar being nudged against her lips. 'Iz, what if I was so bad at it that he won't want to marry me now?'

Isolde stopped, lightning raging in her eyes. Echo and

Makenna cast one glance at her before they decided to leave them alone and disappear into the bedroom again.

'That is not what is the problem here.'

Keira frowned, unable to discern what she meant.

'Are you certain he intends to marry you?'

Keira's lip began to tremble. 'You don't think he will? You really think I was *that* bad?'

'No, I think you have been played like a fiddle.'

Keira held her breath, staring at Isolde with incredulity. 'You think he doesn't love me?'

'I think he does not.'

'Well, you are wrong!' Keira rushed to her feet, uncertain who she was trying to convince: her friend...or herself? 'He does. He will marry me. He has as good as given me his word!'

Isolde shook her head. 'In all these years, I did not watch you grow up to be such a fool, Kiki.'

Keira clamped her jaw shut and looked away, refusing to meet her eye. Instead, her gaze fell on a collection of bottles and containers on one of the shelves.

A new addition – a vintage oil lamp – stood amongst them, and Keira faintly remembered her grandmother's stories of djinns and wishes. What if...she could take it all back?

Slowly, Keira began to gravitate towards the shelf, her mind churning. There would be a price, she knew that. But even so, was there a price she was willing to pay to make it so that the last hours had never happened? Or to have August pay her a visit later that night to make good on his promise?

Behind her, Isolde sighed. 'I know you wish to see yourself mistress of Thornfell Manor again, and that having August's hand in marriage would secure that, Keira, but there are some circumstances where the price is too high. Do not pay it.'

'You are wrong about him,' Keira murmured, forcing back the last of her angry tears.

'I hope I am,' Isolde said, still speaking to Keira's back. 'But *that lamp* won't help you make him love you. Leave it be, Keira.'

Keira retracted her hand as if she had been burned, glaring at Isolde. Her expression was strained, alert, and Keira's gaze flickered back to the lamp. Was it...could it really be the lamp of a djinn that stood before her? Were her suspicions right?

'Use this change of events to free yourself from this unhealthy infatuation instead, Keira,' Isolde said over her shoulder, heading back into her room. 'Cut August loose.'

Then she closed the door behind her, leaving Keira alone in the space, pondering her words. She definitely needed to do something with the situation, but giving up on August would not solve anything. She would simply be without him. Without dreams. Without any hope for her future.

With that in mind, Keira turned and grabbed the lamp off the shelf, promising the nibble of guilt in her gut that she would make it up to Isolde later – she was merely borrowing it after all – and headed outside, her spirits rising. With the lamp tucked against her chest, her despair gave way for eager certainty that, by the end of the night, August would be hers and that what had occurred earlier would be as if it had never happened.

4
ENGAGEMENT

Keira placed the lamp upon the mantelshelf of her fireplace and settled into an armchair, pulling her legs up to her chest, without ever taking her eyes off it.

A djinn.

A demon spirit.

Isolde had been too wary for it to be an ordinary lamp. What else could it be?

All her nan's old stories came rushing back to her, and these days, djinns tended to be exactly that. Stories. Fabled creatures that the grown-ups told their children by their bedsides to stop them from leaving the house at night. But Keira never went far. She had, in fact, never been further than the palace ruins of Theveserin where the Tyrant Emperor and his court of vices once ruled.

Keira shifted her gaze towards the window as if she could see through the woods to the ruins in the distance. It was once the home of the Cardinal Seven; each djinn so corrupted and malevolent that they were described to be the sins incarnate: lust, greed, indulgence, indolence, pride, wrath, and envy. The tyrant himself so prideful that it caused the war and his eventual demise.

A woman had been his Achilles' heel in the end. Saint Helena, whose beauty left him blind to the rebellion rising against him. His court was never seen again after the opposition stormed the castle, yet the myths would have it that the tyrant escaped, bound by a witch to forever walk the realm in the shape of a stag. Which was how the annual hunt had come to be, and a stag its most symbolic prize.

Whoever shot one first would be the champion of the village for the year to come and free to pick whomever they liked to marry. If August had not asked her to meet him, she would have had half a mind to hunt for the stag herself. Perhaps she would have been better off if she had.

Her gaze drew back to the oil lamp on the mantel. Since the reign of the Tyrant Emperor, djinns had been hunted, and few – if any – had been seen for decades, a fact many regretted whenever they harboured a heartache or lost a loved one, pleading to the heavens for one simple wish.

Yet here a lamp stood. On her mantelshelf. Its foot was of delicately ornate porcelain and copper, its lamp chimney made of glass that rose like an elongated rose bud from its oil burner. Could it really be? Or was she letting her desperation get the better of her? It was prettier than other tired-looking oil lamps she had seen, but to think that it could house a spirit was stretching her imagination rather thin.

She rose to her feet and took the lamp, turning it between her hands, her reflection mirrored in its polished surface. Either it worked or it didn't. It seemed a small risk to take for the chance to erase the incident of the day. For the chance to wish for August to finally ask for her hand in marriage.

She reached for the pin.

But would it be real? Would it be without cost?

An image of her mother and father flashed before her eyes. Happy and entirely consumed with one another. Their love like a flaming star. And now they were both ashes. Because she had wished it.

No. She put the lamp back again.

Nothing came for free. She knew that.

Shivering, Keira took a couple steps back and walked through her cottage, passing her tattered furniture, and paused by the windows, gazing out between the decorative iron grates on the outside. When her parents were alive, the small cottage had once belonged to their groundkeeper. From here, she could gaze over the tops of the trees in her garden and spot the lights shining from Thornfell Manor, perched upon a steep hill covered in acres of corn. Her former home.

She had made such a fuss when her parents told her that they were to leave it. To move somewhere else and start anew. She had made more than a fuss, actually.

She had been quite mad. Furious even. And she had raged that she wished that they would leave without her and never come back. Then she had run off to Isolde, cried against her shoulder, and fallen asleep in her bed. When she returned the next morning, it was to find all three of her family members dead.

Murdered. Without a trace of the murderer.

The days after were but a blur. She remembered the coffins. The funeral processions. And August's parents, who showed up on the grounds of their ancestral home, ready to reclaim the house with their young boy on one side and her council-appointed guardian on the other. He had sold it back to them, the whole estate, and thought himself very clever, since he had secured the groundkeeper's cottage and the Thornfells' protection for her in the transaction.

No. Wishes are not free, Keira thought and shook her head, wrapping her arms around herself against the memory. They always cost something, and right now, so close to having everything she desired, she would not risk it. Faith would have to be enough. Faith that August loved her and would make good on his promise to her. That they would talk about and move past what had happened, together.

With that in mind, Keira pulled on a cloak and rushed into the night, heading to the town's local tavern.

It was the first night of the hunting season. All the hunters were sure to be gathered there. August too. After today, surely, he longed to see her as much as she longed to see him, to make sure she was okay and to discuss what had happened. Perhaps they could make another attempt at intimacy. One where she felt... more secure. Less... Her mind trailed off from the unpleasantness that coiled inside. Instead, her mind conjured a fantasy of him returning the gesture, and by the time she reached the tavern, she had quite convinced herself that what went down that morning hadn't been as bad as she thought. If only she didn't think too much of it.

It seemed the whole village had gathered within the small space as she stepped inside, the smell of stale ale and raw meat wafting towards her.

Boisterous men chatted with the ladies and waved over the barmaids manoeuvring the thick crowd in their mini pouch aprons, serving refills of wine and pints of locally crafted beer. Fathers patted their sons on their backs and mothers introduced their daughters. Glasses clinked together and chairs were shoved out of the way to give place for the trophies – the prey of the day – and the men that had shot them. August was between them – the men, not the trophies – yet, as her eyes fell on the hind beside him, she could not help but picture herself, bound and shot.

Diverting her gaze, she locked eyes with Miles instead. Mockingly, he tapped his lip with a finger and winked, but he did not say anything. Perhaps August had warned his friends to keep quiet after all, but Keira wished hard that she hadn't turned red at the gesture.

'Welcome, all as one!' boomed Mr Meroni, spreading his arms wide. His wife and daughter stepped up beside him, and the Thornfells came to stand beside their son. It was odd to see them amongst such crowds, let alone in the tavern. They typically found themselves far above such places.

'You've all had a look at today's catches. There was no stag amongst them today, but there is still much of the season left to capture the "Tyrant Emperor".' He winked, and some chuckled. 'That being said, we have more to celebrate tonight. August! Where are you, my lad? Come here.' He waved August forward.

Keira's heart thudded a little harder, watching him move to stand beside the large man, the whole room's attention rapt upon him. Perhaps that was why August's jaws were clenched so hard, and why his cheeks had paled a little.

'Congratulations with the biggest catch of the day,' Mr Meroni said, and patted his back. 'And it is not the only prize he has secured on this first day of the hunt.' He turned to the rest of the crowd with a playful twinkle in his eye. Keira felt herself go cold all over, pins and needles pinching her hands.

Did he know what had transpired between her and August earlier that day? Would he proclaim it to the entire room like this?

Miles cast her a glance, but she could not fully take it in. Could not read it. Could not comprehend or think or act beyond waiting with bated breath.

Mr Meroni waved over his daughter, who stepped forward with the softest, widest smile on her face. She bowed to August, who allowed her to place her hand upon his, returning her smile with a polite one of his own.

Keira frowned in confusion. What was he doing? People would think...

Time stilled.

'Today, August Thornfell asked my daughter Gianna for her hand in marriage, and she has accepted him! Please allow me to present the future Mr and Mrs Thornfell!'

Mr Meroni spoke, but the words...the words fell through her. She could not make sense of them. Could not make sense of freefalling while standing still. Could not make sense of the hands clapping, sounding like thunder in her ears.

Her eyes caught August's. He looked away. Miles gaped, like she was sure she was doing. He had not known, then. Had not known that August...was to be married.

It had to be a mistake. A night terror, his parents' doing, or—

The doors swung behind her as she dashed out of the tavern, running as fast as she could down the road leading home. Cutting through the woods for a shortcut, her slippers stomped on tufts of grass, her hem soaking with the wet of evening dew. She rushed over the rickety old bridge, moaning at the harshness with which she crossed it. No sooner had the old cottage appeared between trees crowned in autumn leaves, twinkling at her from the foot of Thornfell Hill, than she exploded over its threshold and grabbed the lamp from the mantelpiece. Merely hesitating for a moment, thinking about her nan's warning, its meaning and what she was risking, Keira drew a shaky breath and turned the pin.

5
THE DJINN

'Well, well, well, G – that's quite a body you've found yourself.'

The husky voice curled itself around her ear like the violet smoke caressing her living room walls. In the darkened space, a pair of amber eyes gleamed, trailing her every move. Keira stilled as the man sauntered closer, not daring to move a muscle as he gripped her chin and tilted her head to the side. Although she had expected it to hurt, his grip was featherlight, like the kiss of a cool duvet in the summer heat.

'What an exquisite jawline.' His forehead creased with the same intrigue that danced into his almond-shaped eyes and spilled across his lips.

He was rather handsome, she had to admit. His dark hair curled over his forehead, and his skin was pale with a peachy hue underneath. The muscles rippling down his shoulders and arms were perfectly sculpted, as were the sharp cheekbones cutting down his face, pointing towards lips succulent with coy interest.

He had the kind of beauty that made her stomach knot. She did not care for it.

'I beg your pardon?' She swatted his hand away, and his eyes widened. Pausing to wonder, the djinn looked around the room, taking in the pillow- and throw-covered furniture, the built-in bookshelves, and the low roof with horizontal wooden beams running from wall to wall, before he turned back to her, comprehension dawning. 'You're not G?'

Keira crossed her arms with a sneer. 'I have no idea who *G* is.'

His lips twitched with amusement before he gathered himself and stepped back. 'Then excuse me, young lady, for my poor informalities.' He bowed. Somehow it seemed to make the overwhelming nature of his presence withdraw, like shadows being called back to their masters, but she watched him warily still.

'I didn't expect djinns to have manners,' she commented when he raised a brow.

'It's not your fault,' he said, studying his nails. 'Humans are always ignorant about that which they fear.'

She scoffed. 'Oh, really? Well, I'll retract what I said. I seem to have been entirely correct the first time around. What sort of manners is it even to talk to a lady without giving her your name?'

'Call me Elijah if you'd like. As for manners, the same can be said of a lady calling a man to her home without telling him what he is there for. Unchaperoned, even! Am I to be used?' His face twisted in feigned outrage as he leaned against the wall, arms crossed, eyes sparkling with mock delight. 'Did you hear precisely which djinn was in that particular lamp and think to have your sweet time with me?'

She blinked and shook her head. 'I have absolutely no idea what you're talking about. I have a *wish*.' She inhaled sharply, her nan's warning blaring at the back of her head. *Djinns will take your whole hand if you give them a finger.* She had not meant to say it so carelessly. Not without taking precautions. She had wanted him to beg for his freedom or something first, and only then would she have offered him the chance to earn it by granting her wish. Now all of that had gone astray.

The djinn prowled closer, as if he knew.

'To be swept away?' he purred.

'To be married.'

'I'm sorry, sweetheart.' Elijah tsked. 'I'm not looking for a bride.'

'To the man I love!'

He yawned. 'How perfectly dull.'

Fisting her hands in her skirts, Keira grinded her teeth against her rising temper, struggling not to let it spill out – he could not help her if he was beaten into a pulp, she reminded herself.

'There is a boy that I love,' she began, steadying her voice. 'Who swore he would marry me. But now he has been promised to someone else, and...and I'm certain it is his parents that have forced him into it. They must have heard what happened and...' She trailed off.

The djinn's eyebrows rose, as if asking her what, exactly, had happened.

Her cheeks heated. 'We shared a special moment,' she said simply, curtly, and refused to meet his eyes.

'Let me see if I get this right,' the djinn said, circling her, pretending to regard her like a professor might his student. 'You've given yourself to a boy who's now made a match with another girl, and because you love him, and because he promised himself to you first, you want my help to make sure he sticks to his promise?'

'Yes! Or, we did not – I didn't give myself to him – but the rest, yes.'

'What an awful situation,' the djinn tutted.

'Exactly.' She nodded enthusiastically, hope bubbling in her chest. His lips twitched. 'So, will you help me?'

'For a pretty thing like you?' He put his fingers under her chin and turned her to face him, his voice low and decadent as it curled against her cheek in a caress. 'No.'

6

SPOILED FRUIT

'No? Whyever not?' Keira blurted out, blinking against her confusion, feeling as if she had just been doused by a bucket of cold water. 'Are there some limitations to your magic? Are you unable to affect the feelings of others or make the impossible happen?'

'What sort of mediocre djinn do you take me for?' asked Elijah, his voice dripping with disdain. 'It is my speciality to free people from their chains – not rope them into new ones.'

'You think I'm trying to rope August into some marriage scheme?'

The djinn said nothing.

Keira blew frustrated air through her nose. 'Fine, be this way,' she said, adding more bravado than she felt. 'But I'm not letting you free before you help me. In fact, I order you to stay within this cottage.' She had no idea if the magic worked that way, but it always seemed to in the stories. She didn't exactly feel good about it either, but desperate times required desperate methods.

The djinn jerked ever so slightly, then tensed. His face darkened, and a dangerous gleam appeared in his eyes, causing her to take a step backwards. 'If that is the case, where am I to sleep?' he asked, his voice low and sultry. '*In your bed?*'

She grimaced. 'How about your lamp?'

'Bed it is then.' He shrugged and made to move upstairs.

'I'll ready a mattress for you,' Keira snapped, pausing him. 'Just stay here.'

Begrudgingly, she pushed past him, then gathered the spare mattress and bedding that she used whenever Isolde stayed the night, and quietly wondered if the witch knew what sort of obnoxious spirit she had kept in her home.

'There,' she said once she'd finished arranging the make-shift bed before the fireplace and beckoned towards it. 'All ready for you.'

'Why thank you, most kind of you,' the djinn said, mimicking her haughty tone, and threw himself down upon it, limbs sprawled out like a lazy cat. As his eyes once again found hers, she could have sworn she heard him purr.

'As a thank you,' she tested, 'might you not come with me to meet August? The village youths always celebrate the hunt in the woods at night. You can see for yourself that he holds very little regard for Gianna.' The expression on August's face during the announcement of his engagement resurfaced in her mind, and she felt even more certain that a pleading look of despair had hidden itself in his eyes when he looked at her. Begging her to understand this was not his choice. Perhaps even begging her to find a way to help him out of it.

'No, *shan't*,' the djinn said, having sprung back to his feet and begun fidgeting with the buckles of his black trousers, the firelight casting flames upon his toned torso. 'It was quite exhausting enough watching you ready this bed for me.' The corner of his lip twitched. Even more so when her eyes strayed over his bare skin. Twice.

Shaking herself out of her reverie, Keira growled and stomped out of the living room. 'Fine! I'll figure something out myself.' She poked her head back around the doorframe. 'I better not find you in my bed when I return.'

'Whatever the lady desires.' The djinn waved her off. 'Should you fail in your endeavour, however, you're more than welcome to join me on mine.'

His words followed her as she marched through the village, stalking her like a thundercloud over her head, darkening with her ire. Striking her with the mental image of the two of them together on the mattress, images of what would have happened if she had been such a girl, if for a moment she had possessed the casual spirit of the Nightladies. Grunting, she pushed away the images and spluttered a few curses until another struck her, this time bringing with it a flutter at the depths of her core, taking her breath away and rooting her to the spot as she pictured his fingers carefully freeing the ribbons of her stays, his mouth tasting the skin of her breasts, and her lips parting to let out a—

Distractedly, she ran her fingertips over the cool silk of her laces, and shook her head, her nan's warning echoing in her head. Not even a minute had passed with Elijah under her roof, and her head was already filled with outrageous daydreams. It had to be a spell by the djinn, for sure.

It continued like that the whole way: The harder she tried to not think of the djinn, the more she pictured him bare skinned before the fireplace. And the more her curiosity grew. But as she neared the woods, the sound of revelling youths finally drove him out of her mind.

As expected, the youths had upheld tradition and brought the celebrations to the lake once the tavern closed for the night.

They stood in clusters, talking, smiling and laughing over their brass mugs and bottles. She moved amongst them, greeting those she knew, yet stayed far away enough not to be invited into a group. Her eyes searched for August, and she spotted his familiar white hair and scarlet hunting jacket in the middle of a larger group. Gianna was by his side, her pretty blue eyes lit with excitement and happiness. One could tell by the way she nodded her head and beamed in gratefulness that they were receiving all kinds of well-wishes and questions about the future. August merely bowed and smiled whenever addressed and appeared to let Gianna fill in the rest. If only Keira could get him on his own...

Walking over to a long table of refreshments, she paused to pick up a drink and observe them from afar. A group of boys was hollering and dancing close by, and even closer were the Nightladies, sprawled over one of their picnic blankets, engaging young men and women in talk.

For a moment, Keira wondered whether or not she ought to pull one of the ladies aside and ask them for advice. If anyone could give her some pointers regarding what had happened in the fisherman's hut and what she should have done, it was them.

However, no sooner had she made up her mind, than she noticed that one of the young men was bothering one of the ladies by pulling at her arms and skirt, taunting her to come dance with him despite her rejections.

Next thing she knew, Keira stood before the Nightlady and pushed the boy away.

'What the hell?' erupted the boy. 'Whatever did you do that for?'

'I–I', Keira stuttered, gaze flicking between the Nightlady and the boy, both equally stunned as she. 'You need to leave her alone,' she uttered, hoping her voice carried more confidence than she felt. The boy quickly composed himself and stepped up too close for comfort.

'Why is that? Would you like me instead?' His expression changed as recognition dawned, and a wide smile spread across his lips. 'Hey, boys, look who we have here!' he whooped, locking his gaze with someone else's behind her. A shuffle of quick feet sounded after, before more bodies appeared in her peripheral vision. She drew a breath.

'Keira! Joined the Nightladies have, you?' Miles chuckled and threw an arm over her shoulder. 'Tell me, was it a rite of passage that went down earlier, or what?'

He clinked his drink against her own, but Keira merely forced a tight smile, realising that the rowdy boys had formed a circle around her. She tried to catch the eye of the Nightlady for support, but she had already disappeared amongst the throng of people. A low chanting began to take form amongst the boys, the words hard to distinguish amongst their slurred voices.

Feigning indifference, she raised her own goblet to their leering grins and forced a cheery smile while trying to excuse herself and break through their ranks.

They only moved in tighter, with Miles' arm slipping from her shoulder as the words became more distinguishable and her heart pounded harder.

'Lady of Pleasure, damdidadidei
Her shame knows no measure, damdidadidadi
Lady of Pleasure, dirty as can be
And whoops, there she goes, for a swim. Damdidam.'

Cold went down her back, the blood in her veins curdling in panic as they reached for her. She pushed against them, but it merely made them grab onto her faster, latching onto her arms and legs, sweeping her off her feet.

She cried out, and August and Gianna looked up along with others, but no one moved as the chanting boys carried her over their heads.

She screamed and batted their hands, clawed and twisted, kicking out. With some satisfaction, she felt a crunch underneath her heel – a nose, maybe – and hoped that it was Miles'. But it wasn't enough.

With a last holler, they tipped her, and her scream slashed through her throat before it filled with water.

They had dropped her into the lake.

First there was a deafening silence as the world stood still, existing of nothing but water and murky darkness. Then there was splashing and soaked fabric wherever she turned, as she thrashed and struggled her way to the bank. After a few failed attempts, where she fell flat on her stomach, water once again rushing down her front and back, she finally managed to stagger onto land, chest drenched with both horror and water. Laughter howled through the woods, ricocheting off the tree trunks, returning to her tenfold.

'Thought you might want a wash, you filthy girl,' Miles hissed beneath his cackle and slapped his thigh.

Keira bared her teeth at him, embarrassment rattling through her bones with the cold.

A hand reached out for her and helped her to her feet, her wet curls dangling down her face and obscuring her view. Flitting between them, her eyes scanned the laughing and ogling crowd for one face.

August.

He still remained beside Gianna, looking stunned, but the expression soon turned to alarm as Keira gathered her skirts and started towards him. Beckoning Gianna to stay, he rushed to meet her.

'What in Saint Helena's name is going on, August?' Keira cried when he gripped her wrist and pulled her away from the crowd.

'Shh, not here!' he hissed, then smoothed his features over and murmured softly to the folk standing nearby that his *servant* had had a little too much to drink and that he would help her make her way home.

'You need to tell me, now!'

'I had nothing to do with this,' August said, looking her over once they were away from the party. 'I'll tell Miles to leave you alone.'

'That is not what I'm talking about, August!' Keira cried. 'What is this rubbish about you being engaged?'

He stilled, his jaw hardening as he clenched his teeth together. 'I don't believe that's any of your business.'

'Any of my business? You promised *me*, August. You said you'd marry *me*!'

'Keira, I am very fond of you. You—I've always appreciated your company, but I think you've hit your head in the lake. I never made you such a promise,' he said, a little louder than necessary, and threw nervous glances over his shoulder, as if he expected someone to be listening in.

The treetops swayed in the breeze and Keira's heart hammered through her chest. 'Maybe not in so many words, but you said— what about earlier today? What about what you made me do!'

This time he grabbed her wrist again and brought her closer to him, his voice low.

'It was a mistake, I admit. We shouldn't have done it. I can't have a wife that so willingly would spoil herself so.'

He might as well have punched her.

Shock marred her to the bone, and her words trembled with the effort it took to speak. 'But...I only did it for you.'

His jaw set. 'I'm much obliged. But for your sake, we ought never to speak about it again. Go home, Keira, before you catch a cold.' August bowed before he returned to stand by Gianna.

7
A DEAL

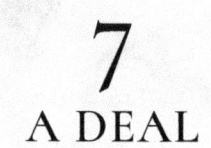

The djinn had been fast asleep upon his mattress when she returned from the revels, his dark locks spilling against his pillow. She did not bother taking a closer look to see if he was pretending, but rather wound her way up the crocket staircase to her bedroom, the drenched fabric of her dress clinging to her legs. It shifted with ice-cold fluidity every time she moved, chilling her to the bone as she reached the bath and found the tub already filled with heated water. She didn't know how, but an inkling told her it was the djinn's doing, and had she felt less miserable at the time, she might even have let it soften her towards him.

For a moment she considered settling in with her wet clothes on. For another she considered drowning in it. Instead, she pinned up her hair, peeled off her layers, and let them splat to the floor before stepping into the hot water.

Absentmindedly, she let her muscles soak and warmth re-enter her body, her thoughts taking her back to the day she and August first met in the Thornfells' new living room. *Her* family's old living room.

Lady Thornfell's gaze had stripped Keira bare as she paced back and forth before her, regarding Keira from top to toe. Behind her, Lord Thornfell languished on the pristine sofa while their teenage son stood by the newly recovered fireplace. Flames cast shadows on his pretty, bored face, bathing his white locks with a gilded hue – save for the one sharing the colours of the fire itself.

'What will we do with her?' Lady Thornfell said, coming to a stop before Keira, drawing her attention back to her stern face. Her forehead creased and her nose crinkled as if Keira were merely dirt underneath it, forcing Keira to cast her gaze down.

'Take it I'm not getting a new sibling, then?' the boy drawled, and his words made her stomach knot.

'Absolutely not!' Lady Thornfell snapped, and the knot eased. 'I will not foster some other woman's brat simply because—'

'There now, my dear. The girl has ears,' her husband said pointedly. 'And lips to talk with. As I'm sure the rest of the village will do if we cast her out.'

Lady Thornfell sighed extensively, but clamped her mouth shut and returned to her pacing. Keira dared not say a word, not even as the lady once again paused before her and grabbed her chin, forcing her head to the right, then to the left. Then she prodded her upper arm, pinched her skin below the bone and, once more, let her eyes glide over the shape of her body.

'She's coming into her womanhood quite nicely. She is what, almost fifteen? She can help man the house and the stables to earn her keep until she is ripe for marriage. Then she'll be off our hands.' She turned to her husband without even glancing at Keira for her reaction. 'The old groundkeeper's cottage was brokered for her, was it not?' The man nodded. 'She can stay there. August, be a dear and take her, will you? God knows I have enough on my hands getting this place in shape.' Lady Thornfell swept her eyes over the pristine living room, over Keira's parents' reading chairs, and their shelves upon shelves of books. Her nose crinkled again.

'As you will, Mother,' August said and stepped up to Keira, offering her his arm.

Keira took it shyly and let him lead her out of the house and down the hill towards the cottage. Keira did not dare look at him, and neither said a word until they had reached the cottage and August turned the big, old, black key to open the door, letting her into the dark, empty space. There was little by way of comfort in the cottage at the time, save for the essential furniture, leaving it cold and empty.

Keira wrapped her arms around herself. 'Thank you,' she stuttered, already prepared to close the door behind her and fall into tears. She would have done so too if August hadn't spoken next.

'Don't take my mother's words to heart,' he said, his sharp facial features softening. 'Her barks are worse than her bites.'

'I do not wish to be...married off to some stranger,' Keira said quietly.

'I'll make sure it's a good match.' August winked, then stepped a little closer and added under his breath, 'Or I'll marry you myself. Then you'll be the lady of the house and can boss my mother around. I would pay good money to see that.'

Keira could not help but giggle. August's smile widened.

'Oh, no. You cannot smile like that. Now I'll have to fend every suitor off.'

She laughed some more, and he dried off a trickling tear from her cheek. 'There you go. You know, your face's much prettier when you smile,' he murmured.

She shyly let the corner of her mouth stay up.

She'd always made sure to keep a smile on her face whenever August was around since. Eager to please him in any way she could. This time, it had cost her. Her reputation. August. Thornfell. Everything.

Despair filled her chest once again, chasing concerns around in her mind, questioning what would become of her next. But the answer did not come to her in the bath, and neither had it occurred to her by the time she moved her tired limbs over to the bed – and stayed there.

Night out, day in, she watched the shadows shift across the wall, burrowed deep underneath her duvet. Now and then, Elijah would find his way up to her room, always sporting a different face than the time before, and let out some form of leer or jibe from the doorway. Never did she respond. Never did she move a muscle, except for the first couple times, when the unfamiliar appearances startled her. Soon, however, she came to learn that his voice was constant. No matter what face he wore, his voice remained the same. Soft, like curling butter, colouring it in a gentleman's accent.

'You know, if you're going to spend all this time in bed, you might as well have a man in it,' he said one day, tossing himself onto the bed beside her. Her skin prickled at his close proximity, but she did not stir.

'No man would want me.'

'You're rather obstinate, but I've seen men bed women with far less to their credit.'

She glowered at him.

'Come now, not even the tiniest of smiles?' he hummed. 'I can't have you moping around if you want my assistance.'

She rolled her eyes and exhaled. 'What if I don't need it? What if I'll just…go to Faerie and find someone there?' Maybe she'd have some faerie wine and forget all about her existence at the same time.

Elijah snorted. 'You wouldn't last a day in Faerie.'

Scowling at him further, Keira merely turned her back on him.

The djinn sighed. 'Alright then, tell me about it. What happened the other night?'

She opened her mouth to answer, but as the image resurfaced – as she pictured how Miles and the others had picked her up and leered, the freezing cold of the lake, and her panicked seizures as dirty water trickled down her throat – the words clogged up and turned her tongue into a knot. 'It impresses me that you think I'd confide in you when you've shown me no reason to trust you.'

No answer. She swallowed. Fighting the rising unease, she pondered whether he would get up and leave. Pondered whether her unease was due to thinking he wouldn't – or that he would.

Although she'd never admit it, there was some comfort in having him there still. Knowing that she wasn't entirely left to herself.

'Trust, I've found, works both ways,' he said eventually. 'You've not given me any reason to trust you either,' he continued, and she felt his weight shift as he kicked one leg over the other. Staying it was then. 'You called upon me to grant you a wish, one that involved altering the course of another, and yet you've not shown me any proof that to do so wouldn't be villainous.'

She turned. His hair was a mop of light brown today, with fine strands shimmering as the sun fell upon him through the window, softening the hard lines of his features. His eyes met hers and held them. Keira inhaled deeply.

'Some of the boys called me a whore and threw me into the lake.'

'Why?'

She looked down, studying the cotton threads of her duvet. How they weaved in with one another. How the eggshell white lit up like snow where daylight hit it. 'They saw August and me. When I...when I took August in my mouth.' Her voice broke and she hid her face so he would not see the tear sliding down her cheek.

'And this...August, was it? Was he there? What did he do?'

'He told me he could not marry a woman that so easily defiled herself before marriage. But I don't understand. I did it for him. I —he assured me we were as good as married.'

Elijah said nothing. Was he judging her? She did not think she could take it if he did...and yet she looked up. To her surprise, his face was wrought with darkness.

'I stand corrected,' he muttered. 'You'd be fine in Faerie. Why do you still desire to be with him if this is his true nature?'

'Because it is not. You don't understand.'

'Enlighten me, then.'

Keira turned to him. 'His parents...they're not good people. Once, his father caught us kissing in the stables. He gave August such a beating for fooling around with the help that his back still bears some of the scars from it. Still, he didn't keep away.' Instead, he had come to her cottage in the night, and laid down upon her floor before the fireplace while she put healing balms over his wounds. Like that first time they'd met, she would never forget the sheen of the fire playing across his skin, his hair, and the heat that curled in her veins at their close proximity.

She had felt things then. Thought things. Things she wanted to do with him, that she wanted him to do with her; things she'd not been able to make herself utter. What had happened in the fisherman's hut...it had been similar to those things, but not like that... Not like—

Her throat tightened at the memory of the pressure, the force of him against it. Tears pebbled in the corners of her eyes, and she wiped them away.

'He loves me; I'm sure of it,' she croaked, more to herself than to Elijah.

But the djinn didn't look convinced, his expression of skepticism reminding her of Isolde's. 'Then why did he say the things he did? Why didn't he stand up for you?'

'He must be confused. Afraid even. He was pressured to say those things, I am sure. His mother and father don't approve of me. My family owned Thornfell before they reclaimed it, and his mother hates that we did. She would do anything to keep me from becoming the mistress of it again. His mother...' She paused, and something clicked into place.

'*She knows*,' she whispered.

'Knows what?'

'After we were caught, we feared Lord Thornfell would tell his wife.' Lady Thornfell had not spoken about marrying off Keira after that first day they met – perhaps realising that she proved too useful as a servant – but neither Keira nor August doubted that she would make good on her threat if she ever discovered them. 'When she never said anything – when she never sent me away, we thought he'd kept our secret.' And the sneaking around had continued.

Elijah raised a brow, shifting in the bed to make himself more comfortable, his leg nudging against hers. 'But now you think he didn't?'

Keira swallowed and nodded, realising how naïve they had been. Of course, Lord Thornfell had told his wife. Of course, she had known. But instead of marrying off Keira— 'She must have married off August instead,' she murmured.

Hurting Keira in the worst way she could, without releasing her from servitude.

August would know by now of course, that their sneaking around had been for nought – perhaps even been told to adhere to his parents' arrangement or see her shipped away. And he would keep his end of the deal, and Thornfell Manor would have a new mistress. Someone who wasn't her.

Keira turned to the djinn and grabbed his hand, tears filling her eyes. 'You have to help me. Help us.'

The djinn's brows furrowed. 'With everything he has done and said, you still want to spend your life with him?'

'I, more than anyone, know what he has endured with his father. How hard he works at pleasing his mother. It must be pretence. With me, August would be free, for once, and I…'

'Would become mistress of Thornfell?'

'And wife to the man I love.' She allowed her gaze to meet Elijah's again, hoping it would convey the burning passion she felt. 'Now all of that is lost. Because of me. Please,' she pleaded. 'Help me return home. It is the only way for me to correct my mistake.' Something startled in his expression, and she could only hope it was her determination moving something inside him. 'I will not give him up.'

Elijah looked away, his features now fully cast in the sun coming in through the window, contemplating. She braced herself for him to turn around and say no again. To reveal that he had only humoured her by listening in jest. But he didn't.

'Fine, I'll help you in this quest of yours. If that is truly what you want.'

She sat bolt upright, relief exploding across her face.

'But,' he warned before she could speak. 'There's one condition. You'll owe me a favour. This is not a wish fulfilment, but a favour for a favour, and I can cash in on it whenever and in whatever way I'd like.'

She bit her lip and folded her arms around herself, her

newfound hope doused. Elijah tilted his head, a question on his face.

'I will agree to your terms, if I can make but one condition of my own.'

His brows raised with surprised anticipation.

'You may not take or ask for my body. It is for August only.'

At this, Elijah threw his head back and laughed. 'Whyever do you think I would ask for your body?'

'My nan told me djinns would take—never mind,' Keira spluttered and snapped her mouth close, mortification coursing through her.

Still chuckling to himself, Elijah shook his head. 'Very well, I will not ask for or take your body, only a favour. That said'—his voice lowered to a husk and a smoulder curved his eyes and lips—'You may soon wish that I would.'

8

PROMENADE

'So, how does this work exactly?' chirped Keira as she came downstairs on her next day off, dressed in a set of her favourite stays and skirts, with a leather belt around her waist and a French braid running down her back.

Elijah, who sat by the kitchen table, one ankle resting upon the opposite knee, lowered his newspaper with a gaze that lingered a little too long on her get up.

'How does *what* work?'

She rolled her eyes, forced back a pleased smile, and picked up a piece of toast. 'This making August come back to me. Making him ask *me* to marry him instead of Gianna. Do we make him jealous? Will you make me prettier? Will you teach me how to please a man—'

'Am I to be the test subject if so?' Elijah cut in, his eyes gleaming wickedly.

She narrowed her own at him. 'Or can you simply snap your fingers, and it is done?'

The djinn, his skin a dark, luscious brown for the day, reached out for his morning coffee. 'I sorely wish so if it would put an end to this painful affair. But since I cannot' – he paused and took a sip – 'let's start with a stroll.'

'A stroll?' Keira frowned, glancing out the window. Beautiful morning light fell over the trees and their leaves starting to change colour. Everyone would be out today, and everyone would be able to see them if they—

Realisation dawned on her.

'To make him jealous! Splendid, I'll go get my walking shoes.'

'You do that,' Elijah said, having once again disappeared behind his newspaper.

E'Frion looked particularly darling in the late summer sun as they promenaded down the road, winding its way between the quaint stone houses and thick plains of grass. Beyond them ran the river, floating by foxgloves crowding the feet of trees and growing up the sides of birches.

E'Frion was covered in flowers, adorning every path, every staircase, every nook and cranny with pink and white, purple and yellow. A flowerbed nestled beneath a window, and Elijah reached down, popped a flower off its stem, and proceeded to tuck it neatly behind her ear. The brush of his fingers left a trace of heated skin, and she bit her lip, shyly diverting her eyes to the passersby.

They were already gathering some attention, although Keira suspected that was more due to curiosity over seeing a new face amongst them than anything else. Even if E'Frion hadn't been small enough for everyone to know everyone, the deep brown skin of Elijah's appearance today was rare even in E'Frion. She remembered her father garnering the same looks, and then her light-skinned mother would, for being upon the arm of her father. Keira cast her eyes to her own skin and the warm undertone underneath it. It had always been darker against August's, but against Elijah's current colouring, it seemed pale. Almost like her mother's against her father's. Nervously, she bit her lip, wondering if they would gather looks for all the wrong reasons, but Elijah merely tightened his hold on her and muttered through the corner of his mouth.

'The need to appear superior is always rooted in a sense of inferiority. True superiority is not so easily rattled by others.'

Keira scowled at him. 'Are you talking of me, or them?'

Elijah nodded his head forward. 'It remains to be seen.'

Coming towards them were August and Gianna, her petite arm upon his, out for a stroll of their own. Spotting them, August's casual expression changed into a glare, gleaming as brightly as his auburn lock of hair amongst the white.

'Miss Keira!' Gianna gasped once they reached them, cutting August off from his own greeting and surprising them all with her vigour. Keira could not ever remember Gianna having addressed her before. 'How good it is to see you up and about. We were quite worried that you had taken ill after that night you–you...' She stuttered for words.

'Took a dip in the pond?' Keira offered, her eyes narrowing. Both Gianna and August seemed to have the decency to blush, although she suspected for two wildly different reasons.

'Y-yes,' Gianna stammered. 'My apologies. I did not mean to bring it up again.' She looked to August, clutching his arm. 'My sweetheart told me you were most upset, and understandably so. I don't know what goes through the minds of those young men at times.'

'One might wonder if they are men at all,' Elijah shot in, eyes on August.

August cleared his throat uncomfortably. 'Miss Keira, who might this man be?'

'Oh, but of course!' Keira breathed, turning to Elijah. 'Elijah, may I introduce Mr August Thornfell and Miss Gianna Melroni? August...and Gianna, this is Elijah—' Keira was about to stumble on his last name, realising Elijah had never introduced himself to her with one, but Gianna blessedly cut her off.

'Elijah! What a pleasure to meet you. We were just wondering between ourselves who this tall gentleman could be. We felt quite certain, didn't we, my dear, that we'd never seen you in our village before?' She turned to August, whose scowl etched deeper into his features.

'Indeed, we have not.'

Keira turned to Elijah, his eyes sparkling with wicked amusement. The two men were about the same height, and still it seemed as if Elijah towered over August.

'How about we amend that and get better acquainted?' Elijah suggested, taking Keira by surprise. Even more so as he gestured towards E'Frion's ice cream parlour, a tiny shop, squeezed in between two buildings, from which the merchant sold ice cream through the window. 'What do you say, my ladies, care for a sundae?'

'Oh, yes, please!' Gianna beamed and hurried ahead, shortly followed by Keira throwing Elijah quizzical frowns. He merely winked back at her, while taking up the rear was August – looking as if he'd had a taste of the dirt his mother kept under her nose.

Elijah bought both women an ice cream, leaving August to get his own, before they strolled a little aside to enjoy their new delights. Except, Keira forgot all about hers as Elijah tilted his head to the side and licked his in a way that drew all their gazes, erasing all other thoughts and words from her mind. Her mouth dropped ever so slightly and so did Gianna's, while August seemed, if possible, more affronted.

'Oh, my!' Gianna exclaimed, turning excitedly to Keira. 'He wouldn't be the source of all the…talk about you of late, would he?'

Keira's cheeks burned so brightly she did not dare glance at August.

'He's a family friend, come to visit,' Keira blurted, her words turning into a murmur as she felt August's eyes burrow into her. *This was such a bad idea.* With her hands shaking, she dropped the ice cream. Beside her, Elijah's eyes followed it to the ground. 'A distant cousin!'

No sooner had the words been said than a carefree wave smoothed out August's features. Elijah looked at her with incredulity, and Gianna smiled sweetly.

'How lovely. I'm so glad you have someone who can look out for you, Keira. August tells me you're like a sister to him, and we so often worry about you, don't we, dearest?' Gianna said, turning to August, her ice cream melting over her glowed hand.

'We sure do.'

'Young ladies living on their own can so easily be taken advantage of.' Gianna sighed and waved her free hand as if she were banishing a curse.

'They can indeed,' said Elijah, eyes like lightning upon August. The latter swallowed and finally hooked his fiancée's arm under his again.

'Come, my dear; your parents expect us.' With one last glance at Keira, August steered the petite blonde away. Both Keira and Elijah watched them leave in silence before Elijah rounded on her, his brown eyes full of sarcasm. 'I guess we might as well go back too, now that you've butchered our plan.'

'What do you mean?'

'What do I mean?' He sighed with exasperation. 'Keira, he was jealous for five seconds before you went and assured him I'm *family*. Which, you know,' he murmured, 'speaks more to how well he's bothered to get to know you after all these years, if he so readily believed it.'

Keira did not pay these last words any attention. Instead, she looked past him at the retreating figures of August and Gianna. 'Was he truly jealous? What does that mean? Does he want me?'

Elijah scoffed and turned on his heel, heading back to the cottage whether she planned to follow or not. 'He wants you, all right,' he said darkly.

'Then I am right! He was forced into this,' Keira breathed, relief flooding her system. Elijah said nothing while she kept on and merely steered her home.

'What will we try next? Can you make me prettier? More like Gianna?'

'Which one? The one does not equal the other,' the djinn said simply, and dried his shoes on the mat outside her door before he opened it.

Keira paused on the threshold, stumbling at his words with roses blooming in her cheeks. Did he just imply that she was pretty enough as she was?

She stopped by her hallway mirror, taking in her complexion as she twirled a lock of light brown hair between her fingers, and a warm flutter started in her chest. Perhaps she would leave her appearance as it was then. It certainly wasn't the way she looked that had caused such a mess between her and August. But they needed to think of something.

Sighing, Keira plopped down into a chair while she watched the djinn pick a book from her shelves and settle down on his mattress before her fireplace to read.

She wanted to ask him questions.

She wanted to know what his magic could do, beyond filling baths and conjuring coins to pay for ice cream, and she wanted to know more about him. Yet, her tongue seemed glued to the roof of her mouth while looking at him. With his perfect jawline and long lashes, he was like a portrait, keeping her mesmerised as he licked his fingers and turned the pages. Her eyes could not seem to let his movements go.

'Had your fill?' he murmured, glancing up at her from his book, and her cheeks heated.

'Of what?' she spluttered. He merely raised a brow in challenge, his mouth twitching ever so slightly. 'I wasn't looking at you, if that's what you think.' His smile cracked wider. 'I was merely weighing out options for the next step forward!'

'Sure,' he hummed, returning to his reading. 'And what conclusions did you draw from your…rumination?'

She harrumphed. 'Nothing. Save for going back in time and fixing my mistake, I'm at a loss.'

Elijah shut his book with a disgruntled sigh, the amusement gone from his features. 'Why do you keep calling it *your* mistake?'

She blinked. 'Because I was the one who took him in my mouth. I was the one who was *terrible* at it.'

'I highly doubt that.'

'How would you know?'

He raised a brow. 'Did he *look* like he didn't enjoy himself?'

'I–I wouldn't even know how it'd look like even if he did.'

'Well, now that,' Elijah said, his voice a caress against her ears, 'is easy enough to see.' His mouth pulled at the corner, and with his smile, her mind flashed with images. Images of him licking, devouring, and feasting on a woman's body. Her sighs. His hooded eyes full of heat. Then the images shifted, and his eyes were closed. His head tilted backwards, his throat exposed, and his lips parting into—

Keira let out a shivering breath as the images faded, her throat dry, her mind ringing with the echo of a male groan. With his lips tightly pressed together, Elijah leaned back on his mattress and returned to his book. A look of utter amusement and glee danced across his face.

She could have scowled at him again, but what he had let her see...

That's what she wanted.

It would not matter how she looked, what her station was, or anything else at all, she realised, if only she could make August feel like that. And she could not deny the cry of yearning in her own body, to be a woman capable of making him – to make anyone – be at her mercy like that, either.

'There is nothing left for it then,' she said and rose from her chair, her determination catching Elijah's attention.

'What?' He arched a brow expectantly.

She sat down beside him. So close she could feel nerves stirring under her skin and goosebumps rippling along her arms.

'You must teach me how to please a man.'

9
CHECKMATE

'Between the...scrotum and anus?' Keira asked.

'Yes, that's where you'll find the perineum,' Elijah replied, moving a chess piece.

'And men like that?'

His mouth curved wickedly. 'We sure do.'

Keira inhaled sharply. 'What else is there?'

'There are all the regular erotic zones, of course, which you'll also find on a woman,' Elijah said, counting on his hand all the places that might pleasure a man. 'The earlobe, the neck, the nipples...' He held up one of the wooden chess pawns, letting his thumb run over its rounded head, and her skin tightened. 'Then there's the Adonis belt and what follows below. But really, you are asking all the wrong questions.'

Keira set down a chess piece of her own – it might have been a knight, although she had long since lost track – and raised a brow. 'Oh, really?'

Elijah leaned forward, coy interest flickering across his face, cast in light from the fire. Night had once again descended outside while they'd talked and played chess, throwing the living room into heady darkness. She much enjoyed her cottage at day. But at night, with Elijah around, it had become something else entirely.

'The ultimate way to please a man is to learn how to please yourself first.' He leaned back again after his turn, appearing triumphant about making her face burn worse than the smoky wood in the hearth. 'Pray, do tell, how experienced are you at touching yourself?'

Keira's hand slipped as she set down her next piece, causing several to spin off their places. 'I don't believe that's... proper to ask of a girl,' Keira spluttered, raptly trying to put all the pieces back in place.

'I don't believe anything about this conversation – this arrangement – is proper per your social conventions.'

That was fair, but Keira scowled at him nevertheless as she repeated her move.

'Even so. We're not discussing *that*.'

'Then we'll make no progress until we do,' he said, and set down his queen, blocking in her king. 'Checkmate.' Keira blinked at the pieces while he observed her with a barely concealed grin. 'The night is still young should you want a more...practical lesson.'

He had barely said the words before new images rose in her mind, this time of a hand reaching for the spot between her legs, and her body writhing with pleasure. Her back arched as the fingers rubbed a particular spot, the imagery so vivid that she felt a jolt at her core and startled to her feet, fumbling with her skirt and nearly knocking the chessboard off the table. 'Whatever. If you can't take this seriously, I'll be taking my leave,' she huffed and grumbled. 'Good night.'

'Make sure to practice while you're up there,' Elijah called after her, receiving a snort in return.

Yet, once in bed, the deafening silence offered no distraction from his advice. Heart pounding, the words repeated themselves in her head until it was all she could think about; the room, the space, and the objects in it—all were tediously bland and out of focus compared to the spot aching below her navel. She shifted, the sheets caressing her sensitive skin.

She hadn't wanted to admit it, but she felt embarrassingly inexperienced at even such a simple notion as touching herself. Even if she did and elicited the slightest of pleasures, it was usually by mere coincidence. A coincidence she struggled to replicate. But she couldn't deny that she wanted to.

Keira swallowed, her fingers clenching and unclenching at her side. If she just—she shifted and exhaled, then shifted once more, and with the movement, her hand moved underneath the duvet, coming to rest against her chemise between her legs.

She held her breath as the tips of her fingers trembled over the cotton. Nerves stirred underneath the fabric, and her breath caught further as she pressed down, feeling something pleasant. Soft. And something at her core thudded as much as her heart. Letting her fingers slide a little, she considered the sensations in her body again. Nothing changed. Not for the better, not for the worse. She shifted her hand a little more, feeling... Hesitant. Uncertain. Stupid.

She toyed with the flesh between her legs, and then... Nothing.

Impatience. Frustration. She was blocked.

Groaning, Keira grabbed her duvet and pressed it to her face, muffling her disgruntled grumbles.

A determined knock at the door made her still and sit up straight. 'J–just a minute,' she stuttered, rearranging her duvet and her hair, as if those actions would douse the heat flushing through her body.

'Either you let me in now,' said the djinn's gruff voice on the other side, 'or I'll break this door down and give you a helping hand.'

'It's unlocked!' she blurted out, mortification heating her face from her chin to the roots of her hair. Her bedroom door swung open, yet Elijah didn't step inside. Instead, he stood perfectly still in the threshold, fists tightened at his sides, strain marred in every feature of his handsome complexion, now back to the dark-haired, tanned version he'd appeared as upon their first meeting.

'Well?' she quipped, raising her brow expectantly at him. 'Why are you just standing there? Can I help you with something?'

'The question, I'd say, is whether *I* can help *you*?'

His gaze, the look he sent her—The heat in her face travelled down her spine, pooling between her thighs at the intensity of it.

'It goes against my every instinct,' he drawled, finally stepping into the room, 'not to...alleviate you from your struggles and... release you this instant.'

The heat in her nether regions shot back up top. *He'd sensed her.* Sensed her trying to...satisfy herself. Sensed her frustration when she failed.

Slowly, Elijah leaned forward and grabbed the frame of the bed, a devious smile creeping up his face. 'You know, if you want me to show you, you need only say the word,' he purred.

Keira opened her mouth but found herself at a loss for words, thinking of the images she had seen before. The spot between her legs suddenly wet and needy. His gaze deepened with something dark and decadent, and his knuckles whitened further. Inexplicably, it made her toes curl under her duvet and her feminine parts pound even more.

'No,' Keira breathed. 'I think I'm good.'

'Thing is, I think you're right,' Elijah said, letting go of the metal bedframe to sit on the edge of the mattress. His eyes never left her face. Her lips. 'I think you'd be very good.'

Once again, images and sounds filled her mind. Of his hands moving underneath her nightgown. Of her breathy moans as she rode his hand and their writhing bodies entwined with the duvet.

'It wouldn't be proper,' she breathed.

His gaze never left hers. 'No, we established as much.'

'I would feel awkward with you watching, worried what you'd think of me.' The heat in her cheeks grew at the thought, but so did the itch to put her hand down there.

His voice grew thicker. 'I do not know any real man who wouldn't...enjoy it. Savour it. Wish it was his hand instead.'

She swallowed, her mouth entirely dry, as if all the wetness in her body had gone—

'I'll get you some water,' Elijah rasped suddenly, clearing his throat before heading downstairs.

Left in the bed, Keira pulled the duvet a little closer to her chest, her core pounding with her heart as she chastised herself for being so easily influenced.

This must have been what her nan had tried to warn her about. The seductive powers of the djinn, drawing her in like a moth to a flame.

She needed to stay level-headed, she thought, and straightened her back. She could not afford Elijah to influence her like this.

August. She needed to think of August.

No sooner had she managed to calm herself, however, than Elijah reappeared with a glass of water and a plate of something smelling suspiciously like heaven. To her surprise, she found it was a plate of chocolate chip cookies.

'Here,' he said, giving her the glass before settling down next to her in the bed with the plate on his lap. 'They'll help with the craving.'

She had half a mind to call him a liar a moment later, when he handed her a cookie and licked his fingers after. Slowly. Deliberately. He could not help himself, could he?

Catching her stare, he grinned wickedly.

'Just...trying to diffuse the tension,' he said, eyes twinkling.

And yet her body felt like a furnace, the craving being more than she could bear.

She bit into her baked goods, savouring the tastes of salty and sweet. *'I do not know any real man who wouldn't...enjoy it. Savour it. Wish it was his hand instead.'* She glanced at him, but he was thoroughly occupied with his own cookie.

'Tell me,' he started, 'how *did* the good people of E'Frion learn about you and August's...activities?'

That doused her cravings.

'I told you,' she grumbled, 'they saw us through the fisherman's hut's window. And they weren't ambiguous about it before dumping me in the lake.'

'Why there? Why not meet him...somewhere more private?'

'It was supposed to be private. His friends were meant to be out on the hunt.'

'And yet they happened to be outside the window at that time?'

'Yes,' Keira said, regarding him. 'Why do you ask?'

Elijah shrugged and broke his cookie in half. 'No reason. Quite the coincidence, isn't it?'

'Perhaps they thought my horse was a stag and went to examine it,' Keira muttered, although she couldn't help but wonder...why *had* they been around? Had they known? No, it had been her and August's secret. Had they followed them? Whyever would they if they did not *know*?

'What's this obsession with the stag anyway?' Elijah asked, suckling the moist core of the cookie. Keira could not help but stare, her brain struggling for words as she spoke.

'They believe it to be the Tyrant Emperor.'

There was a flash of something in his eyes, a humourless curl of his lip. 'People still remember that old myth? It's a hundred years old.'

'You'd be surprised what we hold onto to make things interesting around here,' she said. 'You know of it, then? And him, the Tyrant Emperor? He was a djinn, wasn't he? Like you?'

Elijah nodded, and a muscle ticked in his jaw. 'I knew of him. Was glad of his demise too.'

So, the emperor was truly gone then. Keira gazed out the window, towards the woods. 'I wonder, if the myth had been true, would living as a hunted animal all these years have mellowed him?'

'Some leopards don't change even if their spots do.'

She turned back to him, voice sharper as she said, 'Yet, you want to change me?'

'Not change, uncage. Your spots are perfect. Except for your game of chess.' He said it effortlessly, matter-of-factly, like it didn't completely throw her off guard.

Then her mind caught on his final words, and she thought of how Elijah had manoeuvred every single one of her moves, always staying two steps ahead, just like—

'Elijah!' She clasped his hand.

'What?'

'The game. I know how to win August back now.'

Elijah's forehead creased. 'By losing?'

'No.' Keira's smile merely widened. Yes, Elijah had beaten her at their game, but it had also given her an idea. Maybe, just maybe, there was time still for Keira to beat Lady Thornfell at hers. 'Tomorrow, I'll capture the stag.'

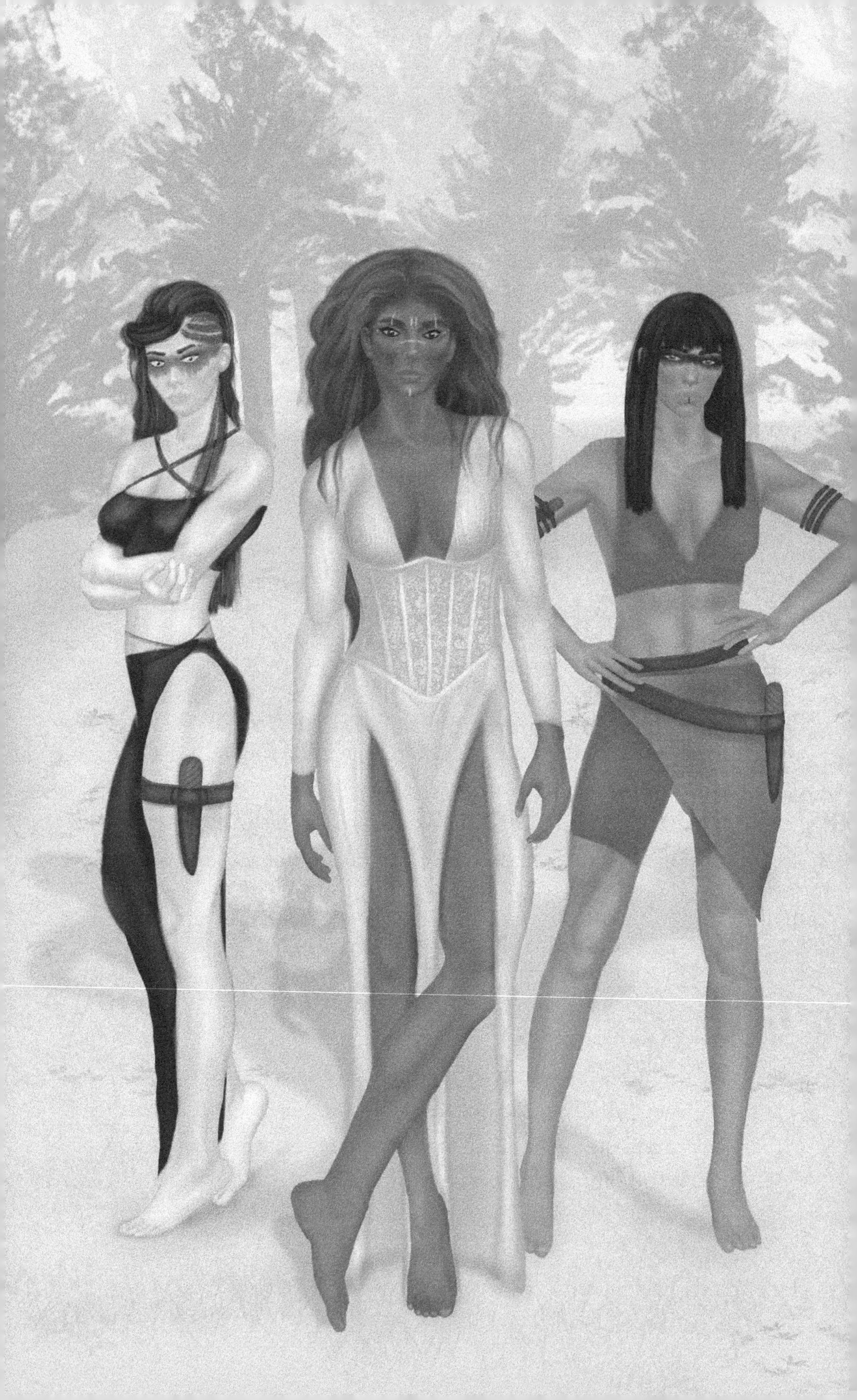

10

HUNTER

The sun was already high in the sky by the time Keira finished her work and managed to drag Elijah out of bed the next day. He'd been particularly troublesome, complaining about some chess fanatic keeping him up all night.

'And then she suggested we'd go hunting for a mythical stag!' he exclaimed dramatically as they rode underneath the trees with the sunrays glinting between the leaves. 'How do you even plan on taking it down?'

'How does any man take down a stag?' Keira asked, signalling that they would halt in the clearing ahead.

'In the most strenuous ways, I'm sure.' Elijah yawned, flicking a bit of magic between his fingers. Once more, Keira rolled her eyes, then dismounted and fastened her horse to a tree. 'How has a lady such as yourself learned to do it?'

'My father taught me,' Keira said. 'He used to take me hunting before he passed. Taught me that to hunt, one ought to find a spot far away from the horses, down-wind, where one can wait for the stag to pass.'

'And that's why we're stopping here?' Elijah asked after fastening his own horse and followed her into the woods.

'Precisely.'

They walked a little further in silence, until they caught the sound of rustling bushes, and Keira held her hand out.

'What? You think it's here already?' Elijah mused, so close to her now that she could feel his presence directly behind her. She closed her eyes at the tug it caused in her body, at the fluttering sensation crawling up her skin. 'Does that mean we'll get back to the cottage early?'

She was about to turn and tell him that they'd never catch it if he kept talking, but what stepped out of the bushes wasn't the stag. Instead, it was a couple Woodland Witches, with Isolde in the lead.

'Keira,' she said, eyes on Elijah. Subtly, her hand came to rest on the sheathed dagger at her hip. The other witches tensed with their bows. 'What are you doing here, and with…whom, may I ask?'

'This is Elijah. He's…' Keira cleared her throat, her voice turning low. 'He was the djinn in your lamp.'

This time, Isolde's eyes did shift over to Keira, but there was no surprise in them, as if she had already discovered the lamp gone and guessed that Keira had taken it.

An apology ached at the tip of Keira's tongue, yet she couldn't quite get it out past her shame, and she opted for a half-baked excuse instead. 'He's helping me capture the stag. So that I can win August back.'

Isolde's gaze cut to the djinn again, her voice sharper than the blade at her hip. 'Is he now?'

Elijah cocked his head. 'Don't worry, my lady; I'll make sure no harm comes to her.'

'I'm afraid if she continues down this path, not even you can prevent that,' Isolde said, her voice full of warning as she met Keira's gaze again. 'Don't walk it, Kiki. Turn and give up this chase while you're still able to.'

'It's my choice, Iz,' Keira murmured, tightening her grip on her father's old stalking rifle fastened over her shoulder.

'Then I can't help you.'

Giving Elijah one last scathing look, Isolde beckoned to the other witches to turn, and Keira and Elijah watched them disappear amongst the trees. Keira's stomach churned. She hated disappointing Isolde, and she hated being at odds with her even more.

'You don't need to do this, you know,' Elijah said, once they were gone.

'It's the best way to get August back,' Keira said, raising a brow at him.

But he merely looked back at her, his gaze full of meaning. As if asking how bad it would be if she didn't. She didn't want to answer that. Wouldn't know what to do with herself if she chose to let August go. Just stay in this village as a servant forever? She wanted more in life.

They walked a little further in silence, until they spotted a small cave at the foot of a mountain. They settled on either side of its walls, crammed so tightly that their knees brushed each other.

For a long while, Keira watched the quiet woods outside, while Elijah watched her.

'What?' she snapped when her skin felt a little too tight.

'You're in a mood today. I thought we were...getting comfortable with one another last night.' He winked.

She shifted against the rock wall. 'Well, you thought wrong.'

Fact was, they'd gotten too comfortable last night. All night she'd struggled to get him out of her head, images of his eyes, his mouth, his tongue – and what she supposed he could do with it –

invading her every dream. Even now, his closeness made her skin felt like it was on fire.

'Are we merely going to sit here and wait then?' he asked at last, and Keira hissed at him.

'Yes. It is better to wait for the stag to come to us, rather than go trudging through the woods for an eternity. But it won't come if you keep talking. It'll be able to hear us from miles off.'

'Such a shame,' Elijah muttered to himself, glancing about the cave. 'It would have been a practical place for a *lesson*. You know, on touching yourself? But if it can hear us talking...it'd definitely hear the sounds I'd have you make.'

She couldn't help it. Her eyes cut to his, her lips parted, and a stirring spread through her body, heating the spot between her legs.

She clenched them closer together, and Elijah's smile grew wicked.

'There is no point hiding it from me,' he hummed, then leaned his head against the rock wall. 'I sense it all.'

'Is that a djinn thing?' she asked, and nearly shuddered at the thought. Perhaps it was a good thing most of them were extinct. Elijah seemed...trustworthy enough, his arrogance and flirtatiousness aside, but she doubted every demon spirit would be like him.

'You could say that,' Elijah quipped, his voice short enough that she had the sense that he didn't want to talk about it. Which only piqued her curiosity more.

'Tell me about yourself. I hardly know anything about you, yet you already know so much about me.'

'I thought you didn't want us to chat.' His mouth curved into a half-smile, yet the humour still didn't reach his eyes. She rolled her own and sighed, setting her sights on the woodland area outside the cave. It was perfectly still, without an animal in sight, and she wondered if perhaps it was too quiet. If they should have moved deeper into the woods to find the stag.

'How do you plan to kill it?'

Picking up her rifle, Keira mimicked loading it and shooting. 'Straight to the neck.'

'Cutthroat little thing, aren't you?' Elijah said, making her snort sarcastically.

'It means it'll die within seconds. No suffering.' Just like her father had taught her. And she wondered, in that moment, whether *he* had suffered or not, when a slight rustling sound caught her ear and they both stilled.

There in the clearing appeared the stag, magnificent and mighty.

It was larger than any stag she had seen before, its antlers wide and far-reaching; an intricate work of art crowning its head as if it were the king of the forest. Or an emperor.

No wonder the legend had taken the shape it had.

With her heart pounding in her chest, Keira aimed her rifle at the animal turning its head left and right as if looking for danger – unable to see it staring it in its face.

Her finger readied to pull the trigger, and then—

Elijah rose and slipped on some rocks, causing such a ruckus that it startled the animal straight back into the bushes.

'Whatever did you just do?' she cried out incredulously. It had been half a miracle that the stag had shown in the first place so soon and with all their chatter, but now…? Now she felt certain it wouldn't go near this place for days. Frustration tore at her at the thought. She did not have days.

'Apologies, I just wanted a better look,' Elijah said, at least having the decency to look slightly embarrassed.

Harrumphing, Keira picked up her rifle and strode out of the cave, moving further into the woods.

'We'll be at it all night now,' she complained. 'And by *it* – she twirled on her heel, pointing at him as he opened his mouth to speak – 'I do not mean a *lesson*.'

'It'd certainly make for more fun,' Elijah said pointedly and strolled past her, as elegantly and soundlessly as a cat. She took him in. His grace. His pure control of his body. So different from the stumbling buffoon she'd sat with back in the cave. So different that she could not help but feel suspicious.

'Did you do it deliberately?' she asked.

'Do what?' He shrugged and turned, clearly feigning ignorance.

'Scare it away!'

'I don't know what you're talking about. A djinn may stumble, you know.' He continued into the woods.

She shook her head and growled at him. 'But you didn't stumble. You startled it on purpose. Why?' Whatever reason did he have to do so? Unless he didn't want her to capture the stag... She paused. 'Are you sabotaging my attempts to get August back?'

Elijah barked a laugh. 'You manage that perfectly well on your own.'

'Whatever are you talking about? If you're sabotaging me—' She hissed and grabbed his shoulder, forced him around—and stepped back. His eyes glinted dangerously, full of challenge.

'Have you considered that your "hunting skills" may be the problem?' He stepped forward, forcing her backwards until she bumped against a tree.

'My hunting skills are perfectly fine, thank you,' she spluttered, narrowing her eyes. The tree pressed against her back.

He smirked, his gaze once again assessing her in a way that made her skin flush. 'To kill, yes. To kill, I'd say they're rather admirable. But not to catch.'

'What are you suggesting?'

'I'm suggesting that you've hunted August to death. That perhaps' – Elijah stepped so close now that she could feel his breath against her neck, her chin, the corner of her lips – 'you've hunted him so hard, he no longer cares to hunt you.' He brushed his thumb along her chin, tilting her head back to meet his gaze. 'Not as he should.' He let silence fill their closeness, letting his breath caress the bottom pillow of her mouth. Then he stepped back. 'A good hunter hunts the prey. A *great* hunter lets the prey believe itself to be the hunter, until they're caught in the snare.'

'I don't want to trap him.' Keira sneered. 'I—' But as she spoke, Elijah waved her away.

'Yes, yes, I know. You want to marry him, love him. You're soulmates. And yet'—he spread his arms wide—'you don't see him out here hunting the stag, do you?'

He left her speechless, continuing in the direction the stag had gone.

Keira didn't realise how far they had gone until she saw a tower rising in the distance, and it dawned on her that they were swiftly approaching the Tyrant Emperor's old palace – or what was left of it.

The site of the palace ruins was just as she remembered it.

Vast and magnificent, one could just about make out how it had looked in its glory days, before Mother Nature claimed it, its extensive gardens stretching far beyond the main building.

Keira stepped onto the grounds, sensing Elijah behind her. He'd gone awfully quiet, taking in the remains of what might once have been perfectly trimmed hedges and trees placed in formations, encircling delicate fountains that had long since broken and wasted away under the pressure of roots and foliage. Now, the trees grew wild, stretching their branched arms in the direction of the palace itself, as if they'd once been rebels about to storm it, caught in time and turned as one with the forest that had grown around them.

'The Palace of the Cardinal Seven... Did you ever see it in its glory days?'

'Briefly,' Elijah murmured. 'It sure looked better than this, though.'

She didn't doubt it. Many of the minor buildings had fallen to decay, save for a circular temple speckled with minty green foliose and the pale palace building itself, its elaborate stone carvings still visible through the layers of overgrowth.

'It's not too bad inside.'

Elijah paused in his steps. 'You've been?'

'Yeah,' Keira murmured, stepping between the pillars and up the small steps of the palace threshold. 'I used to ride here often as a child. It was my personal playground.' She pushed at the giant door. Slowly, it creaked open, revealing the vast hall inside.

Pillars upon pillars lined it from one end to another. Some were chipped, and almost all were wrought in ivy and green growth, framing entries to different parts of the palace, adorning the space not occupied by a large staircase. It led past a giant, ornated window – the layers of dust so thick that the sunrays barely found a way through, save for the places where the glass had cracked and shattered.

'I always imagined being a princess in these halls,' Keira said, taking in the room. In every crack and crevice there were ropy vines and other thick foliage creeping through, hanging over railings, and decorating the space with their eerie beauty. Not even birdsong could be heard within them.

She stumbled at that. Once again, it was too quiet, and she realised the djinn had not replied yet.

'Elijah?' She turned, seeing no one behind her but the empty grounds of the palace. 'Elijah!'

Muffled sounds caught her ears, and she rushed around the corner, seeing Elijah being hauled away towards the woods between two—

Keira gasped. It couldn't be. No one had seen one in years. Yet there they were, two creatures from Faerie, dragging Elijah between them.

'Elijah!'

'Keira! Run!' he shouted behind hands attempting to stifle him as he tried and failed to fight them off.

One of them turned, throwing a spinning blade towards her, and a sharp sting followed.

She hissed, clutching her arm, then pulled at her rifle, aiming it the best she could with her wounded shoulder. 'Let him go!' she shouted.

The other fae turned to face her, sharp teeth gleaming in his wicked smile. 'Put that down, human girl, before you—'

She fired, and the fae dropped to the ground.

Stunned, the other fae stumbled backwards, glanced between her and Elijah, now dumped on the ground, and then took off into the woods.

Keira rushed over, pulse still pounding in her ears, to find Elijah untying himself from coppery ropes. Beside him, the shot fae thrashed and writhed, his golden skin turning ashen grey as he gaped towards the sky before he stilled completely.

'What–what happened to him?' Keira stuttered.

'Iron,' Elijah mumbled, glancing between the fae and her rifle in awe. 'Keira, did your father use iron bullets?'

'I suppose so. Why?'

'Because iron kills the fae, like copper redirects and prevents magic.'

'Copper…' She looked at the binds circling him on the ground. 'That's why you couldn't fight them off. And the base of your lamp…'

'Is why it can hold me. But that doesn't answer the bigger question.' Elijah frowned.

'And what's that?'

'Why did your father keep weapons against the fae?'

11
TOUCHED

'You know, as a child, I'd heal abnormally fast,' Keira said as Elijah dabbed the wound on her arm with a cotton pad. 'I used to pretend like I had magic. Like you.'

They'd returned to the cottage and were sat upon his mattress before the fireplace, the warmth of it heating their skin in the dim light.

He smiled softly; his own scratches were already healed. 'It does come in handy, like that old rifle of yours.' He paused, glancing at her ever so slightly. 'So...why do you think your father kept weapons against the fae?'

Keira shrugged. 'I don't know. But my parents always did warn me about magical beings, djinns included.' She cut him a look that had him grinning so devilishly that it should have been illegal. Especially considering the way it made her stomach flutter. 'I wouldn't be surprised if half the village has iron bullets in their chambers, if only in fear that the Folk would cross the wall of Faerie.' She scrunched up her lips and mused. 'Why *did* the Folk try to capture you?'

'I'm...indebted to the Spring Queen. I guess she's getting impatient.'

'The Spring Queen?' Keira gasped, then swallowed as Elijah began wrapping her wound, his fingertips brushing against her skin. 'She's real?'

The Spring Queen had been rumoured to be the last of her kind after the war against the Tyrant Emperor and the hunt for magical creatures. The last of the fae, sitting on her throne all on her lonesome even to this day. Although Keira supposed, from what she had seen today, that wasn't entirely true.

'She most definitely is,' Elijah said, and a muscle ticked in his jaw. 'There,' he added, putting the final touch on the linen wrap around her arm, as a way of distraction. She allowed it, her attention preoccupied with the burn of his gaze.

'Thank you for rescuing me today. I guess your end of our deal is fulfilled.'

'It was hardly a favour.'

'I'd beg to differ.' He cupped her chin, and for a moment she wondered if he would lean in to give her a kiss for her troubles. Her heart skipped a beat at the thought, and her breath caught. But he merely shifted his hand to move a lock of hair behind her ear.

Then he started putting away her medical kit and pocketed the cotton pieces used to clean her wound. 'Although,' he groaned, 'I don't know how I'll live down the shame of having needed rescuing from a human.'

'Oh, shut it, you,' Keira growled, and hit him with his pillow. He chortled and lay down on his side, stretching his long legs along the mattress. She could not help but wonder what it would be like to be entangled with those legs, and her cheeks heated once more.

'You could always hold up your end of the bargain, you know.'

She glanced at him with a challenge in her voice, matching the hum in her chest. 'Teach me how to please a man.'

He scoffed. 'So that you may use the skills to please August while he does nothing to please you?'

The words cut her, but not nearly as much as they also seemed to cut him, the tartness bleeding into his voice. Somehow, it softened the sting.

'Fine,' she said, putting on an air of indifference as she rose and headed towards the doorway. 'Then you may remain indebted to both the Spring Queen *and* me. I will learn, with or without your help.' She looked back at him with her hands on her hips, but her bravado faltered as she realised he'd followed, standing so close that it forced her back against the wall.

'I have no doubt you will,' Elijah crooned and leaned over her, one hand supporting his weight on the frame behind her head. Her breath caught, feeling his on her skin, watching the closeness of his lips. 'Once you've learned to pleasure yourself.'

'I best go up and try then, shouldn't I?' Keira taunted lowly, hoping her voice didn't betray how much he affected her, before she slipped out from underneath him and waved him off, stumbling her way up the crooked staircase to her bedroom.

'Remember, if you're stuck, all you need is some expert fingers.' He waved back, to which she responded with just a finger of her own. She could not help but smile as she heard him chuckle behind her.

Once in bed, however, her mind would not still, and she found herself unable to think of anything but Elijah's parting words.

Barely half an hour later, she made her way downstairs again, dressed in her sleepwear, and paused at the threshold of the living room, picking at the doorframe.

Inside, Elijah lay shirtless on his side on the mattress, head resting on his hand, eyes upon the hearth. The firelight devoured every inch of his exposed skin and muscles, until she cleared her throat and he looked up, his expression sober and wide awake.

'I...can't figure out how to do it.'

Quietly, he beckoned her down on the mattress with him. When she did not move, he raised his hands. 'I promised not to take or ask for your body, remember?'

Hesitantly, she moved closer and sat down beside him with the hearth warming her back, her legs curled up underneath her. 'Okay. Tell me.'

He arched an eyebrow at her tense, locked-up position. 'I can show you better than I can tell you. And I promise,' he added as she bit her lip, 'your nightgown will hide everything from my view.' His hand started to reach for hers.

'Might you not tell me something about yourself?' she blurted out.

He paused and looked up, dark, full lashes framing his beautiful eyes. They were a fine sea-green colour for the night, with specks of brown that turned into gold with the flickering light. 'Like what?'

'I don't know.' She chuckled nervously. 'I–I just realised I still don't really know you, and...' She exhaled, gaze falling to her lap and her hands folded there. 'You're a mystery to me...still.'

'I like peaches,' he said, rather randomly, and she snorted. 'And anything rich and decadent.'

'Why am I not surprised?' She rolled her eyes.

'I suppose that's why I enjoy your company too.'

A soft smile tugged at the corner of her mouth, and she turned her face to the fire. 'But I am neither rich nor decadent.'

'There are different ways of being rich,' he whispered, in a voice that seemed to wrap around her. 'Rich in money. Rich in hope. Rich in beauty. Bodily rich.' He rubbed a flap of her nightgown between his fingers, his hand tentatively brushing against her hips. Heat surged from the spot and flooded her body. She could not take her eyes off the piece of fabric, wondering how it would feel if it was her between his fingers.

'As for decadent... Well, it intrigues me, really.'

'What does?'

His eyes locked with hers. 'With August, you're like a predator hunting after her prey, and yet you do not recognise that they have taken your claws and made you into their pet.'

Her breath caught, and at once it felt like those penetrating eyes could see straight through her. As if he already knew everything about her, even though she did not. She had not thought about it herself, and yet it tickled something at the back of her mind. Something that told her that what he was saying was true. But what it meant, for her and August, she wasn't quite sure. Nor did she manage to stay on that trail of thought as Elijah took her hand in his and brought her fingers to his lips, allowing them to brush against them. She stopped breathing.

'May you allow me to help you find your claws again?' He pressed one of her fingers harder against him so that its nail left a pale line down his lip and chin. If she had had literal claws, she would have drawn blood. Staring as if transfixed by the movement, she nodded meekly, and he lowered their braided hands around her waist and pulled her down to the mattress with her back against him, as if they were two spoons fitted together into one. Her nether region pounded. Then he steered their hands to the inside of her thigh and began circling their fingertips.

'I'd like you to touch yourself here in any way that brings you pleasure,' he murmured against her ear, a trail of jitters lingering in the wake of everywhere their fingers touched. Part of her suspected it had more to do with his touch than hers, and when she felt his fingers ease up around hers, she held on tighter, keeping his hand entwined with hers as yearning chased through her.

'Don't,' she whispered. '*Show* me.'

He did not object or retreat from her; instead, he shifted closer, his fingers once again tight around hers.

'You do not need me,' he said against the back of her head, yet his hands were steering hers closer to the hem of her dress. Briefly, their fingertips nudged the soft edge and her breathing halted.

'Whenever you're ready,' he whispered, his thumb toying with the border.

'Tell me one more thing,' she murmured, heart thrumming while waiting for his reply.

'I once had a rather large family,' he said at last. 'I miss them.'

A slice through the heart, and the image of her own family surfaced. 'What happened?'

'We were separated when the Tyrant Emperor fell, and the hunting of djinns began. They captured us, then scattered us across the realm. I have not seen my family since.'

'I'm so sorry. I miss my family too.'

His hand squeezed around hers. She could not help herself, and glanced over her shoulder, straight into eyes burning with the heat of a thousand suns. Whatever she had thought to say – whatever she had thought to ask – melted away, and instead, she said, rather breathlessly, 'I'm ready.'

The pressure against her hand was tentative at first, before it steered her underneath the hem of her gown. Her nerves shook with anticipation as her own fingertips travelled closer to the pulsing centre between her legs, her neck craning, her lungs exhaling as she felt his knuckles brush against her inner thigh.

The first fingers brushed against her sensitive opening, and a bolt of electricity flared through her. One by one, he took each finger and steered them in different directions, showing her all the different ways to elicit pleasure, rapidly increasing her pulse pounding through her body and mind. Some strokes made her shiver; others made her shudder. Some made her groan and moan, and a select few made her beg to be shown more.

'You do not need me,' he repeated, breath warm against her neck. His thumb flicked over a sensitive spot, like a button, and she gasped, arching her back, thrusting her bum against the hardness of him. 'You only need to recognise the power you hold.'

His hand settled on her hip, fisting the material of her gown. That's when she realised she was on her own. Kneading and massaging. Chasing the rising urge within, rolling her hips with it as she would in a saddle. And whenever she hesitated or faltered, whenever she turned with imploring urgency in her eyes, he was there, sliding a finger with her own into the heat of her, steering her back on course. Fanning that need – that drive – to see the build-up coming to a close.

In the heat of it, before she could let herself go completely, she glanced back at him, his features shrouded in shadows, only his eyes clear on her, not judgemental, but breathless. Stunned. Mesmerized. By her. And for the first time in her life, she felt what it meant to tip over the edge.

12
PREDATORS

Mr Croft raised his head as she strolled by after her morning shift at the Thornfell Manor, and he wasn't the only one. Everywhere she went, the villagers seemed to do a double take. Conversations stopped midsentence and gazes trailed after her. A woman at a flower stall offered her a free rose, gesturing in a way that implied that it would complement her beauty.

Perhaps it was the extra little spring to her steps, or the fresh glow to her skin that she had awakened with. Or, perhaps, it had a little something to do with the smile she could not seem to shake every time her mind wandered to the pleasures she'd felt the night before – and this morning, alone in her bedroom.

Her skin heated a little at the thought. At first, she had woken with a bang of dread, worrying about what people would say if they found out, what they would have said if they had seen – if faces had once again watched her from the window and laughed. Those faces attempted to enter her dreams too, but no sooner had the faces appeared than Elijah's did as well, chasing them all away until there was nothing but his burning gaze left in her mind. The memory of that gaze had been enough to make her fingers reach between her legs again, repeating what he'd taught her with the memory of his words and the sound of his voice still fresh in her mind.

'Keira!' someone called, and she startled out of her daydreams, rushing to compose herself and extinguish the scorching heat now covering her whole face. It was rapidly doused, however, as she turned to see August coming to a halt before her, out of breath.

'Keira – I wanted to speak with you about the other day...' He panted, straightening his collar. 'I—' He paused and took her in. 'You look radiant.'

Her cheeks pinched as her heart did a surprised somersault. 'Why, em, thank you, August.'

'I must admit, I did not expect to see you so happy after...' He trailed off, looking as if he was moving into some internal sort of conversation with himself, eyes still taking her in.

Her smile faded, her mind catching up to the meaning of his words. *After the announcement of his engagement.* After the humiliation and degradation and abandonment she had suffered when all she had done was comply with his wishes. Ire set her blood to boil, and with it, Elijah's words about claws drifted back to her. She squared her shoulders and scowled. 'Yes, well, I do not need *you* to be happy, August.'

He startled.

'No, of course not, forgive me.' August bowed, then looked around to see if any eyes were upon them before he stepped closer and took her hand. 'Although, I'm not sure the same can be said for me.'

She frowned.

'Keira...' Her name on his lips was like the softest petal of a rose. 'I can't help but think that if we had not been caught that day...'

He shook his head and stepped away, leaving her aching for the rest of his words. What? What then if they had not been caught? The air went out of her. Would he still have been with her? If her reputation was not tarnished while his was intact? If she was not "defiled" and he a conqueror? Somewhere in the back of her mind, the embers of her anger still sizzled. Hissing at the injustice of it. But it was soon quenched by her regret that maybe it was, after all, her actions, her choices, that had led them apart.

August glanced around them, scratching his neck. 'How is that relative of yours? Is he still...visiting?'

'Yes,' Keira said, recalling a glimpse of the djinn fast asleep on his mattress as she left the house. 'And he is well, thank you. He decided to stay back at the cottage today. Perhaps we'll go for another walk later.'

'Splendid,' August said. 'We're all to go to the tavern tonight. I hope to see you both there.' He bowed once more, tipping his hat to her, eyes full of emphasis.

Keira dipped her chin in return and watched him leave before she picked up her skirts and rushed back home, spirit elated, to tell Elijah that whatever he was doing was working: August was showing her attention again! And although, technically, he had invited Elijah out with them too, something told her that'd just been a courtesy. After all, it would not do for her reputation to be seen unchaperoned after everything else that had happened. But based on his words, she felt certain that it was *her* who August truly wanted to see.

She picked up her pace, stopping only to hold open the gate and smile brightly to the mailman bidding her a good day as he left, before she dashed into the cottage, calling the djinn's name.

But even as she called it twice, no answer came. The kitchen was vacant, and neither was he in the living room. She pursed her lips and marched upstairs, certain he had taken some liberties with the bath or even her bed while she was gone, but the soft reproach she had prepared died on her lips.

He was not there either.

Her skin prickled and she flew back downstairs, grabbed his lamp, twisted the knob, and rubbed the base, a creeping realisation settling in her bones when nothing happened. The lamp fell onto his mattress with a clink.

Elijah was gone.

He had left the house. But how? When? *The mailman.*

Had he not had a particular mischievous twinkle in his eyes? She ran outside and up to the gate, gripping the wooden planks until her knuckles turned white, looking for him.

There was no one in sight.

And there was no point in running after him, she realised with resignation. He could be anyone and anywhere by now. He could be a man, woman, or child, or a bird flying south for the winter.

She stumbled back to the cottage and let her eyes wander the rooms once more even though she knew he was gone.

Despite her orders to stay—

She palmed her face and sagged against the doorway, its old paint flossing onto the floor.

What a fool she had been.

Ordering him to stay must have been about as effective as ordering him to fulfil a wish. He must have pretended like it worked, so that she would keep her guard down.

But why now? He'd had plenty of opportunities to leave before if he'd always been free to do so. What had kept him here before now? What had changed?

She was struck still as it hit her.

A shiver went down her spine and what little joy had gathered in her chest the last day plummeted in a ball of despair into her stomach.

She had pleasured herself. And she had allowed him to watch. No worse, she had even let *him* join. *Give a djinn a finger...*

She squeezed her eyes shut at the memory of his fingers coaxing her delicate parts. Of her heavy breaths and his whispers in her ears.

Heat once again rose into her cheeks, but it was a different heat from what had burned within her this morning. What had fuelled her actions the night before. A shameful heat. A despairing heat. And suddenly the way he had looked at her, the way everyone had looked at her, distorted in her mind. Twisted into something disgusted rather than admiring.

She had been frivolous with him, and now...

Now, he too had left.

She waited until nightfall, but he did not return. She'd taken a nap, one that turned into a fight with her duvet as she twisted and turned, sighed, groaned, and grunted in exasperation. One minute her fingers itched to reach down between her legs, to give herself the release her body craved; the next minute her mind filled with memories of his eyes upon her, what she now thought must have gone through his mind instead, and the mortification that ensued at having misread his expression so entirely.

Once she gave up on sleep, she tried to wash herself with a bath, but it seemed to have the opposite effect. She heard echoes of laughter and her own scream from when the boys had dumped her in the lake, and somehow the bathwater seemed to wrap her in more humiliation rather than rinse it off.

Despite this, she put on her best outfit, and worked on convincing herself that it did not matter what Elijah thought of her.

August had still shown interest and even expressed a desire to see her. She also remained confident that he would not care one bit that Elijah was not there to come between them.

So, when Elijah did not show, she put on a cloak and locked the cottage, heading out into the night towards the village and the tavern.

It was emptier tonight than it had been the first night of the hunt.

A few people were at the bar, while others sat in groups around tables, talking eagerly with drinks in hand, enjoying meals prepped with today's catch. August's friends had taken up one fourth of the room, their voices drifting above everyone else's. She felt their eyes upon her as she entered the room, crawling along her skin, raking over her body. It was so entirely different from the experience of walking through town this morning, proving that perhaps that, too, had been merely her own imagination. A foolish misinterpretation.

Her heart sank a little further into her stomach, as did her optimism, and she settled by the bar on her own to order a drink, wondering how literal she could make the proverb "to drown one's sorrows."

'Well, hello, Keira,' Miles said, coming up beside her. 'Barely recognised you looking all...dry.' He chortled, a sound shortly echoed by his friend – the boy who had harassed the Nightlady – coming to stand on the other side of her.

'Miles,' Keira said, gripping her beverage and preparing to leave.

But Miles held out a hand, pausing her. 'Oh, come now, Keira. We're just having a bit of a laugh. I'm sorry. Let's start over. Pray, are you here on your own or are you waiting for someone?'

'I don't think that's any of your business,' Keira said, settling back onto her stool, her eyes flickering to the other patrons in the room. She could have sworn someone mouthed "Nightlady-in-the-making" and watched her while they did so.

'Oh, but I'd hate to see you wait for no reason,' Miles droned on, 'especially if it is August you're waiting for. You know, he has already picked his lady for the night. But my friend here'—he jutted his chin towards the other guy beside her—'is all free. What say you?'

'No thanks,' Keira said curtly, and she started chugging her pint, waiting for them to leave, until the glass was nearly empty.

'Alright then; don't say we didn't offer.' They made to leave, but Miles paused as his friend moved ahead, and leaned in closer, murmuring under his breath. 'Take my advice, though, Keira: quench that thirst of yours for August. It makes you look pathetic.'

'I could say the same to you,' she snarled back. 'Tell me, do you really think me a *whore*, or are you just upset it was my mouth around his cock and not yours?'

Surprise flashed through Miles' eyes at her words, but he only laughed loudly, as if he had said something particularly clever – or she something particularly stupid – and wound back to his table. She heard him and his friends tittering and turned away, leaning her forehead against her hand.

Perhaps she shouldn't have said that...and yet, it'd had felt so damn good to do so. Good, yet exhausting.

Saints.

Suddenly she felt so tired. Heavy.

Perhaps it had been a bad idea to come after all. The throng of people had increased, and the air had turned stuffier and warmer as a result. Maybe she ought to go out for some fresh air. But her legs didn't feel particularly keen on moving, and her stomach curdled at the thought.

Fearing that she might vomit once she stood, she kept still, attempting to block out the loud noises that made her cringe and wish to fold in on herself at the same time.

More shapes and voices were coming up to her now. Guys she did not know. Men asking if she was with someone. Asking if she was a Nightlady. Poking and pulling at her, asking her to come with them. Leering when she spilled the last of her drink and all she seemed able to do was sway in response or stagger against them, clambering for something to hold her upright.

She knew she was standing, and yet it felt like she was freefalling. Fear travelled down her numb spine, the only movement that seemed to occur in her body. Everyone around her had gone blurry, their laughing faces blending until they were all teeth and little else. It was like watching them through a haze, one she could not find her way through.

But someone else did.

Someone came through the crowd and stepped up to her: someone tall, with fine hair so light it looked like snow. She knew his facial features. Knew the auburn lock of hair that glinted amongst the white.

Relieved, she stumbled towards him, and he caught her against his chest. The men around erupted into cheers, but August ignored them, holding her close so that it looked like they were merely dancing. There was something strange about his eyes that she couldn't quite place. She was so unbelievably tired.

Her head fell to his shoulder, lolling against his chest, and she was vaguely aware that she was being held up more than she was standing on her own.

'Come, Keira,' August said, his voice warped. 'Let's get you home.' Even if she had wanted to protest, her muscles would not move, and she could do nothing else but let him lead her out into the night.

13
PREY

The room swirled and spun in on itself.

Her gaze flickered around, catching small details that she tried to hang onto. The bookcases. The mantelpiece. The djinn's lamp upon it.

Her cottage. At least they were in her cottage.

A flare of a flame and the fireplace was being lit. The young man shifted away from the hearth, his silhouette basking in silvered light from the windows. His pale hair vivid in the darkness.

'August,' she whispered as he came to pick her up from the chair he had put her in. 'I don't feel so good.'

'You'll be alright, Keira,' he murmured, lifted her, and shifted a little before he knelt on something soft and white.

Elijah's mattress. The mattress of the one who'd left her.

But August had come.

She clung onto him, her hands pulling at his shirt as much for balance as the need to keep close to him, her face nuzzling against his, her lips grazing his skin. She needed something. Him. Reassurances. Stability. She wasn't sure. For a split second, she imagined kissing him – contemplated the idea of them testing what she had learned in his absence, wondering if that would make him stay – but even the thought had her insides reeling and she tumbled out of his grasp and onto the djinn's mattress. The room spinning with her rising nausea.

'You said you'd marry me,' she whimpered, squirming onto her back. After all that had happened, he was finally here with her again. In front of the fireplace. And yet it did not feel right.

He shushed her and pressed something against her lips. His fingers. They moved to his chest, and it took her a moment before she registered that he was undoing his sleeve buttons, undressing himself. A sound, something akin to a protest or need – she wasn't sure – escaped her as he pulled off his shirt, revealing fine, naked skin, gleaming in the firelight.

'August...'

His body leaned over hers, his fingers prying the front laces of her stays loose. Shaking her head, she pressed a hand against his chest, weak fingers clawing against solid muscle, but he only brushed it away.

'No...' There were so many things that they needed to discuss; things she needed to know. Had he come back to her? Was he still with Gianna? Why wouldn't the room stand still?

'It'll be alright, Keira,' he repeated, and her head spun as her lungs were freed and extra air flowed into her body.

August dropped the stays beside him, and for a moment she merely lay there gulping down air, letting her lungs expand and her skin cool. Then she felt him pulling at her skirt.

No. Not now. Not... Ever? Certainly not tonight, with her body heavy as lead. Where was Elijah? She tried to angle her head, but it only made the room spin more.

Her chemise slipped off her next.

'No,' she muttered, more decidedly. Trying to shove him away again. Her lips fumbled for words. Any words. 'I'm not...ready.'

Once again, as if she had not spoken at all, he merely towered over her and put his arms around her, pulling her up into a seated position. She tensed and made herself heavier, until she felt the warmth of a large shirt being pulled around her shoulders. Her arms pulled into the sleeves.

He was dressing her, she realised. In his shirt.

She could have cried with relief.

Soft lips brushed a kiss on her temple before he lowered her back down again and pulled the blanket around her.

Something eased in her chest, but she could not connect what, could not decide whether it was safe to feel relief. Her fingers reached for August, trying to locate where he was, but everything was darkening – her world was spinning off its axis. It caught for a moment on an object being set on the floor in front of her, and then he was there again.

His lips moved next, but she could not catch the words he spoke nor protest as he slid underneath the blanket with her, pulling her close as she trembled throughout the night.

14
DEVOURED

Night chased her unconscious mind. Boisterous laughter followed her wherever she ran. But she did not wake but for a few times.

Some of them were mere moments of fear, fear that August had taken what he wanted. She woke and lashed out, beating against the walls keeping her trapped. Yet the strong arms only tightened around her, and then she was pulled under again.

Other times she woke and sat bolt upright, her stomach and chest heaving before she could prevent them. The contents of the former splashed into the bucket made ready.

Someone sat up behind her, gathering her hair in a bundle. Then she fell back again once done, sweat beading along her skin, eyes upon the fireplace and the flames, each one blazing like the pain coursing through her.

When she finally woke at dawn, Keira stirred against solid arms once more, her body aching and her eyelids fluttering open. Next to her, his head sharing her pillow – or perhaps it was her sharing his pillow – lay a perfectly familiar stranger.

She had never seen him before, and yet she thought she might have. The lines of his face were much like those on the first day he'd appeared before her. His tousled hair much like the hair he'd had when he plopped down on her bed and agreed to a favour for a favour, only now it was a lighter shade of brown, like the creamiest of caramels. His pale, sun-kissed chest rose with even breaths against her shoulder, and although she felt like they might soon open, his eyes remained closed, his long, dark lashes brushing the tops of his cheeks.

She bit her bottom lip, resting her eyes on his, thinking back to the feel of them against her temple from the night before.

He was not August, like she had thought, and more surprisingly, there was no disappointment following the realisation. Quite the contrary, a small voice pointed out, she possibly felt more at ease than if it had been. She contemplated the panic and resistance she had felt at seeing "August" undress, and the way her body had relaxed once she realised that he was only trying to help. Except it wasn't August who had come to her rescue. It was the djinn.

As if he could feel her gaze upon him, Elijah shifted and woke, the colour of his hair darkening, his jawline changing. Another face, another him. But she could not help but wonder if she had just seen the *real* him. The version of himself that he kept hidden away from others.

'Hey...' he murmured. 'How are you feeling?'

'A bit bruised and battered,' she admitted and winced as she tried to move. She glanced between them, at their close proximity. She was wearing his shirt, the only cover between her body and his. Their legs were entwined, and she could feel his skin, warm and rough, against her own where her stockings did not cover them.

'Did we...' She hesitated, acknowledging the intense throbbing in her pelvic area.

His countenance darkened. 'No. I would never. But someone sure hoped to. I brought you home before they had a chance.' He sat up and pulled his trousers towards him, so abruptly that his absence beside her felt like being tossed into the lake all over again. 'Do you remember who it was? Do you know who would hurt you like that?' he asked, pulling on his trousers, jaw set for war. His eyes gleamed with the intention of murder.

She thought she did. She remembered Miles coming up to her before everything went unclear, and his friend standing behind her. He could easily have slipped some herbs or something into her drink while Miles distracted her. It wasn't unheard of. But it often ended badly enough to shatter someone's life. If there was any truth to her suspicions, she'd been lucky.

Her shudder seemed the only answer Elijah required. 'When I get my hands on them...' he growled and made to stand with the promise of violence in his every movement.

'No—' She grasped his forearm. It was warm and muscular under her touch. Both glanced at her grip. 'No, please,' she said more softly and fell back upon the mattress, exhaustion already making her head swim. 'Stay.'

He hunched down and stroked a lock of hair away from her face.

'Are you certain? They don't deserve to get away with this.'

'They don't...' she whispered, her body shaking with the effort. 'But I don't want to be alone. Please.'

His features softened. 'Fine. But at least let me find you something to eat. Get your strength up.' She nodded in acceptance and this time let him rise, listening as he disappeared into the kitchen.

For the remainder of the day, he hustled and bustled around the house to take care of her. Bringing her food and water, opening the windows for a fresh breath of air, and closing them again before she could catch a chill. Whenever she needed an extra pillow, he was there, and sometimes she even fell asleep to the feel of his fingers stroking through her hair.

She did not empty her stomach again, and by the time night had fallen and the first fire of the evening was lit, her nausea had lifted too. It almost felt like nothing had happened, except for the sense of violation and the fear of what could have happened still churning through her body.

'I thought you'd left me,' she whispered after a while as they sat in silence watching the flames crackle in the fireplace, backs leaning against the sofa behind them. He kept his arm around her, his fingers stroking her shoulder, as if he was afraid that she would collapse without his support. They stilled now, as she spoke, and she nearly regretted it. 'I thought I had done *it* wrong and that you'd never come back.'

'You couldn't have done it wrong, even if you'd tried.'

She sipped her tea, mixing the warmth rushing through her with the warmth of the liquid. A log collapsed in the fire, sending sparks into the chimney.

'Ordering you to stay doesn't really do anything, does it?'

He shook his head. 'No.'

'Where did you go?'

'I was keeping an eye on you.' His gaze flitted to a table where a vase with a single flower sat. The one given to her by the woman at the flower stall. Keira realised now that the woman had not spoken, only gestured, so as not to reveal herself – or himself. 'Then I had to take care of something for myself.'

She did not pry. After everything he had done for her since the night before, she supposed she owed him some privacy. Yet, there was another thought she wanted answers to, something that had poked at the back of her mind when she watched him sleep.

'You were the one who helped me up from the lake, weren't you?'

He nodded. As she knew he would. She'd recalled it over the course of the day. The familiarity of those light brown locks. The line of his chin this morning. She had caught them in her peripheral vision as he helped her up from the lake, but had thought nothing more of it. Until now.

'Then I'm glad of it. That the order did not work. And that you came back.'

'Believe me, it would have been against my own desires not to.' He inclined his head, and his lips parted as if to say something else, yet he did not. Instead, his gaze swept over her mouth, and he fell quiet while the shadows of the flames chased across his face. The air grew warm, but not from the fire. A burn began in her chest and spread across her shoulders, down her stomach, and pooled between her thighs. Her throat went dry, and she would have asked for water except she did not think she could bear the thought of him moving an inch away from her. It was funny, really. If anyone could have seen them sitting like this, it would have been considered an outrage.

The thought brought back an onslaught of memories from the night before. The leering, the whispered words. The judgemental glances and the...

Shame washed over her once again, and she clamped her legs tighter together. What had happened to her...had it happened because of the things she had done? Had it happened because she had given in to her body's desires and acted...promiscuously?

Beside her, Elijah growled. 'If you let those short-sighted, narrow-minded village halfwits hold you down, I'll snap my fingers and erase the whole lot of them.'

Her mouth dropped open. 'You can do that?'

He didn't answer, his jaw clenched and his gaze firm upon the fireplace, leaving it hard to tell whether it was the flames or his ire that burned so fiercely in those eyes of his. Like they'd burned two nights before, when he gave her the first lesson. Like they'd burned when he'd stepped into the tavern to save her. That's what she had seen. Concern for her and a protective promise of retribution warring with one another in a way she'd never seen in August.

She swallowed and watched the flames, feeling heat return to her body, rising up her skin. A boldness, an urge, tickled her spine, and she needed something to be done with it. She glanced to the window and realised the shutters were closed. Had he gone and done so during the night? It did not really matter, she realised. What did, was that no one could see...

'Elijah?'

'Mmhmm?'

'Your next lesson...what would that happen to be?'

'Well,' he started, his next words fading on his breath as he appeared to catch something in her expression. To read her desires like he always seemed to read her. He cleared his throat. 'Well, once you've learned to please yourself, the next lesson would be to...let someone else...pleasure *you*.' He spoke the words tentatively, like someone testing the ice lest they'd plunge through. She *needed* him to plunge.

'How would I go about doing that?'

'You order them to.' There was a rasp to his voice, as if his mouth had gone dry too. Someone would need to wet it.

'Then,' she coaxed, voice barely but a quiver. 'Pleasure me.'

He sat unmovable, searching her face. Perhaps for any sign of uncertainty. Perhaps to halt time so that she could change her mind. She would not.

Instead, she twisted her torso and leaned back against the seat of the chair next to the sofa, her chest heaving above her drumming heart, her pulse thundering in her ears.

'You did say not to let them keep me down, did you not?'

'I did.' He nodded.

'Then, I do not think orders should need to be made twice. Do you?'

She could practically see his shudder and sucked in her lip at the unfamiliar surge of triumph it gave her.

'No, I should think not,' Elijah said breathlessly, before shifting ever so slightly so that he was leaning forwards on his knees rather than sitting. With his eyes locked on hers, he pulled her closest leg towards him and ran his fingers along the edge of her knee-length stockings while his other hand slid underneath her thigh. 'Allow me, then, to start by removing these.'

Bit by bit, his fingers rolled down the soft cotton, her breath quickening with every inch of skin he touched. Once her leg was liberated, he moved on to the other. This time he broke his gaze with her, but only to nuzzle the sensitive skin of her inner thigh with his nose and breath as he pulled down the last stocking. Her own breath hitched in her throat and escaped between her parted lips in shivers.

Then his hand slid underneath the hem of her shirt and hitched at the lines of her undergarments. His eyes locked with hers again, waiting for her order to stop; to remove his fingers from her skin, burning underneath his touch. She would not give it, and he pulled her undergarments down her legs and chucked them aside with her other discarded clothes.

The moment they were gone, Elijah set her legs apart and moved between them, his head levelled with her thighs. Only the gentleman's shirt remained between them, shielding her nakedness from his view.

At once, uncertainty flared through her, and her forehead creased.

He did not miss it.

'A man worthy of you would seek to give you every pleasure he possibly could, but only if you allow him. Do you allow me?'

'But...do you *want* to?' she stuttered, eyes dipping to her pelvic area, unable to keep embarrassment from creeping into her voice.

His forehead smoothed with amazement. 'More than anything else.'

She sucked in a shivering breath and inclined her head, letting the exhale out in an even worse state.

Once again, his hands went down her back and cupped her buttocks, pulling her hips out and forward past the shirt, leaving her entirely exposed to him. And his expression...

His expression set her whole soul aflame.

He licked his lips, eyes gleaming with ravenous need. She swallowed, devouring every inch of his face, every flicker of lust dancing across it, revelling in the feel of his fingertips digging into the crevices of her hips. Relished in his hands kneading her skin, her pelvis top, and the slanted surface of her abdomen, her breathing increasing with every stroke. Finally, as his fingertips reached her nipple, he dipped his head and repeated his act with the ice cream during their promenade by dragging his warm, wet tongue over the outer lips of her opening.

She cried out. Her hands fisted into the mattress. And his tongue kept on moving, kept tasting every inch of her, dampening his mouth with her wetness. Once she felt the edge of his teeth, she bucked, unable to keep the moan from ascending out of her lungs as he proceeded to suckle her softly.

He groaned with and tightened his hold on her.

She was fire. Writhing and coiling against him.

His fingers dug into her flesh while his tongue kept devouring.

She whimpered.

His tongue flicked again and again against her sensitive spot, curving like a finger, coaxing her to come. Coaxing the building pressure to burst through her body.

Just when she thought it would, he pulled away and slid his fingers into her instead. Keira gasped and tensed her body against the violent bolt of pleasure that slammed into her, and her head tipped, exposing her throat. At once his face was beside hers, fisting her hair and pulling her head further back, his lips tasting the slim column of her neck.

'He's a fool to let you go,' Elijah whispered, trailing his tongue featherlight over her skin, kneading her sensitive spot with the heel of his palm. Her body strung tighter, and she groaned with the tension rising in her body, feeling the shivers of pleasure all the way down to her curling toes. 'I'd never. I'd always hunger to give you more, to satisfy this bottomless craving.' He buried his face in the nook of her neck. '*Fates*, even your scent is enough to drive me mad.'

With every move of his fingers inside her, she knew the urge well, but she also felt something else. The hardness of him, pressing against her hip through his trousers. Her eyes opened wide, catching on his, heavy with heat and yearning.

'The things I want to do to you,' he murmured. 'Tell me, Keira. Tell me what you need.'

Her lips parted with a raspy sound slipping past them. 'More.'

At once, he returned to his spot between her legs, and his tongue, torturously slow and steady, elicited one trickling moan and one deep-plunging tremble after the other.

'Saints!' she breathed, digging her nails into the mattress, the table, him – anything she could grab a hold of. She could feel the edge, feel it right there, each quickening roll of his tongue bringing her closer; and one final, torturous swipe pushing her over.

Her cry was soundless as she collapsed onto the pillow, her body convulsing in ripples of pleasure. Tears gathered in the corners of her closed eyes, and she stayed still, as if her mind was struggling to gather its shattered pieces. She could feel him beside her, his breath hard and muffled as if he was laying face down against the mattress, his fingers still tight upon her. She would bruise, but she did not care.

Then he let go and pulled down her shirt, covering her, before he moved up to share the pillow with her. His breath caressed her neck as he whispered, 'Not everyone who can please you will be worthy of you, but anyone who is worthy of you will aspire to please you.'

She turned to him, still half-delirious, scepticism warring against the thought of anyone else doing what he had just done, doubting that anyone else could.

As if he read her mind, Elijah cupped her cheek in his hand and kissed her, long and deep. His tongue swept her mouth in a similar way to what he had just done below, turning her legs to mush.

'I shudder to think what the third lesson is,' Keira whispered once he had let her go and she had managed to catch her breath. The djinn smiled his diabolical smile and stroked her cheek and her neck, resting his fingers against her collarbone and heaving chest. She burned for him to continue further.

'*That* I'll show you when you ask me,' he murmured, 'to break my promise.'

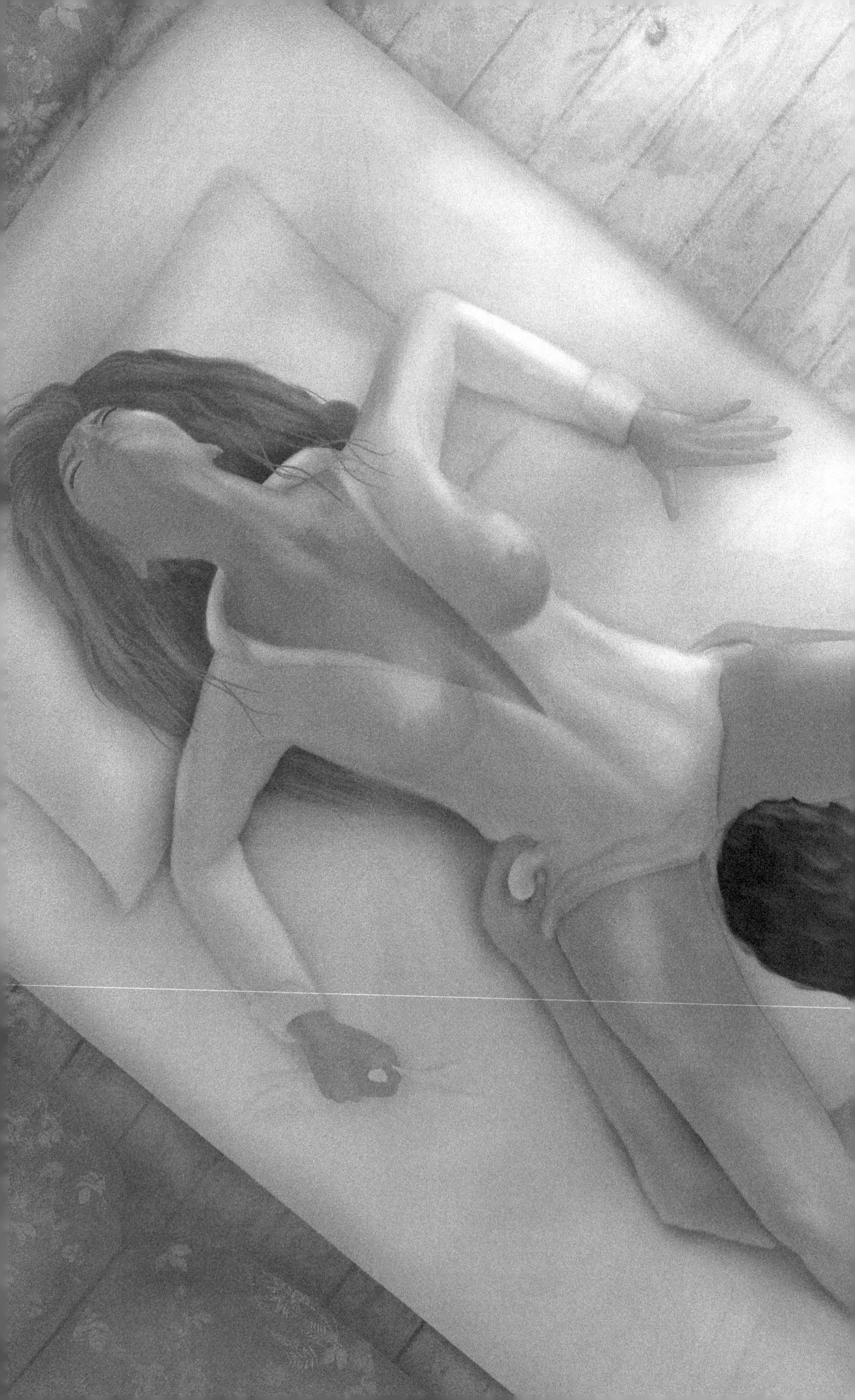

15
PEACHES

'What excellent peaches,' Elijah said, holding up a particularly plump fruit to the sun. The seller turned to him with pride, an expression that rapidly morphed into dumb shock when the djinn spoke next. 'Reminds me of a particularly fine lady's bum I was so lucky to hold in my hands the other night.'

'Come now, *Cousin*, I'm sure Mr. Burton does not want to hear about your escapades!' Keira spluttered loudly, pulling him away from the stall before pushing him down the road, her cheeks burning and ears ringing with Elijah's laugh.

'Oh, I'm quite certain he would have loved to hear all about it. In fact, I'm quite certain the *whole* village would envy me if they did.'

Face entirely aflame, Keira gave him another shove, but could not help the smile stretching her lips, heating her cheeks. She was not so sure they would, but she felt certain the people of E'Frion would have one or two things to say, had they known.

As if she could feel their eyes upon her, she warily glanced at the villagers passing them by and chewed her cheek. Most did not acknowledge them. A few tipped their hats at her. But there were some who watched from the corner of their eyes, murmuring as they passed them by. Her stomach clenched.

'I thought they might talk. After what happened at the tavern. I feel like I can't toss a rock around here without someone judging me for it.'

'That's the small-town mindset for you,' Elijah muttered low, dipping his chin as they passed the baker and his wife out for a stroll. 'There's a whole world, whole realms out there, where society has progressed and evolved.'

'I wish E'Frion would as well,' Keira murmured, pondering what sort of realms – what sort of worlds – Elijah would have seen, wishing she could have seen them with him.

'I'm rather surprised at how little it has. Theveserin used to be more fashionable, even here. It's almost like the realm has reverted in time and become more reserved... Like England, back when Queen Victoria came to the throne after George the Fourth.'

'Who are they? What's "England"?' Keira mused, scrunching up her nose. Elijah's lips twitched and he looked for a moment as if he would lean down and kiss her for it. Her heart skipped a beat at the thought.

'I'll take you there someday, if you'd like,' he grinned, offering her his arm instead. She took it, wrapping herself against his side.

'Gladly.' Keira scoffed a laugh, ruefully certain in the knowledge she would never be able to leave E'Frion. 'Let's leave straight away, shall we?' She beamed up at him but found that his own smile had faded.

'As soon as I get my affairs in order,' he murmured, gaze travelling past the village, towards Faerie.

Towards the Spring Queen.

Her mind flashed to a conversation they'd had after the second lesson, when they had talked about how they were once again even with who had saved whom, and he had assured her that she would probably get a new chance at saving him from the Queen of Faerie again soon enough.

'Why are you indebted to her anyway?' she had asked, her fingers fiddling with Elijah's as they lay upon his mattress. They'd been talking long into the night after her second lesson, her body curled into his with the fire crackling.

'I made a mistake once...it ended up costing us both, dearly,' Elijah whispered, looking at her as if he'd rather not say more. There was a shame there which made her chew her lip, recognising it, and she recalled how quickly he had agreed to help her when she spoke of her own mistakes. Knowing a thing or two about regret, Keira had chosen not to prod further, but she kind of wished that she had now, her mind running loose with the possibilities.

Had the Queen of Faerie done him a favour of any kind? Had they been involved? Keira hadn't thought that she would care, but the squirming worm inside her told her that she did.

'You alright?' Elijah asked, assessing her expression.

'Yes.' Keira huffed a breath, attempting and failing at seeming upbeat. 'I think I've rather had enough of this walk, though. I'd much prefer to go back to the cottage and—'

She stopped herself, but when she dared a glance at the djinn, his eyes had already gone molten.

They had barely left the house for two days since the night at the tavern; days spent talking and practicing, passing them by with the moon and sun both. She'd experimented by herself, he'd helped her discover more things that she liked, and one time she'd even demonstrated what she had learned – with him as her audience. The way he had looked at her alone had been enough to make her come, and she'd had to bite her lip not to invite him to join her.

Keira swallowed.

Around them, the birds sang within the trees, and her heart fluttered with them.

Elijah had been right.

She had already caught herself wishing, not once, but twice that she hadn't made him promise not to take her body; all of it aching to learn lesson number three. But she'd asked it for a reason, she reminded herself. However, much fun she was having with Elijah, he was still a djinn and August was human. What they had was still a bargain, an arrangement, while August and Thornfell were her future. And her body was to be his when they married. At least *that* was something she could still offer, however deep into the rabbit hole of debaucheries she had otherwise fallen.

Still, as she looked up and saw that their feet had carried them back to the cottage, her core throbbed with the same anticipation and impatience it had done in the morning, when she'd urgently suggested they would take a day to stroll about the town. To distract herself from jumping the djinn.

'Pray say,' Elijah said as they reached the door, turning to her with a purr in his voice that curled her toes. 'Should we have another session tonight? Just to make sure you haven't forgotten anything during this day of abstinence?'

Heat flooded her body, sending goosebumps along her skin and a drought down her throat, stealing her words. In her mind, they were already before the hearth, breathless, heaving...naked.

As if he knew, the playful gleam in Elijah's eyes – green for the day – rested upon her, until they shifted above her shoulder and darkened.

She turned, seeing August approach, walking through the gate of her white picket fence.

'Keira,' he greeted her, casting a glance at Elijah. 'May I have a word with you, in private?'

She turned to the djinn, catching in his gaze a caution – a message – she could not quite read. She frowned and the look disappeared. Inclining his head to the both of them, Elijah withdrew into the cottage and Keira turned back to August. He was still observing the retreating djinn, a look of contemplation marring his polished face.

'Did your relative not have brown eyes the other day?'

Her heart skipped a beat. 'I wouldn't think so, considering they are green,' she said quickly, then added, 'Where's Gianna?'

To her surprise, he seemed to shrink a little under the bite in her voice. 'She's not with me. She will not *be* with me anymore.'

Keira's brows rose. 'What do you mean?'

'Apparently, people saw me taking you home the other night...' Once more, his eyes flickered to the cottage behind her. 'And it's caused a lot of problems with Gianna's parents.'

Keira stilled. She had not even considered that others would have seen Elijah taking her home looking like August. Nor had she thought about the fact that August himself would know that he had not. Judging by the look in his eyes, it had already roused his suspicion that something was off, although she could tell that he did not quite know what yet. Should she tell him the truth? No. August had thought less of her after what little *they'd* done. She could not stand the thought of his reaction if he ever learned what she had done with *Elijah*. Besides, the hostility in his eyes would be little compared to what she would see if he learned what Elijah truly was, to how the whole village would react at the realisation of having a djinn amongst them. Despite being a pain in her "peachy" behind, Elijah did not deserve their wrath if they did.

'That's odd,' Keira said, a little too lightly, feigning her ignorance. 'Someone must have misunderstood. Have you told them it's not true?'

'To be frank, I drank a little too much and was out cold that night, so I couldn't be certain. Besides, it led to the story about what you—about what we did, umm, that day, being brought to their attention.'

She swallowed. If the whole town now knew what had happened between her and August in that fisherman's hut, it was a done deal. Both their reputations were certainly ruined forever. Not just amongst August's inner circle, but throughout the whole village. Suddenly, the many eyes she had felt upon her as she and Elijah walked through town had a whole new meaning. And if someone saw her speaking to August, it would only be a confirmation of what they now believed to be true.

'I should go inside,' Keira stuttered, and made to turn.

'Gianna's parents broke the engagement.'

She stilled.

'And Mother thinks you and I should...' He came closer, reaching for her. 'Come together. To save both our reputations.'

'How romantic,' Keira snapped, jerking her hand away from him.

'Come now, Keira,' August murmured, trying anew and pulling her closer to him, enveloping her in his scent of leather and rosewater. 'You know you've always been the one. Mother would not permit it before. They forced me to court Gianna. But now, now we are free to be together.' His features softened to that same imploring expression he had worn in the hut that day. It tugged at something within her, and yet there was a resistance holding her back. She turned to the cottage, but there was no sign of Elijah watching them from the windows. She turned back to August, his smile having hardened ever so slightly.

'Don't make your mind up yet. Come for a dinner with me. Yes?' His brows slanted.

Swallowing, Keira found herself nodding. 'Okay. One dinner.'

His lips lit up into a grin. 'Excellent!' Putting his hands in her hair, he planted a kiss on her forehead, but he did not step aside after. 'I implore you to remember, Keira,' he added in a whisper. 'You can have everything you ever wanted now. Me...Thornfell.' His nose brushed down her temple until his lips were placed over her ear. 'Imagine what we could do in that large house, you and I.' His thumb pulled down on her lip, leaving salt on her tongue. 'More of what we did in that small hut.' He winked at her.

She almost gagged, which wasn't really the reaction she had expected. Rather than the familiar flutter of butterflies, it felt like her guts filled with squirming worms. She watched him leave before returning to the cottage, her swarming thoughts brewing up a storm.

In the kitchen, Elijah leaned against the countertop, turning a peach in his hand.

She eyed the fruit and felt the familiar flutter of wings and pounding of yearning in her body. She did not know when he had taken the fruit, much like she did not know when he had taken some of her affections for August. It made her bristle. 'Ought you not to have paid for that?'

'Ought you not to have made *him* pay for what he did to you?' asked Elijah, taking a bite, turning the fruit over with his tongue. She felt her own mouth water.

'That is none of your business.'

Elijah scoffed, anger flaming his already apparent irritation.

'It's only a dinner, what do you care? This is what we've been working towards!'

He kicked off the bench and strode up to her, cloaking her in his shadow. 'This is not—' he started, but then caught himself. His muscles tensed at their close proximity and his breathing raced with hers. She could have sworn she heard his heart galloping in his chest, their heaving moans from nights past echoing in the quiet room.

'Fine,' he snapped, bringing the fruit to his lips again. He nibbled it slightly and ripped some of its flesh with his teeth. Juice coated his lip, beckoning her to lean forward and lick it off. She could not take her eyes off him. 'Enjoy your dinner.' He stepped aside, leaving a cold space of air.

But she was not going to let him off that easily. 'I don't understand you. You should be relieved.'

'Ecstatic.' Elijah shrugged, clenching his jaw.

'Your end of the bargain is practically over!'

'And you'll be owing me a favour,' he said, sauntering into the living room, before he turned back on her, holding out his fruit. 'That said, should you not find dinner to your liking, you know where to come for dessert.' He winked and took another bite. 'I'll even serve it to you for free.' Then he tossed himself onto his mattress and out of view.

Groaning, Keira rushed upstairs and slammed the bathroom door closed, throwing herself upon the edge of the bathtub to grumble.

No sooner had she sat down though, before her eyes slid over the porcelain object and her mind wandered to an image of her and Elijah in it together, naked and wet, surrounded by foam. Her on top of him, rolling her hips like she did when she went riding, and his head leaned backwards, lips parted, moaning her name.

She cried out and leaped off the tub, shattering the illusion in the progress.

Panting against the ebbs and flows of desire coursing through her body, she grabbed the sink and stared at herself in the mirror, her pupils dilated, nearly erasing all the golden-grey of her irises.

What was happening to her? Was she falling in love with Elijah? No, it couldn't be. She loved August, always had. Always would. Had the djinn put a spell on her? She had to admit, after all this time, she still knew very little about how the djinn's magic worked or even about the djinn himself. But would Elijah do that to her? She doubted it. She...trusted...that he hadn't.

Finally, Keira remembered what Isolde had said. How sometimes, one would fall in love with the idea of a person, rather than the person himself. *That's what's happening,* Keira sighed. She was smitten by Elijah; yes, she could admit that, but it was only the idea of him she enjoyed. The idea of the pleasure that she had already come to associate him with. It was merely a feeling she was drawn to, not the djinn himself. There was no future with a djinn, like there was with August. No chance for that life with a happy, quaint family she had decided upon for herself. There was only lust. And once she knew what to do, once she got a grip on all his *lessons,* the bodily experience would be exactly the same with August.

As she kept telling herself these words, her pulse slowed and her breathing steadied, and she had almost managed to collect herself when Elijah's voice rose from the floor below.

'If you'd like to do something with that pent up frustration of yours, we could always change the dessert into an appetiser!'

16

LIES SERVED

Despite his evident annoyance with her, Elijah offered to walk her to the tavern and would not hear a word of her objections assuring him that she was perfectly capable of walking the short stretch by herself.

'It's not *that* long since someone tried to take advantage of you while you were on your own,' Elijah said. 'I'll walk you.'

And that was the last he said of it, as they both strolled into the village in silence, him seemingly lost to his own thoughts, her seething with the things she wanted to say and wished he would say with equal measure. Yet, none of them were said by the time they reached the tavern.

'Here we are then,' Elijah said, pausing before the building, looking at it as if he could see through its walls. Warm light and laughter sifted through the iron-gated windows. Keira stared at it, thinking of the night she last found herself here, her hands clammy at the thought of going back in.

'How come you saved me looking like August that night?'

He shrugged. 'Thought you'd be more inclined to come with

me,' he said at last and kicked a pebble, turning to face the direction they had come from, the trees' shadows already cloaking most of it in darkness. Guilt churned in her stomach, but she wasn't exactly sure why. Only that she hated seeing him like this.

'Are you alright?' Keira asked, fidgeting with her sleeve.

'Peachy,' Elijah said, his jaw clenching.

She scoffed a breath, frustration rising. 'Fine, well, I better go inside so that he doesn't think I stood him up.'

'Wait—'

Before she realised what he was doing, he'd grabbed her, pulled her into the shadows, and pushed her up against the tavern wall.

'Elijah!'

'I just want to remind you of what you deserve,' he whispered. Slowly, his hand reached up to caress her face, tucking a lock of hair behind her ear. 'Make him work for it. Make sure he makes you feel like you're a goddess walking upon this earth before you ever take him like that again. Make sure he makes you feel like this...' He leaned in, catching her mouth with his. She stilled, her breath caught as their lips locked and their tongues moved, causing her heart to hammer through her chest. If someone walked by...if someone spotted them... She couldn't find the strength to care. Couldn't find the will to focus on anything but the way he made her world spin off its axis, filling it with need. Tempting her to have him and take him right then and there.

And when he pulled away, it was like a rug had been pulled from underneath her feet.

Just like before, he looked like he wanted to say something more, but then his expression changed, as if he'd given up on the thought. 'I'll see you at home,' he murmured instead, then turned and walked away into the night. Leaving her breathless and yearning for more by the side of the tavern.

Groaning, Keira rolled her eyes and went inside, trying and failing not to turn around and look after him. Hoping he would turn and look back after her. Yet, as the door swung shut, he did not, and she continued into the tavern on her own. August, however, was nowhere to be seen.

Remembering what kind of rumours were going around about them – rumours that had reached Gianna's parents – Keira refrained from asking Mr Meroni whether he had seen him. Instead, she picked a table and hoped that he would show sooner rather than later.

The more time ticked by, the more Keira was left feeling a fool. A few other people were having their dinner at the tavern, and she could feel their glances wandering over to her table. Her skin crawled and she pulled her shawl closer around herself, fighting the urge to run out of there. Perhaps she should. Perhaps she could even catch up with Elijah, tell him what a big mistake it had been to go.

She hid her face in her hands. *Elijah.*

Every part of her ached.

Not with hurt because August hadn't shown, but with longing. Longing to be with the djinn again, and it confused her. No matter how many times she looked at the menu or spun her spoon between her fingers to distract herself, she was unable to think of anything else. Her mind kept returning to the cottage. To him.

It was ridiculous.

And yet...

In one swift motion, Keira rose from her chair, the scraping of its wooden legs against the stone floor catching several patrons' attention. Awkwardly, she tried to smile her apologies, but the smile quickly became strained as the door opened and August strode in. Now everyone's attention turned raptly upon them.

'Keira, darling!' August exclaimed as he rushed towards her

and took her hands, kissing both of her cheeks. They burned after, not from the kisses, but rather from the glares around them: from Mr Meroni's scowling expression at the back of her neck, from patrons whose mouths had dropped open. It did not matter what she and August were to one another: to the village they were now as good as coupled up. Once again, it made her feel trapped and not at all as excited as she had expected to feel.

'I'm so sorry I'm late,' August said, beckoning her to sit down before ordering the best meal and drinks the house had to offer from the waitress. 'I lost track of the time hunting.'

Keira blinked. She had expected him to talk about Gianna or, at least, everything else that had come to pass since the first day of the hunt, but as he launched into recounting his wild chase through the woods, she soon came to realise that he wanted to draw a line over it all and pretend like it had never happened. At least for now. She guessed she could try to do that too. *For now.* But could she ever draw a line over Elijah?

'It was the most gigantic stag I've ever seen,' August said, taking a sip of his ale before he continued. 'Could've been the emperor himself, I tell you. Unfortunately, I lost him. By the time I realised, I'd become quite lost. I don't think I've ever been in those parts of the woods before. After a bit of wandering though, trying to make my way back here to you, I stumbled across the ruins. It was much easier finding my way after that. Have you ever been? To the ruins, I mean?'

'Hm? Oh, yes. I played there...as a child.'

'You don't say,' August murmured and arched a brow, his golden eyes intense across the table. He cut his meat and chewed it slowly, watching her with interest. It made her stomach curl, and she could not fathom why. Why he caused such a reaction in her now, when one such look from him before had been enough to make her heart sing.

'I've never been inside the ruins themselves. Have you?'

She nodded, repeating what she'd once tried to tell Elijah. Before the fae had taken him. 'Plenty. It looks worse on the outside than it does inside. Some of the furniture is still there... Old beds and vanity mirrors. I found what looked like an apothecary in the dungeon once. Glasses filled with herbs and potions.'

She had imagined Isolde would have loved it, but she had kept it a secret while practicing witchcraft to see if she too could become a witch. She remembered it now.

Aside from her fast healing that had made her rather adventurous and reckless, sometimes, as a child, she had made the occasional odd thing happen. A flame to grow in size or spiral out of control over here, a pinecone and stick figure to animate and walk over there. Somehow, she'd outgrown it all though, until the incidents were mere faded memories, having chalked them up to a wild imagination, and slowly accepted that a future as a witch wasn't in the cards for her.

'The royal baths are also still there,' she said after some thought, picturing the empty pools in her mind. 'They're massive. If the village decided to chip in and fix it up, I'm certain it would have made quite the public bath.'

'How astonishing!' August hit the table. 'You are much braver than I thought, Keira.'

She frowned yet smiled. 'I was. When my mother and father were alive. They always used to say I was a bit on the wild side. My nan said I had a spirit in me that could not be tamed.' Her voice faded, thinking of Elijah's words. *'You're like a predator hunting for her prey, and you don't even realise that they have taken your claws and made you into their pet.'*

When did she stop being fearless? When did she stop roaming the woods and start caring one too many times of what other people thought?

'Your mother and father, were they from here?'

She frowned. 'No, we moved here when I was young. You know this.'

'Yes, but I mean, do you know their heritage?'

She shrugged. 'Mother could have descended from the Winter court I suppose, but father definitely descended from the Summer court.' His heritage was the one that had given her the warm colouring of her skin and the dark, exotic look of her facial features, and the curves to her hips. Her gaze locked with August. 'How is your mother dealing with the thought of having a *mixed breed* ruin your lineage?' She didn't know the truth precisely, but Mrs Thornfell would brag to everyone who would listen that they had descended from royals.

'You let me worry about her.'

But she had done that before, and he had done nothing when his mother had made a move. What if his mother suddenly changed her mind again? What if the Meronis changed their minds? Would he leave her once more?

She realised then looking at him – at the ease of which he sat and enjoyed their food, not even in a rush to apologise for what he had put her through like it did not matter – that it actually did not. It did not matter whether his mother or the Meronis changed their minds, or even if he did.

It did not matter...because she could not stand looking at him.

Could not stand how everything was always about him and his needs, and that he had never once cared about hers. That he had not checked up on her, taken care of her, or comforted her after everything *his* need for her to pleasure him had put her through.

It did not matter what *he* would choose or do.

The only thing that mattered was that she had doubts, that she no longer trusted him. There were no longer enough reasons –

Thornfell Manor or no Thornfell Manor – for her to choose him when…when she had begun to find trust and comfort with someone else. Someone who had given plenty of signs that he would choose her if she asked him to.

Elijah.

She rose, taking him by surprise.

'I'm sorry, August. I can no longer accept your hand in marriage.'

He gaped at her. 'What?'

'I'm not okay with what you did. What you allowed others to do. I no longer trust you, and quite frankly, I no longer even like you.' She tossed her napkin on the table. 'I wish you well.'

Before he could protest or call after her, she rushed out of the tavern, exhilaration fluttering in her chest, pumping triumph and excitement through her veins.

She was moving on. It was a relief. A relief unlike all others, to let go of what she had – up until now, she realised – forced herself into believing she wanted. Perhaps Isolde had been right all along. Perhaps she'd never loved *August,* but the idea of him. Perhaps she was truly seeing him for the first time, and in doing so, she was seeing someone else more clearly.

She knew now that no house, no traditional security, could hold a candle to what she was starting to feel when she was with Elijah. To the possibilities, the freedom and empowerment, unfolding before her instead.

Her feet paused on the crossroad. One path would lead to the woods, the other to her cottage. She wanted to tell him. Yearned for it. Yearned for his reaction and what could happen between them after. Yet, something held her back. A small inkling of doubt still.

He'd given her signs, of that, she felt certain. Signs that he would choose her. That he wanted to be with her. But she had been wrong before and August had even said those things outright.

Perhaps Elijah saw her as nothing but a friend. A maiden he'd struck a deal with. She had pretended to be indifferent to him for so long that perhaps it was what he expected. Perhaps he would pull away once he learned that she wanted *more* with him, and she didn't know how to know for certain. Except...

There was one person who could give her advice on what to do next, the only one who knew her better than herself; the one who'd already caught her going astray once.

Turning her nose towards the forest, Keira made haste towards the territory of the Woodland Witches. Even if Isolde had no advice about the djinn, Keira could, at the very least, trust her to celebrate that she was ready to move on from August. Perhaps she would kick up a feast, and Keira would drink and dance wildly and loosely with the witches all night, only to return empowered and ravishing by Elijah's bedside in the morning, brimming with courage. She was of no doubt that he would use her absence as an excuse to steal her bed, and if he had – her lips twitched – she would join him in it. But not before she had undressed before him. Not before she had put his hands upon her naked body, guiding them to where she wanted them.

The very idea almost made her turn on her heels and head back to the cottage immediately, but the appearance of several small octagonal huts stayed her course, and she made her way between the moss-covered stone walls towards Isolde's cottage.

No one was home as she entered, but Keira helped herself inside like she always did. She had come and gone plenty a time, and Isolde had made it clear ever since they'd first met that her home was Keira's and that she was welcome anytime she liked. Even if it meant Isolde would return from full moon rituals to find Keira sleeping in her bed.

Casting her eyes upon the pantry, Keira felt her stomach growl – she had not touched the food August had ordered at all – and hastily made herself a meal. Isolde's pantry was always full of the most delicious meats and cheeses, bread, cakes, butter, and, of course, caskets upon caskets of wine. Screw propriety to the wind – if she was continuing down the road of debauchery, she might as well go all the way.

Grabbing a bottle of wine with one hand, Keira broke off a piece of cheese with the other and nibbled on it while scurrying around for all the things she wanted to put together. Once her arms were nearly full, she decided to pull the curtain aside and see if she could spot Isolde through the window.

But there was no window on the other side.

Instead, there was a portrait, its frame so rich it would have made more sense to be found in a palace rather than a small witch's hut. Seven silhouettes could be seen underneath the dust-covered surface, and Keira hoisted down the portrait and brought it out into the main cottage space for a better look at it.

Premonition tingled in goosebumps down her skin as she brushed aside the dust, her eyes immediately catching on a familiar face framed with creamy brown hair, perfectly combed and split down the middle. *Elijah.*

Next to six other divine people.

One looked arrogantly lazy but handsome. A second scowled from the back. The third, in the middle, was sat leisurely on a throne, his haughty chin resting on his hand. The next two's wickedly cruel countenances were worse than the others. And then the last one was a devastatingly familiar woman.

'Try the scrying mirror once more, Makenna,' Isolde called over her shoulder as she entered her hut, then paused at seeing her visitor. Lastly, her eyes fell upon the portrait in her hands.

'Keira, what...are you doing here?'

'I came to talk to you about Elijah...' Keira murmured, her voice shaking. 'I wasn't sure if there was much you could tell me, but...it seems you know him pretty well, don't you?' She pointed, first at the man in the photo looking so much like the man that had pulled her up from the lake, then at the brown-skinned female. 'This is you? You're one of the Cardinal Seven?'

Isolde closed the door behind her, shadows falling over her eyes. 'Yes.'

17
LADY INDULGENCE

'Elijah is my brother, Elnatan,' Isolde said, helping herself to a bottle of wine, pouring a glassful. 'Or as close to a brother as anyone can get, I suppose.'

Elnatan. Keira knew that name. Knew it from the legends and what it meant. '*Gift of the Gods?*'

'The one who keeps on giving.' Isolde rolled her eyes. 'At least he thinks so himself. The personification of lust and yearning,' she drawled and downed her glass. 'The panty dropper of many a young lady.' She turned to Keira with a glint in her eyes. 'You know a little something about that yourself already, don't you?'

Keira's cheeks turned aflame. Her mind was already reeling against this piece of information, racing a million miles an hour with what it would mean – what it possibly said about her feelings for Elijah and the effect he had on her – but she forced herself to focus. She could fall apart later when she had more answers. 'And you? Who are you?'

Isolde draped herself over her divan, pulling a plate of cured meats and cheese towards her while swirling the content of her second glass. 'Can't you guess?'

Now that she thought about it, Keira could not help but think of all the time she had seen Isolde indulge in her food, her wine, her women and, on a few occasions, men. Even in a cottage that to the ignorant eye seemed so small and earthy, it was everything that Isolde thrived in. Nature. Comfort. Seclusion. 'You're the Djinn of Gluttony?'

'I prefer indulgence,' Isolde said with a wry smile. 'But yes, my real name is Gale.'

G, Keira realised. The person Elijah had thought her to be when they first met. Even then, he knew Isolde as someone she did not. Did that mean Isolde had always been Gale, or had Gale been posing as her? Had her real friend been made away with?

'Are you the *real* Isolde?'

The Djinn of Indulgence tilted her head contemplatively. 'Yes and no. There was a woman of my line who looked like me and who bore the name Isolde. However, she died of natural causes many years ago, and Echo, her lover at the time, let me take on her identity. As for the Isolde you have known, yes. I am her.'

'Why? Why hide who you are?'

'Would you have trusted me if not? You who knew the legends even before I came into your life? You, who were warned away from djinns since the day you were born? Warned by your dear nana. Courtesy of me, ironically...'

Keira clenched her teeth together. She *had* been warned, but what good had it done? She had trusted Elijah easily enough, albeit she had been desperate, and...Isolde's stories, she realised, had softened her mind towards djinns bit by bit over the years. Romanticising them down to genies and wish-fulfillers. And at her core, she had decided to believe just that. She had been but a child still when she met Isolde, but apparently, she'd been a wiser child than she was now as an adult. She would, as Isolde said, have been more distrustful of Elijah with her nan's warning loud and clear in the back of her mind, rather than a faded memory.

'I didn't think so,' Isolde said and emptied her glass, taking her next sip directly from the bottle.

'I don't understand. I thought all of you were made away with during the siege.'

Isolde's eyes grew distant. 'Most of us were, the good with the bad. Imprisoned in different vessels and spread across the realm. In cold mountain crevices. At the bottoms of lakes. But people are always drawn to the magic of the djinns, hungry for power, thirsty for affection – so many of them were eventually let out and put to service, fulfilling wishes. Wish fulfilment that surely led to misery and death for those stupid enough to let out the worst of my "siblings."

'For years, I searched and hunted after them, determined to bind them and place them back where they belonged, where they could hurt no one – or no one else. All but Elnatan. He found me not long ago, searching for… Then I bound him too. Until you took him.'

'You should have told me,' Keira muttered, hurt seeping into her voice.

'I don't owe you my past, Keira,' Isolde said curtly. 'My secrets are mine to reveal when I'm ready, and in this case, it was safer that you didn't know.'

Keira's voice pitched with bewilderment. 'Safer? Safer how?'

Isolde settled her eyes on the portrait and sighed, her look growing misty and distant. 'I'll have to start at the beginning for it all to make sense.'

Keira merely raised a brow expectantly, beckoning her on.

'As the story goes, our court of vices presided over the emperor's occupied lands a hundred years ago. At least, until Helena came.'

'Saint Helena,' whispered Keira.

Isolde nodded absentmindedly. 'A mere mortal at the time, and still powerful enough to make three ancient spirits fall at her feet. Maybe even more of us, although I cannot speak for the rest.'

Keira looked up at Isolde absentmindedly sipping her glass. '*You* loved her.'

'My brothers and me both.' Her eyes flickered to Keira, and it dawned upon her what Isolde was saying. Brother*s*. Plural.

Her face went cold. Her lips numb. 'Elijah loved her too.'

Isolde took another swig and let the liquid roll in her mouth before she swallowed and spoke again. 'She was sent, you know, to make our house crumble from within. Little did our enemies know that we were already a house in tatters. That the family bond so highly spoken of was neither tied by blood nor loyalty. And yet, she was blamed for coming between us.

'Elnatan did everything in his power to stop it when our "brother" Aeros ordered her execution after learning of her duplicity. He went as far as opening the gates for the rebels, bringing our downfall upon us all. Yet Aeros escaped, cursed out of his own body. It was a bigger hit to his pride than death would have been.'

'And you? Why weren't you bound to a vessel like the others?'

'*I* betrayed *her*.' Isolde fixed her hardened glance on Keira. 'It was the only way to save the child.'

'The—the child?' Keira felt sick. She did not know how Isolde had betrayed Helena, but by the tone of her voice, she did not want to hear about it. Not if it meant Isolde had caused another woman's death.

Isolde tapped her glass with her nail. 'While they were still in love, Aeros and Helena conceived a child. Before Elnatan's desperate actions to save her mother, I stole into the night with the babe and took her far away. I watched her grow until I was called away to find my siblings. I thought I left her in trusted hands, but I lost track of her and the generations that followed. Your dear "Grandmama" did not.'

'My nan?'

'Back then, everyone knew about the child. The Winter Court, who came out victorious from the war, educated their youths and turned her bloodline into a myth. The last legacy of Helena, the key to the emperor's return. Guilds were raised to find and protect her and her descendants. Guilds were raised to hunt and kill them. The woman who called herself your nan was a Guild-leader of the former. Your "parents" were members of it.'

Keira shook her head, the weight of what Isolde was saying dawning upon her.

'Are you saying...'

'They weren't your real parents,' Isolde said and rose, stalking towards Keira. 'Nor was your grandmother your family by blood. They were guardians, tasked to keep safe the last descendant of the Tyrant Emperor. Tasked to keep *you* away from the ones that hunted you.' She towered over her now. Dark and looming. 'And they failed.'

'Failed?' Keira whispered, and suddenly she wasn't all too sure whether Isolde was the Isolde she'd known no matter what she'd said. 'Did *you* kill my family?'

Isolde's glare turned frosty. 'If you truly thought I could, you'd already be out that door.' She beckoned behind Keira, then turned on her heel and paced the small space, moving from one end to the other in four strides. 'No, I did not kill your guardians.'

'Then who did?'

Isolde straightened, back still turned to her. 'My sister Wren, the Djinn of Wrath and Vengeance, before I managed to cast a spell and entrap her with the others.'

'Why? Why would she do that?'

'I don't know,' Isolde muttered, gazing back at her. Her thick, auburn hair fell over her brown shoulder. 'There's only one person who can answer that, save for my sister herself.'

'And who is that?'

Isolde swallowed. 'She who sent her. The Spring Queen.'

18

INTO FAERIE

She did not know how much time passed as she sat in Isolde's hut, absorbing all the new information. At one point, she vaguely registered that Makenna stepped into the hut, looking confused at the tension between the two inside it, and stumbled back out again as Isolde beckoned for her to give them some privacy.

Isolde, who was the Djinn of Indulgence, one of the Cardinal Seven...just like Elijah. The Djinn of Lust.

Her stomach tightened. No wonder Elijah had such an effect on her. Had it been real? Had any of her feelings towards him been real?

The very uncertainty filled her with a need to scream and rage and cry, but instead she was merely numb, unable to do any of those things.

'You should have told me,' she whispered after a while, then added before Isolde could repeat her former excuse, 'You should have told me about Elijah.'

'I *did* tell you not to take the lamp,' Isolde started, but Keira cut her off.

'Don't give me that! You should have *told* me who he was. I let him into my home, my life, my—' *Bed*. Keira shut her mouth, core burning. Even now she longed to return to him and be with him. Was that part of the spell? Would it wear off and leave her cold and empty once he lost his interest in her?

At least Isolde had the decency to look ashamed. 'I didn't know how to explain without having to explain everything and put you at risk. Besides...' She hesitated, chewing at her bottom lip. 'A small part of me hoped that Elijah would be what you needed to get over August.'

This hit Keira like a ton of bricks. Not because it surprised her, but because it had come to pass, and a moment ago, she had been happy about it.

'He was,' she whispered. 'That's what I came to tell you. But now...' Now she did not even know if her feelings for August had truly changed, or if they had simply been meddled with.

'Do you think he knew? What your sister did to my family?'

Isolde shrugged. 'I'm not sure. He told me in passing that he'd ran into your nan once. She chased him off the porch with a rolling pin. It was how I knew where to find you.'

During any other circumstances, Keira might have laughed at the visual of her grandmother chasing Elijah from their home, but now it only filled her with more apprehensions, reminding her how much he had kept from her. He never told her that, and yet he must have known. Must have seen the family portraits in her cottage.

Isolde sighed and rose from her seat, moving to put a hand on Keira's shoulder. 'Talk with him, Keira. And if all else fails, now that you know the truth, let it set you free. The guilt of losing your parents has kept you tied to this place, but it doesn't need to anymore. You were merely kept here, but you don't *belong* here.'

Downcast and exhausted, Keira simply nodded and bid her goodbye, yet as she trudged on in the darkness, the path before her swayed as she made her way back to E'Frion.

Her family wasn't her family, Isolde had kept secrets, and Elijah was more than he had ever let on.

Oddly enough, it was the last of the three that bothered her. Her family had *still* been the ones to raise her, Isolde had always been private, but Elijah...

Part of her wanted to return to him and have him explain everything. Had he used his magic on her or not? Had he been involved in her family's murder? The other part longed to know as well, but also to hear him say that her feelings were real. That what had grown between them was not false, and that she was safe with him. Then she would forgive his secrecy.

But how would she even know what was real?

How would she know that he would tell her the truth and not use his influence all over again, if that was what he'd been doing all along?

She had not even known that her own family had been false. She had not even known who she was.

The last descendant of the Tyrant Emperor. Wanted by the Spring Queen.

The Spring Queen.

Keira paused as she reached the stables, her mind racing a mile an hour.

The Spring Queen held the key. She was the one that sat with all the answers. She was the one who wanted both her *and* Elijah, assuming that was why she'd sent the Djinn of Wrath after Keira's family. What if she sent someone new for Keira? But if she beat the Queen to it and went to Faerie on her own…the Queen might tell her everything she needed to know. Perhaps, if she played her cards right, Keira might even make the Queen of Faerie spill Elijah's secrets too.

Yes, that was what she would do. She would go to Faerie, discover the truth for herself, and then know what to do with the djinn.

It was a simple plan. Easy. What else was there to do? Go home, be the fool, and be played like a fiddle all over again? No, she could not stand the idea. And so, she changed course for the stables without a second thought.

Okay, maybe she should have thought twice about it.

With her teeth chattering and her stomach growling, Keira cursed her impulsivity, realising that she was nowhere close to prepared for the journey, having abandoned both her second platter of food that evening and proper clothing back at E'Frion.

But her anger kept her warm. Her anger had simmered and caught fire on the way, turning some of her hunger into rage, giving her stomach and mind plenty to work through.

There'd been many an opportunity for Elijah to tell her the truth. When he first introduced himself, when they spoke of the Tyrant Emperor and his demise. When he spoke of his family—

She mentally facepalmed herself.

'I once had a rather large family,' he'd said, followed by a sob story she'd so readily believed. Had he known? Had he known that she was the emperor's heir? Had he known what happened to her family even then?

The more she thought about it, the more questions popped into her mind, like a can of worm, making her insides squirm. Just like thinking of her and August did.

Why couldn't anyone be honest with her? Why was she always left in the dark, looking the fool?

Angrily, she dried a tear off her cheek and corrected her grip on her reins – then brought the horse to a pause. Ahead of them towered a tall wall made of roots and wild forestry, tightly braided so as not to let anything through.

The Faerie border.

Dismounting, Keira stared between the horse and the wall.

'Well, I can't very well bring you through there, can I?' she murmured, patting the horse's nose thoughtfully. In response, he blew warm air through his nostrils, warming her frozen fingers. 'And I can't just leave you here either.' What if he became prey to the fae? She turned and gazed in the direction they had come. There had been an inn on the way, but it was much closer to E'Frion than the Faerie border – and she would rather not turn back around, now that she had come so far.

'Horses have an incredible sense of direction,' her father had once said. *'If you get lost hunting, let your horse lead the way, and you'll find your way home again.'*

Chewing her cheek, Keira contemplated her options one final time while the autumn chill settled into her bones. Then she fastened the reins to the saddle so that they would not slip and trip the horse as it walked. At last, she unclasped her cape from her shoulders.

'It's not much, but maybe it will keep you warm until you reach E'Frion,' she said, and fastened the cape around the horse's neck. She shushed it off, but he only stared dumbfoundedly at her – and she couldn't blame it.

Sighing, Keira turned the horse around and clicked her tongue, smacking his flank. It made him startle forward, but it wasn't until she clapped her hands and chased him on that he began to trot away from her and towards E'Frion.

Finally, once she could not see him anymore, Keira turned back to the wall, realising and regretting at the same time why she had put so much effort into sending the horse away: she could not change her mind now.

Rubbing her arms through her thin blouse, Keira slowly yet determinedly began climbing the roots and branches. Just like in her childhood days, some sticks and thorns tugged at her clothes and scraped her skin, but she continued anyway. Now and then she caught on something or nearly fell through, but no matter how long she struggled, she never seemed to make any progress. Panic began to rise at the idea that she would be trapped amongst the jungle of roots and branches for years to come, forever tied up in a web of wood. Suddenly, she realised why so many never returned from trying to enter Faerie, and panic seized her fully.

In a blind frenzy, she pushed and shoved, clawed and slipped, screamed and roared, until her skin and clothes were streaked with dirt and tears.

'Can't…anything…be…easy…in…this…saints…forsaken… world?' she growled towards the rising dawn, just before her foot slipped and she rushed down a particularly slippery trunk, flaring her arm open on a thorn bush nearby. Landing with a thump, she cried out and sagged against another woven nest of shrubs behind her, tilting her head exhaustedly against a thick branch. Before her, the thorn bush was coated in her blood.

'This is all my fault,' she murmured after a while, curling in on herself and cradling her wounded arm against her corset.

If she had not been so naïve, so eager to mean something to

someone...if she had not strayed from the approved path, she would never have met Elijah. She'd be safe and sound in her cottage and—She snorted. She'd also be bored out of her mind.

No matter what Elijah had done to her, at least that was the most alive she had felt in ages. At least he had not judged her or turned his back on her like August had.

She should've gone home and talked to him, she realised, and swallowed. At least she should have heard him out. Now she would die here, alone. Bleeding out on Faerie ground. Would anyone even know where she had gone? She'd passed Miles on her way out of the village and ignored him as he called her name. She would have liked *somebody* to know where she was, even if it were him. Not that he would come looking...

Just as her eyes slipped closed drowsily, they caught on a movement.

Opening her eyes, she caught it again – a slight shiver of the thorn bush, and then the forestry beside it began to shift and rotate until it opened up a whole path for her to walk through. Her mouth dropped open.

Cautiously, Keira rose to her feet, still cradling her wounded arm, and followed the path until she reached a forest glen. Here it seemed as if autumn had yet to fall, the ground still blooming in pinks and lilacs. The trees rose green, wild and tall, with the first rays of the morning sun shining down between the treetops.

They fell upon a majestic castle built around the trunk of the largest tree, with tall green spires and marble walls cut into the finest architecture her eyes had ever seen. If she was to wager a guess, she would have bet her cottage that it was elven made. And was that an elf or a fae seated on its golden steps?

Feeling faint from blood loss and pain, she couldn't be sure that she wasn't hallucinating, but there certainly seemed to be a beautiful boy draped before the castle entrance, toying with a twig.

Once she shifted closer, she realised he couldn't be much younger than her. He looked up, narrowing fine eyes the colour of polished copper.

'Who are you? What happened to your arm?'

'I–I'm Keira,' she said. 'I fell through the wall.'

'That's an odd way to come through the wards,' he said, half of his mouth pulling up at the corner, revealing a dimple underneath prominent cheekbones coated in golden glitter. He was an unnaturally beautiful boy, heartbreakingly so, with an even more unnatural hair colour – looking as if it had been dipped in black ink.

'The wards?' she asked.

'The wards only let through the subjects of the Queen,' he drawled in return.

'I'm not a subject of the Queen – I've never even met the Queen.'

He cocked his head. 'Then I'd run if I were you, while you still can.'

'I can't leave. I need to see the Spring Queen and ask her—' Keira paused. She did not know this boy, and she had heard that one should be careful with what one said to the Folk. Secrets were worth more than coin in these parts of Illnora.

The boy grinned as if he knew what she was thinking, then chucked the twig aside. 'It does not matter what you intend to ask the Queen. She is away.'

'When will she be back?'

'It's hard to say. A minute, a year. Personally, I'm hoping for the latter.' He twitched his brows. 'So, you might as well leave the way you came.'

With half a mind to argue, Keira caught sight of something between the trees and stopped herself.

'Fine, I'll just...leave then.'

'Bye, bye, then.' The boy waved and stretched out on the steps.

Narrowing her eyes at him, she turned on her heel and moved a little back the way she had come, until she was certain the boy could not see her anymore. Then she started squeezing her way through the moss-covered trunks until she came out into what looked like the castle's back garden.

Next to the hedges and geometrically shaped flower beds, there was a giant pond filled with dwarf cattails, water poppies, and lily pads. Something shimmered underneath its surface and pulled her towards it. Keira tried to discern what it was when a tinkling voice caught her attention.

'Something caught your curiosity or are you merely considering a bath?' said a white-haired girl, peeking up at her from behind a water lily, her forearms resting on its lily pads. She had large, doe-like eyes filled with laughter, and a perfect, petite mouth sitting below a slight button nose.

'I–I thought I saw something,' Keira mumbled, staring at the girl. If she thought the boy beautiful, he was nothing compared to her.

'Many seek what they once lost in these waters,' the girl said, swimming closer. 'Their innocence. Their youth. Their *truth*.' She rose and held out an inviting hand. 'I can help you find it again.'

Keira regarded her soft, encouraging smile and found that she would very much like to do whatever the girl suggested. 'Can you really?' she asked, taking the girl's hand.

'Oh, yes.' The girl chuckled, and her laughter sounded so sweet that Keira could do nothing but laugh with her. Then the girl swam back and led Keira to the edge. 'Look,' she said, gesturing to the surface.

Keira half-expected to see the reflection of the girl's naked body and her own poor state, but instead she saw only herself, her face clean, looking bold and brave in a sheer, white getup that would outshine the Nightladies' apparel. Her eyes were rimmed in kohl, sensual and fierce, and there were flowers braided in her hair.

'But...that's me!' Keira breathed, locking eyes with the white-haired girl once more, and the girl's smile turned more secretive and amused.

'It certainly could be.'

'How?'

'By joining me for a swim.'

Keira halted, retracting her hand. 'Oh, I don't know. I've already taken a swim in a lake like this once before. I didn't much care for it.'

The girl's laugh tinkled again. 'Oh, but this will be a swim unlike anything you've ever experienced before. Come with me under the surface and you'll find everything you've ever searched for.'

'You mean...I'll find what I want?' Although, she couldn't quite put her mind on what that was right now.

'Anything you want,' the girl cooed.

Something gnawed at Keira's mind. She knew she was supposed to question what the girl said, but she couldn't for the life of her understand why. With a voice like that, how could she not be trustworthy?

'Will we return? I don't know if I can hold my breath for long under there,' Keira said.

'Of course,' tittered the girl. 'Don't you trust me?'

'I do,' Keira murmured, taking the girl's hand again.

'Then come with me,' the girl sang again, leading Keira into the water.

Cold clasped her feet, yet she didn't stop. Instead, she let herself be pulled, deeper and deeper. Finally, they dipped under, where the water was grey like morning fog, and Keira was surprised to discover how deep the pond really was the further they swam. By the time they reached the bottom, there was already several feet of water above their heads.

Smiling, the girl turned to face Keira as if they were readying to dance, then pulled her close, caressing Keira's face.

'*So pretty,*' said the girl's sing-song voice, echoing inside Keira's mind, and Keira wondered if she was able to see her blush under water. Over the girl's shoulder, Keira could have sworn she saw other white-haired creatures gazing back at them. Her throat tickled a little from the pressure of holding her breath.

Are we returning to the surface? Keira thought, wondering how she would mime the words when the girl's voice once again sounded in her head.

'*Soon.*'

Despite the way her lungs were beginning to cramp, Keira found herself relaxing into the girl's arms. Holding her closely, the girl ran a hand down Keira's side, causing a thrill to rush through her like the bubbles fluttering against her skin. Then she drew Keira closer and put her lips to hers.

The longer they kissed, the more Keira struggled to hold her breath; yet the more she fought against the girl, the stronger the girl held her. With panic seizing, Keira pushed and pulled, until finally, the girl let go, her beautiful gaze now hard and hungry upon Keira's wounded arm.

She bit her.

Screaming internally, Keira kicked and swiped, only to feel more arms and see more hair surrounding her. The girl hung back with a peculiar expression on her face. *'Heir of Sin,'* her voice said in Keira's mind. *'Heir of the empire.'*

But Keira was too occupied with the other creatures rushing in and pulling her down while she kicked, trying to reach the surface. This time, she screamed for real, and water filled her lungs. Her sight darkened at the edges as the creatures dragged her down, clawed her skin, and swarmed her.

Then there was blood and a turmoil of limbs and white hair, swiftly followed by an explosion of light and her lungs filling with air.

Blinking against the harsh sunlight, Keira coughed and retched up swamp water while cradled in someone's arm, squeezed tight against a wet shirt sticking to a muscular chest.

Carefully, Elijah set her down on the grass next to the black-haired boy who merely tutted, once again stood twirling his twig. Then the boy's gaze lifted, following Elijah as he turned on his heel to face the pond and the women sneering at him.

'What are you doing?' Keira coughed, feeling the sting of cool air against her fresh wounds, but Elijah didn't answer.

Instead, he stared at the women, watching as, one by one, their burning gazes shifted into pure hunger and yearning. The one who had dragged Keira down held up her arm, mouthing for Elijah to 'Wait!' just before her eyes glazed over.

Then, the creatures turned upon each other.

Unable to do anything else, Keira stared as they began to caress each other, kiss each other, and devour each other's limbs until their sharp teeth drew blood and they whimpered in pain as much as they moaned.

Without another word, Elijah turned back around, water still dripping from his wet clothes and hair, and picked her up.

'Are they – are they—'

'Quite literally fucking each other to death,' said the boy curiously while tilting his head, watching the frenzy turning the pond scarlet.

'Are you just going to leave them like that?' Keira gaped, staring at Elijah.

But Elijah didn't even meet her gaze and merely proceeded to carry her away.

Looking over his shoulder, Keira took in the last ripples across the now-scarlet pond and the boy left beside it, waving her goodbye with a dimpled smile of amusement on his face. It didn't reach his eyes.

19
THE INN

Elijah carried her all the way back through the ward without a word, each branch coming undone from the others and slithering aside for him to pass. On the other side stood her horse, neighing at the sight of them.

'You found him,' Keira whispered, eyes on her cape still wrapped around its neck. Was that how Elijah had found her? But Elijah still didn't say a thing as he gave her his own coat and helped her up into the saddle. Effortlessly, he swung himself up behind her once he knew she was steady and clenched his arm tightly around her waist. A breath of protest lingered in her chest, but she found she had no strength to expel it.

Neither said anything as they rode, shame and humiliation burning through Keira next to the anger radiating off Elijah.

She had failed. Failed in finding the Spring Queen, failed in discovering the truth, and behind her sat someone whom she did not know at all.

The Djinn of Lust, Lord of Pleasure.

Someone capable of things far worse than she ever could have imagined. And yet, she found that it did not scare her as much as it should have. Rather on the contrary...her body seemed rather thrilled by it, leaning close to him as her teeth chattered from her drenched clothes, her breasts heavy and nipples hard in a way she suspected had less to do with the cold and more to do with the man sitting behind her.

Once they reached the inn, she kept her gaze to the floor and pulled Elijah's coat over her shoulder to hide the worst of her state. Part of her wondered why they had not just gone all the way back to E'frion, the other part rejoiced at the thought of a bed and a bath already – as soon as they were out of prying eyes.

She could feel them on her, taking in the bedraggled state of her clothes and filthy hair, the blood caked with the mud, and she crept closer to Elijah as if his presence could shield her from it. Without a word, his hand settled around her waist, pulling her closer to him. His eyes did not meet hers, but she could see his jaw clench as he listened to the innkeeper.

He booked them two separate bedrooms and let the housekeeper show them to their chambers, but no sooner had Keira said goodbye and been let into her own, than Elijah burst through her door and locked it after him.

'What are you doing?' Keira hissed, hands still fumbling with his jacket over her shoulders. 'People are going to think that we—'

'Why did you go off to Faerie on your own?' Elijah seethed, angrier than she had ever seen him.

She blinked and straightened her back stubbornly. 'That–that's none of your business.'

'None of my business? Keira, you could've gotten yourself killed. You could've gotten us both killed!'

'No one asked you to come!' she exclaimed, spreading her arms wide. 'Why are you even here?'

'Because of you!' His face pinched. She bit back her words and retreated, swallowed them and stared at him, his chest rising and falling. There was an edge to his voice, not one of annoyance but... fear. Had he been scared for her?

No. Keira mentally shook her head. That would mean that he cared. That he might even feel more than that, and she was done fooling herself about such things. He was the Djinn of Lust after all. Messing around with her emotions was his thing... wasn't it?

His breathing slowed and his eye softened. 'I came...because of you.' Regret began to stew within her. 'Please, talk to me. Make me understand. Did...August put you up to this?'

'August? I needed to figure out the truth,' she said quietly, avoiding the intensity of his gaze.

'The truth about what?'

'About my family's murder. I learned that the Spring Queen sent...the person who killed them. And I needed to figure out why.'

'So, you decided to go seek her out? The woman who caused their deaths? The woman who might very well have wanted to see *you* dead?'

Keira's skin heated. She'd already admitted to herself that it hadn't been a good plan. But hearing it from Elijah made her feel even more ashamed.

He stepped closer, voice softening. 'You should have come to me. I would have come with you.'

'Would you also have told me that you'd met my grandmother?'

He looked confused for a moment, before realisation dawned. '*That's* why you went?'

Well, that and the fact he was one of the Cardinal Seven but had never told her. She wanted to ask him about that as well, but part of her held back, uncertain what would happen once he became aware that she knew. Would he enchant her, if he hadn't already? Would he admit it if he had?

She did not get a chance to answer, however, before he asked, 'Keira...do you believe I had anything to do with your family's murder?'

She pressed her lips together, biting her cheek.

He tilted her chin up, eyes examining hers, her heart pounding through her chest. Even now, she wanted him even closer. 'You really think me capable of that?'

'You killed those nymphs, didn't you?'

It came out a little sharper than she intended, and he let her go, staring at her with stunned surprise. Silence spread between them as he ran his hand through his hair at a loss for words.

'Elijah, I—'

'You should go take a bath before you catch a cold.' He cleared his throat. No sooner had he said the word, before the scent of perfumed flowers and hot water drifted from the adjourning bath chamber. She looked uncertainly from the bath to him, unwilling to leave the conversation like this.

'Go on,' he said assuredly, although he still didn't meet her eye. 'I'll be here when you get back.'

'Right,' Keira stuttered, clambering to collect herself – to push down the wretchedness threatening to swallow her whole – and to peel herself off the wall. Somewhat unsteadily, she slipped past him and made her way to the bath, wondering if he would follow. He did not.

The bath was a freestanding copper tub, much like the porcelain one back at her cottage. The heated water stung against her chilled skin as she lowered herself into the bath, then enveloped her in soothing warmth. Tapped – or enchanted – to the perfect temperature.

Once inside, she sighed, resting her forehead on her knees as she wrapped her arms around her legs.

She already regretted her words – regretted how they had come out – but she was not so sure Elijah would be willing to hear it. His expression haunted her mind, and she glanced at her arm, the wound having healed itself, leaving behind faint lines stretching like thin leaves. How or when, she did not know, but it was not lost on her that it could have been so much worse if he had not come, and for that she was grateful. That said, the saints knew he had yet to answer for the things he had kept secret himself.

She bit her lip, staring at the door as if she could see him through it.

She wanted him.

Needed him with every fibre in her body. But she still did not know whether she could trust that it was real. She *did* trust that he hadn't had anything to do with her family's murder; it was a gut feeling, more than anything else, one that was not buried under layers of fear. But there were so many things left for him to tell her still, before she could trust him entirely. She supposed though, he could not do so unless she let him.

Deciding to take the stag by the antlers, Keira gave herself a final rinse, before she rose from the tub and clothed herself in a robe hanging at the ready.

Returning to the bedchamber, she came out of the bath just as Elijah re-entered her room, looking fresh and dry, as if he'd gone for a wash elsewhere or magicked himself clean. Her heart tugged a little in disappointment that he hadn't decided to bathe with her, before she scolded herself for the ridiculous notion. She should have been happy about it. It was easier this way.

'Brought you some food,' he said, and set down a platter with assortments of breads, cheeses, and fruits. 'And a pint of mead. Should help you sleep after...everything.'

The nymphs.

'Heir of Sin. Heir of the empire.'

She shuddered, remembering the water creatures and what Elijah had done to them, and even more so thinking of what he could do to her if he set his mind to it.

'Elijah,' she started. 'About the nymphs...'

'I won't apologise for what I did, Keira,' he said, voice low and quiet.

'You shouldn't have left them like that.'

'And you shouldn't have gone to Faerie without me.'

She exhaled frustratingly. 'I hardly think me going on an adventure—'

'Damn it, Keira!' he barked and spun around to face her. 'They were Eleionomaes. They're practically freshwater sirens. The only adventure they'd have led you on is a one-way trip to the Underworld. Do you understand?' He moved closer, towering over her. A shadow darkened his expression as he did. 'I'd have made them suffer a hundred times worse if they so much as curled another hair on your head.'

Her breath caught as heat thrummed around them. 'Why?'

'Why?' he huffed a laugh, low and dark against her skin, her mouth, as he lowered his face towards hers. 'Isn't that clear to you yet?' He gave her a chaste kiss, soft and brief.

She shook her head. 'No.' Not if it was all a spell. Not if—

He kissed her again, deeply and yearnfully, walking her back towards one of the bedposts until it knocked against her back. Warm and heady, his tongue lay claim on her mouth as if he'd been starved for days. Tasting every inch of her as if making sure that all of her had made it back from Faerie.

She was the same, meeting the strokes of his tongue with her own, letting some of her pent-up frustration rise to be devoured by his need. But it was only need, right? Lust, as was his vice. She tried to convince herself of that, and yet it did not feel like it. It felt deeper. More urgent, as if it was not just their bodies that were desperate to merge, but their souls as well. Yearning for each other. Calling each other home.

When they finally broke apart for air, her breath caught as he continued kissing down her neck, above her clavicle, pausing with his hand on the band of her robe. Their eyes met.

'Elijah...' Perhaps she should have asked him then. Perhaps she should have stopped things until she had her answers. She was still mad at him for all the things he had not told her, and they still needed to talk about it all, but...

'I met your grandmother the last time I was in this realm. I've never seen her since, and I never went near your family beyond that. Do you believe me?'

She nodded.

It was all she needed, for now. All except for him.

She needed him *more*.

And it was that need that had her tug at his neck and grind against him until he groaned and carried her to the bed, placing her on top of it.

Her robe came a little undone, and the air thickened as Elijah caught sight of her nakedness underneath.

'Fates,' he murmured, the sound turning her core molten. Electric nerves firing as his fingertips brushed her skin. 'Do you know what a waste this would be with *him*?' he said, stepping back to unbutton his sleeves. 'He wouldn't even know what to do with you.'

'Him?' she asked, her brain disconnecting as Elijah pulled his shirt over his head, her eyes taking in every defined muscle of his slender torso.

Elijah paused, shirt still in hand, and raised a brow. 'August? The dinner? Keira, about that...'

Her mouth quirked at the corner, remembering now that she never made it back to the cottage to tell him; never made it back to say that she had chosen him. 'Oh right. I never had the dinner.'

His shirt dropped and so did his knees onto the bed. Her heart drummed in her chest as he prowled closer, pulling her to him. 'What, *exactly*, are you saying Keira?'

Her cheeks strained as she struggled to hold back her smile. 'I'm saying'—she wrapped her legs around his hips and pulled herself halfway into his lap. 'That I never had the dinner. I wanted the appetiser.' She ran her hand over his abs and watched in fascination as his skin trembled.

His chest heaved as the words settled with him. 'I'm going to need minute,' he breathed, voice thick with emotions, and the most ridiculous thrill surged through her at realising that *she* had rattled *him*, the Djinn of Lust himself.

She bit her lip. 'Don't take too long. I might run off again.'

'Is that so?' he murmured, gaze sweeping over her mouth, her breasts. 'I think we ought to have another lesson then. Just to make sure you won't.'

It took everything in her not to grin like a silly schoolgirl, even as she trembled with trepidation.

'The third one?'

He regarded her, eyes studying her expression. 'Hmm, I'm thinking something extracurricular instead,' he said, licking his way to the sensitive nook of her neck. 'Something to truly remind you where you belong – or to whom.' His weight shifted over her, pressing her down on her back as he moved her arms over her head.

'And how are you planning to do that?' she whispered, attempting and failing at bravado as she felt his hips press against hers. A shiver went through her body. 'One would have thought you'd shown me all of your tricks by now.'

'All my tricks?' he mused, pitching his voice to sound humorous before it darkened into a low husk. 'Darling, I haven't shown you anything yet.'

Something slithered around her wrists, and she yelped as the bed curtains came loose, holding her in place.

'Elijah!'

Smirking, he snapped his fingers once more, and it was as if all sound from downstairs evaporated – as if sucked out of the room – and she had a sneaking suspicion that no sound from them could be heard outside either. Her whole body tightened at the thought.

'Why did you—'

'Clearly, I'm not doing my job right if you're riding into Faerie to play with nymphs,' he said, shifting down her body and pulling at her robe. 'I know better ways of making you scream if it is violence you prefer.'

She'd surely forgotten how to breathe, blatantly aware of how exposed she was to him and of his arousal, straining against his trousers. 'Will you—'

'Oh, no. Not yet, Peaches. That would be more like a reward, not...'

Punishment, she swallowed.

'Like I was saying,' he murmured, circling his finger around her taut nipple. 'There are other ways of making you scream.'

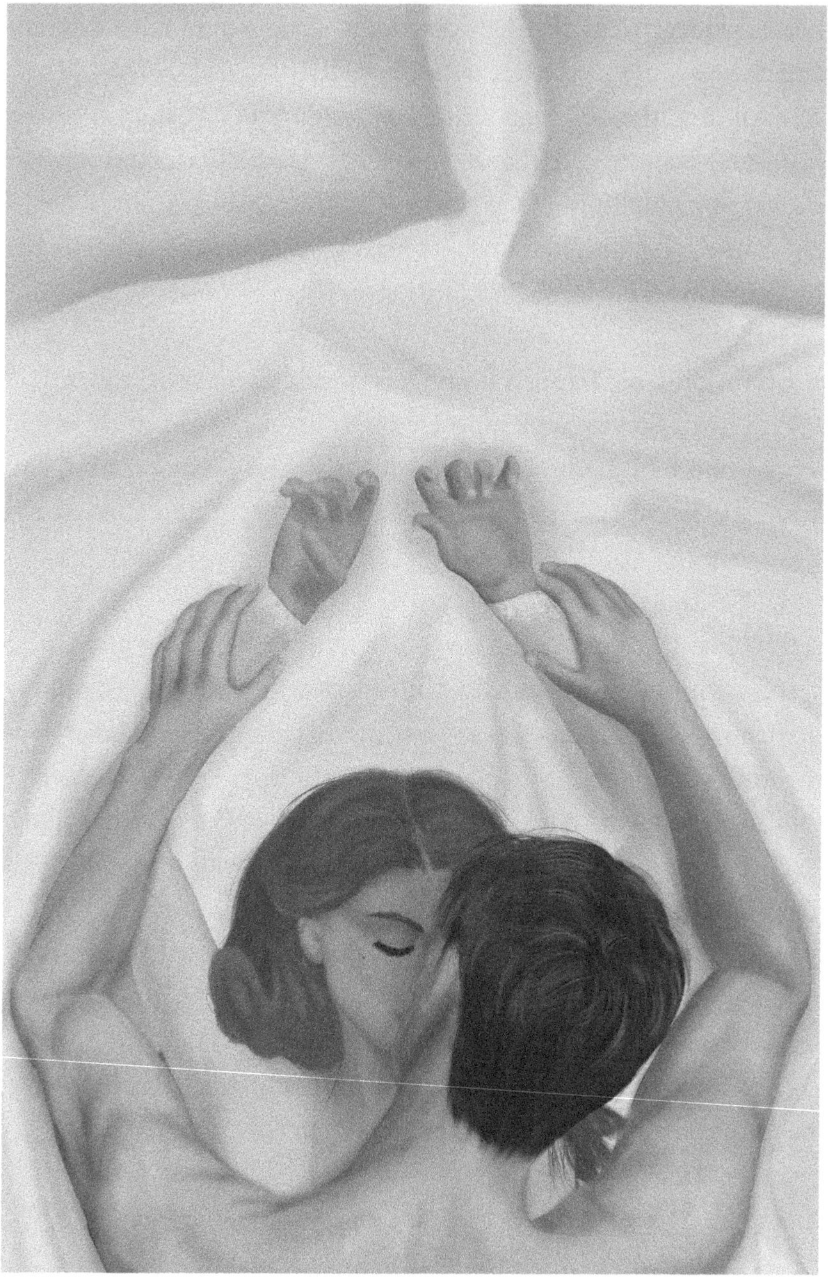

Mortified. She was absolutely mortified, hiding her face behind a pillow. And what was even worse, was that Elijah lay next to her, looking like the cockiest bastard that ever lived.

'I thought it was amazing. Like a *squirt* of peach juice with my meal.'

She raised her head and glowered at him. '*Peach juice* is not enticing.'

'Cantaloupe juice, then? No? Apple juice?'

She threw her pillow at him as he chortled, trying her best not to pay attention to the way his muscles rippled.

He'd kept her on edge for ages – playing with her body and going down on her – until he let her shatter. And shatter she had. All over him. She felt pretty certain she would never live down the humiliation, even now, until he crawled up beside her, kissed her knee, her shoulder, and her cheek, before pulling her into his arms and burrowing them under the duvet.

'Honestly, Keira. It's nothing to be ashamed of. It is, in fact, quite the desirable trait.'

'Really?'

'Mmhmm.' He nodded, kissing her softly while running circling motions on her arm, his fingers lingering on her scar contemplatively.

'Don't you have a room of your own? Shouldn't you be using that one?'

'And leave you here to play with yourself?' He yawned, eyes already closing. 'I don't think so.'

She harrumphed. 'You should have just let the nymphs take me. Perhaps, I'll head back into Faerie while you sleep.'

His hand paused and she met his gaze, deep and solemn.

'Promise me,' he murmured at last, 'that if you go on another adventure, you won't go without me?'

Her heart thudded a little harder at the intensity in his voice. 'You'd come with? Why?'

'I think I'd go to the ends of the world with you, if only to keep you safe.'

Smiling, Keira finally gave in and burrowed closer to his chest, her leg firmly placed between his legs. She could feel him against her, hard and straining, wakening a dull ache at her core. He'd been so patient with her, she thought. Unlike August, he had not asked for a thing in return even though he would take every opportunity to give her the pleasures he could. Part of her wanted to do something about that, the other part pondered whether she would be brave enough, until she fell asleep.

But the ache only grew so violently that Keira woke in the middle of the night, feeling restless and impatient.

Behind her, the djinn lay sprawled out on his back, one arm beside him on the pillow, the other under her waist. His chest was marvellously chiselled, and she traced the lines of his abs down where the duvet had slipped off him, her eyes catching on the bulge straining against his trousers.

Her core throbbed harder and her mouth went dry at the sight, her attention rapt upon the shape of him until the djinn shifted and spoke, startling her. 'Where's your mind at?'

She met his gaze, drowning in smouldering pools of dark desire mirroring her own. His fringe hung in a curtain, dipping loose strands of hair before his eyes. It struck her then that he was keeping the same features he had worn when he had saved her from the lake and the morning after her drink was tampered with. This time, however, his face did not change, as if he no longer felt the need to keep up appearances with her. As if he was choosing to be himself instead.

Djinn of Lust, Lord of Pleasure.

She shuddered, thinking of all the things the title promised, and dug her nails into her skin.

'What do you need?' he whispered.

'I want to see you.' She wanted to do more than that. She wanted to feel him. Wanted to extend the night until they'd done all the thing she wanted to try with him. Her insides aching to the point she was surely going mad.

But all that she was able to do when the djinn made the rest of his clothes disappeared, was stare.

She didn't know what to do with herself.

Whatever the Nightladies had said about the holy grail of male members, his had to be it. Long and slender, it stood at high attention, veins protruding around the shaft.

'May I...touch it?' she asked breathlessly, catching a glint in his eye as she glanced at him. It made her cheeks burn, but his lips merely twitched into a half-smile that made her dizzy.

'You certainly may,' he said, male arrogance playing in his voice. Yet his breath caught as her fingers wrapped around him, and the playfulness in his eyes shifted to something far more raw and needy. She knew it too well.

Unlike August's, Elijah's felt perfect in her grasp, thrumming with power and hardness. She still didn't know anything about sizes or the like, but what she did know was that if Elijah fully claimed her body, she'd never be the same. And her legs wobbled at the thought of it. Even on her knees.

'Keira—' Elijah started as she shifted and placed herself across him, still holding him in her grasp.

'You owe me a lesson on how to please a man,' she interrupted. His mouth closed and his chin dipped, as if he understood that she needed this moment. Needed it after what had happened with August.

Of course he did. He always understood her. Read her and her needs like an open book. Perhaps that was why it felt so different. With August, the thought of doing what she was about to had made her squirm, as if it made her lesser than him, somehow. Tarnished, almost. But with Elijah, the idea made her feel bold. Empowered.

Gradually, she began to move her hand along his shaft. Up and down, then back up again, her insides fluttering as he groaned and leaned back against his pillow, his eyelids closing. She inhaled sharply as she cupped his balls with one hand, watching his slender form go taut like the muscle she held in the other. She caressed it further, listening until his breath turned uneven and ragged. Then she sat back a little more, lowered her head towards him, and waited till Elijah turned his gaze back on her, before she placed her lips around his length – eyes upon him as she did.

A bang of triumph shot through her as she saw the mighty djinn's mask of control slip, and she shifted her attention back to his member, contemplating how deep she could take him. What move she'd make next to make him fold and unravel.

Yet no sooner had she thought this than the memory of what had happened with August washed over her. Soon, with the same crippling uncertainty as she had felt then, her jaw locked, and her muscles trembled. For every taste her tongue had of Elijah, her mind flashed to August.

She was utterly paralysed, caught between the present and the past. And to make matters worse, tears began to trickle pathetically, one by one.

Quietly, Elijah's strong arms pulled her back up to his chest and wrapped around her, lulling her while she sobbed it all out, his lips leaving gentle kisses on the top of her head.

'I'm sorry,' she whispered in the end, when her crying had finally quietened. 'I...I just wanted to please you after...everything.' After all her silliness. After all her mistakes.

In response, Elijah fisted his hand in her hair and gently tugged her head back to caress the column of her neck with his finger.

'First off, you don't ever have to do something you don't want in order to "please" me or any man, ever again. Secondly,' he said, in a voice that made her shiver, 'don't apologise. I'll be inside this fine throat of yours one day – when you truly *wish* it.'

She scarcely dared to breathe, tears still lingering in the corners of her eyes. 'Are you certain?'

He dried her tears, kissing her gently. 'Positive. I have you to myself now, Keira. I don't plan on taking it for granted.'

She shook her head. 'I don't understand. I mean, why me? I'm emotional, inexperienced, imperfect—you said it yourself; they've taken my claws. I'm nothing but flawed.'

'You're impulsive, passionate, and headstrong, I'll give you that.' He smirked. 'You follow your heart, your wants, even when you think you're not. But your only *flaw* is thinking that it is wrong.' He shifted their weights so that she was cocooned in his embrace, her back against his chest. 'Is it infuriating trying to make you see the truth? Indeed. But I enjoy the challenge.' Her breath came out in a shiver as his lips caressed the sleek column of her neck, fanning small embers lapping at the remainder of her humiliation. Replacing it with assurance.

'Is that so?' she mumbled, curiously noting how the rest of her embarrassment seemed to die with his touches. She wanted more of that. More distractions. 'And how would you rise to the challenge after what just happened?'

'We could always go for another meal?' He purred suggestively, nipping at her shoulder with his teeth. She nudged him with her elbow, frowning until his chest stopped trembling with quiet chuckles and his arms tightened around her, one hand sliding over to her breast, the other brushing by her entrance. She inhaled sharply.

'Or, I could play you some music?' His hand began to trace the skin around her nipple, coaxing it to harden, while the other hand began to massage her below.

'Is fornication the answer to everything to you?' she asked demurely, tilting her head against his shoulder, glancing up at his hooded gaze.

'No, but it is in my nature. As I suspect it is in yours. It's why this feels like—'

'Home,' she whispered. The reason she found herself so drawn to him. The reason she could not confront him. Because he spoke a language that her soul seemed to understand, and she feared she would be lost without him. His gaze heated further.

'Exactly.' His movements quickened with precision – above as well as below – causing a sensation to spread through her body, racing her towards a different, deeper release. Keira whimpered, digging her nails into him, her body straining with building wave. Her mind delirious with need.

'*Saints!*'

'They can't help you now,' he murmured against her ear. 'They can't help you at all.'

'My nan was entirely correct about you,' Keira mused, 'you're as wicked as they come.'

Elijah sniggered, nuzzling his face into the nook of her neck, having just whispered in her ear all the things he was planning to do with her once they returned home. But it was only the promise of those things that stopped her from taking the reins herself and steering them back to the privacy of the inn.

They were riding back to E'Frion, with Keira seated in front of him, his hand firmly tucked around her waist. They had not gone all the way yet, but he had played her body like an instrument and made her come, repeatedly. After, he had put her on her back again – this time with his length pressed between them, naked and hard as he rolled his hips, teasing with a pre-taste of the third lesson until she nearly lost her mind. How neither of them had given in was beyond her.

'And what else did your dear grandmama have to say about my kind?' Elijah teased coyly, his hand slipping a little below her navel, rubbing against the fabric of her skirt. 'And let me preface that by saying that whatever sexual prowess she mentioned, mine is far superior to that of the average djinn.'

Keira rolled her eyes, then hesitated a little. 'She always said djinns were demon spirits, and that they're eternally damned. Much like the *Cardinal Seven*.' She almost held her breath, waiting for his response. Although she was coming to terms with the idea of him being the Djinn of Lust, it didn't change the fact that they still had a lot to talk about. But he needed to admit the truth to her first.

Elijah stiffened behind her. 'And what do you think?'

'I'm just hoping she was wrong. I mean...you're a pain in my behind, but I don't like the idea of you being condemned.'

He softened against her. 'It's alright, Keira. I've been to the Court of the Damned before. It is a rather wicked place, with all sorts of frivolous behaviour.' He kissed the back of her head. 'I think you'd enjoy it. We could have as many lessons as you'd like there, straight in the middle of Hel's throne room should you want to. Then I'd show you what kind of pain I'd truly be to this fine arse of yours.' She felt a pinch to her buttocks and yelped, twisting in her seat, prepared to give him a scolding for not taking the conversation more seriously, when the words died on her breath.

There was a vulnerability lingering in his gaze, a fear almost, and it struck her then that perhaps she was not the only one scared of rejection, and that perhaps making such jokes was his way of shielding himself from it.

'Shouldn't you change your appearance before we get to E'Frion?' she asked instead, deciding that if he needed more time to tell her the truth, she would give it to him.

He shook his head. 'I've every intention of courting you once we get there. I won't have people thinking we're related in any shape or form.'

She melted against him, thinking that they couldn't reach the village fast enough.

For the rest of the trip they kissed and laughed, talking about all and nothing until they returned to the cottage and Elijah led the way to the door, the anticipation of what waited inside humming through the both of them.

'Let me go inside and take care of something first,' Elijah said, turning on the doorstep and blocking her from entering.

'What?'

'It's a surprise,' he said sheepishly, opening the door. She raised a brow. 'Did you use my bed while I was at the dinner?'

'That,' he paused, looking guilty as sin, 'is another surprise.'

'I knew it!' she exclaimed and stumbled in right behind him, colliding with Elijah's slim figure as he'd come to an abrupt stop. He stood as though rooted to the spot, his expression dark and morbid facing the kitchen. His jaw was set in such a hard line that she thought he might grind his teeth to dust. And before him, at the kitchen table, sat a familiar figure, who at the same time didn't seem familiar at all.

'August?' she started, and the cruel iciness in his eyes gleamed in a way that she had never seen before.

'Hello, Keira.' He smirked.

'What—who are you?' she asked, because as certainly as she was seeing August's body before her, she knew that he was not him.

'Ah, good, we can skip the pretences, I see,' the man crooned and leaned forward, hands folded on the table. The door smacked shut behind her and she jumped, startled. Elijah jerked, as if he had been prepared to leap forward, but remained a little before her, shielding her with his body. August's eyes hardened. 'I was getting tired of pretending. Allow me to properly introduce myself. I am—'

'Aeros,' Elijah interrupted. 'The Tyrant Emperor.'

20
BETRAYAL

'How lovely to finally make your proper acquaintance, Keira.' The emperor leered. 'It's been rather tedious waiting for you two to return, I must say. Elnatan told me you had a soft spot for *this* body, but I suppose he was wrong.'

Keira stared at the man whose mannerisms were all wrong for the body he inhabited, her pulse pounding in her ears.

'W-why are you here? What have you done to August?'

'August...' Aeros dragged out the sound of the name as if tasting it on the tip of his tongue. His gaze took in the shape of his hand, his slender arms, and flickered to the window where August's pale reflection stared back at him. Then he began to speak, as if reading August's mind. 'The boy went hunting, hoping to take down the mythical stag so he could secure his girl's hand in marriage – how disappointed he'll be to learn of your...divided interest.' His eyes flickered mockingly between Keira and Elijah, and it punched Keira in the gut. August had gone out to find the stag. For *her*.

'He could hardly believe his own eyes when he spotted it. So elated. So relieved. Little did he know he was the prey.'

With the same amusement in his voice, the emperor went on to recount how he had shifted out of the stag's hide, overpowered August, and then possessed his body before he could even notice.

Keira's insides ran cold. 'I thought you were cursed to be a stag forever?'

'The witch that cursed me made it so that upon Helena's death, I'd be confined to a stag's body until my hands were once again stained with the blood of the woman I loved. I was unable to change into another form. Unable to access my magic. Forever hunted. Irony, I believe, is what she was going for.' He shrugged. 'Considering a stag has no hands and Helena would already be dead. I guess she did not account for the bonds of family and how far one's siblings are willing to go for you.' His eyes flicked to Elijah, who lowered his gaze.

A crawling sensation of unease tickled at the back of Keira's mind. 'What is he talking about?'

'He didn't tell you? Well, that's Elnatan and his secrets for you. Days ago, my dear estranged brother sought me out in the woods, carrying bloodied cotton, which he applied to my hooves. Swearing he would make up for his mistake. Swearing he would help me restore our family to its greatness. The blood belonged to Helena's heir, liberating me from my curse. Allowing me to jump bodies.'

Cold washed over her. Days ago…the cotton pads. She had seen Elijah pocketing them after cleansing her wounds from the day they went hunting. The day he startled the stag so that she missed her shot – the same night they'd had their first lesson… before he'd left the cottage.

'Keira, it's not—' Elijah started, but she merely stared at him as the extent of his betrayal sank in.

Had everything been just a ploy? To win her trust? For what, to free his brother? And last night...her skin grew cold and warm and uncomfortable.

'Don't lie to the girl, Elnatan,' Aeros drawled. 'It is rather pointless with all that is to come.'

'You don't need her. Let her go.' Elijah's voice was low and hoarse, tinged with the same emotion as when he'd berated her for going to Faerie on her own. *Fear.*

With the emperor's eyes flicking between them, Keira could feel her own fear rising, and it was all she could do to keep from trembling as Aeros rose and stalked towards her.

'Oh, but you know that isn't true, Elnatan. Only she can open the palace. Only her presence can reveal the place where our siblings are kept. Besides,' he said, and reached for her. 'She is my insurance policy. I want her by my side when I take back what's mine.'

'Don't touch her!' Elijah rushed forward, but the emperor merely threw his hand out and pinned him to the wall.

'Elijah!' Keira gasped, before the emperor's sleek fingers clenched around her chin, examining her face. Her skin crawled at his proximity and the look in his eyes.

'You look so much like her; no wonder my brother has taken a liking to you. He was always rather good at sleeping his way towards what he wanted. Be it with my wife, or the Spring Queen.'

'I never slept with the Spring Queen,' Elijah growled.

'Semantics.' The Tyrant Emperor shrugged. 'He sold her his servitude in exchange for my annihilation. Whether it was a physical or metaphorical bed – you got in with her nevertheless, did you not?'

Only subjects of the Queen may enter the ward, Keira thought, the words echoing in her mind.

The Tyrant Emperor smirked. 'Of course, she won't like it when she discovers you played her.'

Keira frowned.

'Oh, he didn't tell you?' He glanced amusedly at Elijah shaking his head, pleading softly.

'Elnatan was tasked to find you and bring you to Faerie. Instead, he brought me to you.'

The chair flew at the library door and ricocheted in broken pieces across the floor.

'Well, at least we'll have firewood,' Elijah murmured before he sighed in exasperation. 'Keira...Keira!'

Ignoring him, Keira rushed forward and threw herself at the door again. No sooner had they returned to the old ruins, before the emperor had locked them up in the palace library to keep them out of his way, sealing it shut with his magic. No matter how hard she pulled at the handle or pushed against the wood with her shoulder, it would not budge.

'He can't just leave us in here!' she shouted, banging at the sturdy surface with her fist before she hissed, retracting her hand. This time having surely injured it.

'Here, let me,' Elijah murmured, taking her palm before she could protest, and healed the ache away. She did not thank him. Did not stop to think about the last time he had nursed a wound of hers. Instead, she avoided his gaze and rushed over to the window, debating whether she could make the jump. Clearly, she could not, what with the ground being at least two floors down.

'Keira... It's not like you think.'

She felt him reach for her, but with every word, Keira retracted further into herself, rebuilding her walls.

Too many secrets. Too many half-truths. Too many lies.

Once again, she had chosen to be intimate with a man who'd led her behind the light. This one who'd nearly seduced her into giving him everything, and for what?

'Instead, he brought me to you.'

He'd just humoured her. Kept her on a string for his brother, or the Spring Queen – maybe even both. Having his bit of fun while he did it too.

Her skin burned with the memory of how close they had come the night before. Of all that they had done.

I came on his face even, she groaned internally, even as her body tingled at the memory.

So stupid.

She should have talked with him. She should have forced him to tell her everything the minute she learned who he truly was.

But just like with August, she had been swayed by pretty words and empty promises. Avoiding the truth even though it was staring her in the face.

August.

The memory of their dinner resurfaced, and she recalled how his strange mannerism had put her off. How repulsed she had felt by him, even then, and how she had applied that to her feelings for him in general.

But it had not been him. It had been the emperor seated before her, digging for details about the palace. About her. And on top of it all, her feelings had been influenced by Elijah.

Her chest twinged, once again uncertain about her feelings for both him and August. Once again uncertain about what had been real and what had been pretend.

All she knew was that August's body had been possessed

because of her. If she had merely accepted him when he first asked, he would not have gone out to secure the stag. The guilt of that knowledge was almost worse than the hurt from Elijah's betrayal, and she promised herself she would do everything she could to see August safe. But Elijah?

Perhaps jumping out of the window would hurt less.

She wrapped her arms around herself, taking in the library. It was a beautiful space with bookshelves built into white walls, mosaic tiles, and a black spiral staircase leading down to the second floor with an empty pool, and she felt certain she would have enjoyed it despite various signs of decay had the situation been different. The entire way over here, her mind had been in pieces, reeling with the information that had come to pass and the fact that the Tyrant Emperor was before her, forcing her through the woods while using August's body as leverage. Once or twice, she had considered screaming for the Woodland Witches, but there was no telling what the emperor would do if they heard and came to her aid.

Once outside the ruins, the emperor had forced her to open the doors, their shoes clapping against cracked tile floor as they moved down the hall and up the majestic staircase leading to the second floor. A giant ballroom waited on the other side, with two-floor windows covering one of the walls, stretching from one end to the other. Immaculate frescoes of gods and demons painted the others, but it was all a blur as her gaze flicked about, pausing at a grand table set with fine dinnerware with gold and glass goblets as if the palace still expected to host a large party. As if it had been frozen in time, since the day the palace was sieged, and the Cardinal Seven were imprisoned.

She had seen them then – the copper vessels that held them, placed on pedestals – just before the emperor locked her and Elijah up in the library.

'Keira...' Elijah's fingers touched against her arm, bringing her back to the present, and she closed her eyes against the tingles that spread throughout her body. 'Please, we need to ta—'

'No,' Keira bit back, retracting her arm, before she spun on her heel and pushed past him. 'We need to get out of here.'

'We...can't. His magic is too strong.'

She narrowed her eyes at him. 'Then use your magic and stop him before he attacks the village.'

Elijah raised a brow. 'Even if I could, we still need to talk.'

'So, people are just going to get harmed while we chat?'

He raised the other. 'Why do you care about them anyway? Those people have been nothing but terrible to you.'

'Yeah, well,' she scoffed, 'people can surprise you.'

Catching her glare, his voice softened. 'Keira, you have to listen to me, I didn't—'

'No, I rather think I don't!' Keira snapped, beckoning to the door. 'The *Tyrant Emperor* is out there – in August's body – prepared to do gods-knows-what, and...' she paused staring at him, chest aching. 'And you helped him do it. You've been helping him this whole time.'

'But I haven't! That's what I'm trying to tell you! Aeros is twisting the truth. He lies!'

'And you don't?'

His forehead crinkled as bafflement filled his gaze. 'When have I—'

'When you didn't tell me who you were, Elijah! Or should I say *Elnatan*?' she spat out. The effect was immediate.

Elijah straightened, realisation dawning on his features that she knew what the name entailed – that she knew far more than the emperor had revealed – and the air thickened around them. Her heart pounded harder.

'How *long* have you known?'

'*Gale told me,*' she whispered. 'Before I went to Faerie. You played me for a fool.' She hated how the hurt snuck into her voice. 'You strung me along and went behind my back to lift the emperor's curse. Why?'

'I had my suspicions after you told me about the hunt and the mythical stag. I needed to know for myself whether it could be true. If it was, I could not risk anyone killing him...not before I'd made things right. But I never played you for anything, Keira.'

To that, Keira laughed bitterly. 'No? What about the images you've been putting into my head?'

'Images?'

'Yes, of me and you doing...things! Before the hearth, outside. In the bath!'

'In the bath?' he crooned with a bit of a chuckle, looking from her to the stairs. Eyes twinkling. 'Do tell me more.'

She scowled at him. 'Don't play coy. You messed with my mind. You made me feel things I otherwise wouldn't. You toyed with me!' She pushed past him, but Elijah grabbed her and forced her to face him, this time entirely serious.

'Keira, I didn't—'

'You lie!' She cried, tears pebbling in her eyes. 'You've bewitched me so that I would want you instead of August.'

'Me?' Elijah scoffed, surprise marring his expression as he let her go. 'It is you who's bewitched *me*. It is I who can't stop thinking of *you*. Desiring you. Contemplating all the ways I want to be with you, repeatedly. Yes, I saved my brother, but that was *before* I fell in love with you!'

She stood still, gaping at him, as if rooted to the spot. 'You're not serious—'

'No?' His expression heated and darkened. 'I was in *agony* when you went to meet with August. If anything, it is you that has been toying with me.' He stood so close now. So close, that it was just him and her and the impenetrable air of heat around them. 'I'm here, ready and willing to be yours, and you refuse to see it.'

'Prove it,' she snarled.

He grabbed her chin and pushed her back up against the bookshelves, barely giving her the chance to yelp before his mouth was upon hers.

His kiss was more brutal than anything he had done before.

Starved. Feasting. Devouring. Angrily bruising her lips in all the best ways. Conveying with every crush of his mouth, with every swipe of his tongue, what she had known in her heart before she learned who he was; that he wanted her, as much as she wanted him.

It broke her further, because she knew she couldn't trust it. Knew it wasn't enough.

'I wanted to give you the benefit of the doubt,' she whispered, voice thin against his lips as they came apart, 'but you've been manipulating me the whole time.' She had to believe it. For once, she had to believe it. She couldn't be the fool falling for the sweet words of men over and over again.

Elijah growled against her mouth, grip tight on her chin. 'I've never done anything to you beyond helping you free yourself.'

She sneered. 'Is that what you call it? August wanted to *marry* me! I was prepared to let him go because, for some reason, I could not stop thinking about you. Now I know what that reason was. A mere spell of a djinn.'

Elijah paused and opened his mouth but closed it again and shook his head instead. It annoyed her further. Particularly when he stepped away from her.

'My future could have been secured, if it hadn't been for you! I'd be back at Thornfell again; I'd have a family – it would be like the past never happened!'

'He doesn't even deserve you!' Elijah roared, turning back

around on her. 'He took advantage of you and then left you in the gutter. That's what he did.'

'He told me he regrets it. He told me he loved me!' Saints, she hated how desperate her voice sounded. Desperate to believe her own words. Desperate not to let Elijah burrow himself deeper into her heart.

'He is a man! Human men will tell you anything you want to hear if they know it'll allow them to wet their stick.'

She glared at him.

'And he would continue to do so if you were to marry him, but he would *never* be loyal to you. Never value you,' Elijah rattled on, erratically pacing the floor while trying and failing at calming himself. 'He'd never *worship* you. Not in the way you deserve.'

'As if *you* would,' she snarled under her breath, her voice vibrating with her suppressed rage and need. Need, because no matter how mad she was with him, his words *did* settle into her heart. Stroking that yearning within her in a way that only he could.

She gasped, feeling the floor disappear under her feet as Elijah hoisted her onto an abandoned desk, placing himself between her legs as books toppled over the edge.

'Let me take you to church and find out,' he growled. 'I dare you.'

She inhaled sharply, feeling her pulse thundering through her body, pounding in her core. It was there, in his eyes, a promise. A promise that if she said the word, if she asked for it, he would give her the kind of pleasure that would have her screaming his name.

This was different than before, more than a lesson; something that would take her beyond the edge and into a gaping pit of decadent darkness.

Heat pooled between her legs, warring with the wrath already chasing through her body. She wanted to lash out at him. To make him hurt the same way she was hurting, and to make him spill his secrets. She also wanted him. Terribly. Achingly.

Despite the emperor and everything else she wanted to trust him. Yet, she knew that he would only hurt her further. Would only leave once he'd had what he wanted, like August had done.

She just needed to prove it to herself once and for all.

A sort of chilling calm blanketed over her as she realised what she needed to do, complete with a charged thrill of anticipation skittering down her back, along her arms, and into the very tips of her fingers. If men wanted to use her, so be it. But she would return the favour if that's what it took to get the truth.

No sooner had she thought it than her fingers curled against the edge of the desk, nails digging into the wood like claws. Her eyes narrowed and she moulded her lips into a sneer. 'You *lie*,' she crooned.

'What?'

'You've had your chance for weeks. Instead, you've been preparing me for someone else.'

Disbelief marred his face. 'Unbelievable.' He laughed under his breath and stepped away, but the sound was void of humour.

'What's unbelievable is that you never manned up to claim me for yourself. What did you do when you watched me pleasure myself? Did you picture me with August?'

Colour drained from his face.

'Did you picture our sweaty, heaving bodies writhing against one another?'

'Stop that!'

'You talk a big game about freeing others' desires, and yet you're the least free of us all,' Keira edged him on, her ears ringing, her skin prickling with electricity chasing down her limbs and in the room, around and between them. 'You're a dog on a leash. A mere genie in a bottle.'

'I'm warning you, Keira, stop,' he growled, once again standing in front of her, their faces inches apart.

'Or what?' She leaned forward until she could feel his warm breath on her skin, brushing her lips against his as she spoke. 'You'll finally take me? I'd love to see you try.'

His mouth crashed into hers, hard and bruising. Like the tide, his tongue pushed through, conquering every inch of her mouth, clashing with her own. Her arms wrapped around his back, and he pulled her body closer until their fronts collided, bundling up her skirt until she felt the hardening shape of him press against the fabric blocking her centre.

A bolt shot through her, turning her legs to mush.

A bell rang at the back of her mind, warning her that perhaps she would come to regret this; that she was acting too rashly again, but it was drowned out in a wave of pleasure as he reached under her skirt and slipped his fingers between her legs.

Moaning, Keira arched her back and grasped the nearby bookshelves, her breaths struggling between his movements.

Already, she could feel the rise of delicious pressure building, persuading her to let go. To lose control. But she needed to keep her wits about her. She needed to control the situation.

'Wait,' she breathed, mustering the will and strength to pull his hand away and grasp the back of his head, forcing him back by his hair. Raptly, she set her lips to the nook of his neck, tracing the base of it with her tongue.

He groaned and pressed against her hands, now fumbling to unbutton his trousers, then startled as she reached down and wrapped her fingers around him. The feel of his hardened, silky-smooth form left her equally breathless as his eyes locked with hers, full of fire.

Another warning she chose to ignore.

Instead, she pushed down his trousers and pressed their bodies closer, her hips barely resting on the edge of the desk, her legs wrapped around his waist.

A moment of unspoken words, shared with just a glance.

Her eyebrow, raised in challenge.

And then...

Keira cried out and arched her back as he slid into her, the stinging pain burning like cold fire as she adjusted to the feel of him inside her. As they broke whatever was left of her hymen.

Tentatively, Elijah waited before he pulled out again, his gaze hard upon her, almost accusatory. His jaw clenched as if he was struggling.

It was then she realised that he was pacing himself so that it wouldn't hurt her as much, and that it was as much control as he could master. It nearly undid her.

'More,' she whispered, and he obliged. Once more, he slid in, slow and steady.

Her breath hitched, but she did not wince. Did not give him any other sign that it hurt, until finally, the pain gave way to a different kind that left her pining for more.

Sensing the change in her body, the slackening of her muscles, Elijah lifted her off the desk and lowered her to the carpet.

'Does it hurt still?' he asked while taking off his shirt, his voice clipped.

'No.'

'This wasn't how I wanted our first time to happen,' he mumbled, his muscles shaking from restraint under her grip. There was a knot in her chest at his words, but there was no use having regrets now.

'Yet, it is happening,' she whispered. They might as well make the most of it.

No sooner had the words escaped her before he thrust into her anew, more forcefully, filling her world with stars. His muscles rippled as he sank into her, bending one of her legs for better access.

Wide-eyed, Keira gasped and arched against him, moaning through the waves of pleasure following the way he moved. She knew then that he had been holding back. That nothing they had done before this would come close to what they could do.

'Elijah,' she breathed, grappling for the floor, the desk, his hair. Tears of ecstasy gathered in the corners of her eyes at every luscious movement he made. Phantom claws sprouted from her nails, and she raked them down his back, eliciting a string of curses from the djinn.

'You drive me mad; do you know that?' Elijah groaned and buried his face in the nook of her neck. 'Absolutely insane.'

He rolled his hips, eliciting gasps that travelled all the way to her navel.

She was *so* close.

She had to do it now, as he rested his forehead on her shoulder, before she lost herself to him and forgot entirely.

'Is it true?' she breathed, panting through the rise and falls in her body, tensing her muscles so that he could not move without an answer. 'Is it true we can't get out of here?'

'Your wish might've,' he said between strained breaths, his muscles trembling with frustration, with the need to plunge deeper and take his yearning out on her. She shuddered at the very thought of it and how much she wanted it. Insatiable, the both of them. 'A master's wish trumps any magic.'

The moment she let him, he pounded into her again. Hard. So hard – so meticulously – that she could only hold onto him as he chased her higher, higher, and higher until—she fell over.

Not just over the edge, but the end of the world. Into a sea of pleasure, screaming his name.

Stars lingered under the roof until the ripples of pleasure phased out and he rolled over to lie beside her.

Both shivered in silence, panting against one another until his head came to rest against her shoulder and her body tensed.

It didn't go unnoticed.

Instantly, he looked up and searched her face, examining it for any trace of displeasure or pain, confusion and concern marring his every feature. 'Are you okay?'

She let the silence fall before she spoke, her voice low and damning. 'I guess men really will tell you anything you want as long as they believe they'll get to "wet their stick", be they human or not.' Shifting away from him, she sat up and pulled her skirt down to cover herself.

'Keira—' he started, perplexity clear in his voice, triggering her pent-up anger.

'You broke your promise.'

'Keira!'

'No,' she snapped, twirling on him before he could change her mind. 'I wish for you to get us out of here. I wish for you to get us out of here, to help me get August's body back, and then for you to disappear with the rest of your "family" for all I care.'

He winced and shook his head. 'Keira, don't—'

'I *wish* it!'

In an instant, he was gone. Vanished into thin air.

She looked around the space, but he was nowhere to be seen.

With unease rising, Keira began to wonder if he'd simply left her, when a click sounded from the hallway, and the door sprang open. Elijah stood on the other side, fully clothed, his face cloaked in shadow. He did not meet her eye as she marched past, nor did she attempt to meet his.

21
POSSESSION

No sooner had they left the library before Elijah moved into another room, a chamber of dark lavender-blue walls and golden interior. As her eyes settled on a large four-poster bed with bluebell satin covers, incredulity rose within her. Was he planning another go? More astonishingly, her core fluttered at the thought. But Elijah seemed to ignore the bed completely, determinedly passing without looking at it, heading for the richly carved dresser instead.

'That door over there leads to an inverted tower,' Elijah said gruffly as he pulled out a drawer and roamed through the clothes within. This had clearly been his chamber. 'It'll take you outside. You should leave, get somewhere safe, and I'll handle my siblings.'

Keira looked to the door and dismissed it with a single scrunch of her nose. 'I'm coming with you,' she said, turning back to him as he pulled out a couple daggers, inspecting their shiny copper blade. To her, at least, it looked like they had been perfectly preserved amongst the folds of his clothes.

'I won't have you anywhere near him,' Elijah growled, shutting the drawer.

'And I won't take orders and leave August alone with the likes of you,' Keira retorted, crossing her arms.

They stared at each other, neither backing down. Her heartbeat was in her chest, one part begging for him to give her a reason to fight him, the other hoping he'd say a few magical words that would make everything right. That would make the ache in her heart go away.

Something flashed in his eyes, as if he was thinking along the same lines. His lips parted to speak, and she braced herself, pressing her arms further into her chest.

'Fine,' the djinn shook his head at last, and her heart sank watching him head for the door. 'But you stay behind me. And when I tell you to run, you bloody run.'

She could adhere to that, Keira thought, her conscience stinging at the bite in his voice. *At least for now.*

Moving as fast as they could without making a sound, they snuck down the abandoned overgrown corridors in silence, heading for the ballroom. Now and then, Elijah would pause in open doorways, taking in what was left of the room, his features haunted as if watching the ghosts of his past move before him. Maybe he was. More than once, Keira wondered whether one of those ghosts was Helena, her gut wrenching at the thought, the stickiness between her legs itching further, making her shift uncomfortably from one leg to the other. She didn't think he had noticed before he turned back at her, tugging at his shirt.

'You can dry yourself off with this if you want,' he offered, and her cheeks heated.

Still, she refused, dabbing her legs in demonstration with her own skirt instead, the coarse fabric brushing against skin still sore and tightening the knot in her stomach.

Shame. Every ounce of goodness from him made her feel more shame. But she doubled down and ignored it, unwilling to inspect it further.

'Alright then.' Elijah shrugged and continued onwards, guiding her around a maze of fallen plaster, missing pieces of floor, and mould. 'Careful where you step; the ground can be treacherous.'

She stared at him, remembering all the times when he had used that same voice to guide her towards her point of pleasure and release. Bitterly, she stuffed her appreciation of the past down and pushed past him, ignoring his warning, feet stomping through dried roots and flattened plants. 'You could say that again.'

'Keira...' The imploring tone of his voice held her back. 'You shouldn't have used your wish like that.'

'Whyever not?' She scoffed. 'Did it complicate your grand plans to restore your brother's empire?'

'I didn't tell you who I was, because for once in my life, I wanted to see if someone could love me for me – not my powers. I helped my brother, yes, but only because I wanted to reunite my family.' He came up to her, face open and honest. 'Can you blame me? I'd been alone for years. Most of them spent in a lamp. I was so desperate for company that I made it my duty a long time ago to make things right. I betrayed him, Keira—'

'With Helena, I know. I know what you felt for her, what you did.'

'Exactly. And I was to be the dutiful brother and make up for it. To make it up to them all. I even promised him. But you'll make a traitor out of me again. I do not regret it.'

She stilled, turning to face him.

'You shouldn't have used your wish, because I would have done it even if you had not wished for it. Get us out, I mean.' He covered the distance between them and put her hand upon his heart. 'I sold you my loyalty with my body long before tonight.'

'You're a whore,' she purred venomously, before pushing away from him, anger spilling into her voice. 'And you've made a harlot out of me. I will not be your poor little consolation—' Her breath hitched as he yanked her arm and spun her around, pushing her against the wall, his face livid.

'You may be as upset with me as you'd like,' he snarled. 'But I'll never hear you call yourself by those words ever again. Not for following your desires. Not for stepping into your own sensuality and allowing yourself the pleasures of your sex. The pleasures you deserve!' The last words rang between them in the silence that ensued, both their chests heaving.

His eyes dropped to her parted lips, to her neck and swollen breasts. Her heart drummed in her chest, traitorously yearning with the rest of her body for his gaze to turn into touches, touches that would slip under her skirt. For *him* to slip in underneath it.

Tears prickled behind her eyes as the last hours came crashing down upon her along with frustration and regret. Why couldn't she just hate him? Why did she need him so much?

'You weren't supposed to betray me,' she uttered as the first tears fell.

She'd trusted him. Trusted another man, been intimate with him, only to find that he had lied and gone behind her back just like August. And now she had given him her virginity as a way to prove a point. 'Why did you lead him here?'

Elijah cupped her face with his hands and dried her tears. 'It was never my intention to stay. I was going to take him – take them all – away from here. But I couldn't just leave you after that first night when you'd been so brave with me.' She sucked in a breath, recollecting their first lesson in the heat of his gaze. 'And when I came back to say goodbye, you needed me.'

After that, he had stayed. For her. Had gone to Faerie, for her. Anger gave way to ebbs of guilt.

She *knew* her words had hit Elijah hard. She also knew she had provoked him to break his promise, although she had not explicitly asked him to. And yet she could not get past the anger and hurt that threatened to swallow her alive.

Elijah let go of her face and handed her one of the copper daggers, wrapping her fingers around its handle. 'If anyone tries to attack you, you use this.'

'You'd want me to hurt your family?'

'If they hurt you, they're not my family,' he said, gaze ablaze. Her eyes burned at that, and he pulled her closer to him again, kissing her forehead. 'I'll fix this,' he whispered. 'I'll fix all of it.'

A familiar cry ripped through the air, making them jump apart and stare down the hallway.

Colour drained from Elijah's face. 'Was that…'

'I think so,' breathed Keira. They looked at one another. Her mouth opened, wishing to say something – anything – but her words remained absent, her heart still scorched and afraid to open. Elijah read her expression and dipped his head in understanding, taking her hand instead as they rushed in the direction of the sound.

Four people stood in the ballroom now along with the emperor, all of them emotionlessly staring at the hunched figure in the middle, trembling on the floor.

Isolde.

Her fiery red hair hung in messy curls down her face, the paint of the Woodland Witches washed down her cheeks with her tears. Gaping wounds ran down her brown arms, caked in blood. Still, her eyes betrayed no fear, no hurt, as she stared up at the emperor in challenge and loathing.

'Where's my body?' snarled the Tyrant Emperor.

'It's gone,' Isolde hissed in return, baring her teeth.

'Where is it?' the emperor roared and slashed the air. A large cut appeared on Isolde's cheek, blood trickling over her skin like it did from the wounds on her arms.

'Stop!' Keira cried out, running into the room before she could halt herself.

'No!' Elijah shouted behind her.

Ahead, all six heads turned in their direction, alarm spreading in Isolde's widening eyes. 'Keira, run!'

No sooner had she spoken than the emperor clenched his fist and, as if he had cursed her, Isolde's body twisted with a sickening crunch and she screamed, her mouth gaping towards the roof.

Keira froze in her spot, feeling the eyes of the other four vices devour her with peaked interest.

One of them was clearly the youngest, his eyes green and narrowed with something bitter. However out of place, she felt a familiar twinge of jealousy rise like bile in her throat, and her head exploded with images of August and Gianna, of watching the men of the town ride out for the hunt, and of Elijah and Helena together.

Desperate to look away, her eyes caught on another male vice instead, his skin even darker than Isolde's, looking mighty bored. His appearance settled the burning envy within her and replaced it with a sense of heedlessness. It fuelled the ire she felt looking at the other two, neither of whom looked back at her. One was a silver fox of a man with eyes that shone with hunger at the sight of Isolde collapsed on the floor before him, and the other – the fourth of the siblings – was a woman, her beauty wild like a raging storm flashing its lightning over treacherous seas. The wicked smile on her lips never reached her eyes, which were wrought in rage, and as they fastened on the person behind Keira, even her smile receded.

'*Elnatan,*' she hissed.

Down on the floor, Isolde made a faint jerk and a swollen eyelid cracked open. *Not dead,* Keira thought.

Finally, the emperor squared his shoulders as his brother came towards them, stepping before Keira. 'I thought I ordered you to stay put?'

'Your heir found more persuasive ways of convincing me to do otherwise,' Elijah drawled. 'Good thing too. I'd imagine you'd like to know where your body is before you beat our sister into a pulp.'

Keira stiffened behind him.

'She could tell me herself if she desires to live; instead, she insists it is gone.'

'It is,' Elijah said. 'The rebels made away with it once it was left abandoned. Whether it was dumped at the bottom of the sea, burned, or dragged after a carriage, it is gone.'

'Then she will pay for it with her own!' The emperor roared, raising his fist.

'Or you can take mine,' Elijah said simply, tilting his head. Everyone stilled, even the emperor – everyone except Keira.

'No!' She grasped his hand and pulled him around to face her, hissing below her breath. 'What are you doing?'

'Keeping my promise,' Elijah said, his expression void of emotion. 'You wished for me to save August. This is how. When Aeros changes bodies, you take August and run. You leave all of us behind. Never to see us again, remember? That is your wish.'

Despite his words, Keira's fingers clenched harder around his as she gazed over his shoulder, at the emperor in August's body, at August's eyes narrowed in suspicion – as if expecting Elijah's offer to be a trap of sorts. August who had not known. August who had been overpowered. Was he still in there?

Overpowered.

Her mind stuck on the word. Was that it? Did Elijah believe he could fight off his brother? Glancing back at him, she could have sworn she saw something akin to confirmation in Elijah's eyes, but she strained herself not to let the relief show on her face. With the slightest dip of his chin, Elijah faced his brother.

'Release the boy and take my body instead,' he said. 'Do we have a deal, brother?'

The emperor sneered. 'Why would I take yours?'

'Because you can't shapeshift into your former body with the one you're wearing. Besides...you know you've always wanted my gifts. With them, you wouldn't need me to get you female company... With them, you might never have lost Helena.'

A feral, taunting smile spread over Elijah's lips at the same time as white-hot rage and embarrassment swept over the emperor's.

'I'll enjoy squandering your love-sick mind until there's nothing left,' Aeros said, and August's shadow began to grow behind him. It took Keira a moment before she realized it was the emperor himself, turning into his djinn shape, rising from its bodily cage.

'Come have your go,' Elijah answered, his back straight, his arms beckoning the emperor towards him.

As the emperor left August's body completely and shot forward for Elijah's, the human between them keeled over on the ground and groaned, clasping his head.

'August!' Elijah called after him.

The white-haired boy looked up, first at the four spectators, then at the djinn writhing and fighting against the emperor's possession. Confusion marred August's face.

'August,' Elijah called again and slid his dagger across the floor, his features starting to shift, his light brown hair darkening to pitch-black. 'Take Keira and get out of here!'

Finally, August's familiar golden eyes settled on Keira,

widened, and, as if he acted on impulse, grabbed the dagger and staggered to his feet, running towards her. He collided into her, almost knocking her off her feet, before pulling her out of the room with him. Stumbling after, Keira tried to protest, but the words died on her breath as she threw her head around, catching a last glimpse of Elijah, his slim shape lengthening into a taller, dark-haired man. Cool, calculative ice glazed over the pleading urgency in his gaze, and Keira's heart froze, realising that the Tyrant Emperor had won – and that Elijah had lost.

22
AUGUST

They flew down the giant marble staircase, leaping over missing steps and cracks filled with budding greens. Her breath caught in her throat as she looked back, second-guessing, hesitating, wondering if she should turn and go back. For Isolde. For Elijah. But every time she slowed down, August tugged at her arm, until they reached the first floor and the palace's main hallway.

As they burst outside, morning light momentarily blinded their eyes before they threw themselves into the woods and kept on running in the direction of E'Frion. Tall grass tickled her legs and fern leaves brushed her arms.

'Wait! August, wait!' Keira called and finally stopped, digging her heels in so that he was forced to a halt.

His hair, normally so neat and perfectly combed, swayed in disarray, mirroring the turmoil of his expression. 'Keira, we must go! Djinns – demons – they have returned!'

'I know, but we must help Elijah.'

'Keira, you don't know. Monsters! They are—' He paused and

froze in place, truly taking her in, as if he had not really registered that she was there. Not really.

'You...I remember you now. In your cottage, with the—and the one who took my body. You...you've known?'

'Y-yes,' Keira stuttered. 'I know they are djinns, but Elijah is...' *different.*

She looked back to the palace, wishing she could tell August what her heart knew to be true, even though her mind wasn't quite ready to admit it. There were *things* Elijah had kept from her, yes, but even so...

At once, August wrapped his arms around her, hugging her so close that she could scarcely breathe.

'It's alright. I'm here. We'll break their enchantment. Don't worry, Keira. I'll take care of you.' He stepped back and took her hands, giving them a slight shake as he looked deep into her eyes, his forehead creasing. 'You're safe now, alright?'

She opened her mouth to speak, but he merely clasped her head between his hands and kissed her forehead. 'You're safe with me.' Then he pulled at her hand again, urging her to follow towards the village. But again, Keira barely went a few steps before she halted, pointing behind her. 'No. August, we have to help Elijah. I won't leave him.'

'Keira, you're not thinking clearly.'

'But I am! He needs me and I love him!' The words were out before she could stop them. Before she could even weigh the truth of them. Once they were out, however, she realized that they were. The truth. She wasn't certain when it had happened or how – whether it was as Elijah sacrificed for her, or when he'd held her as she cried at the inn – only that it had. She had fallen in love with a djinn.

'What will they take, grandmama? What will the djinn take if you give them a finger?'

'Your heart. The djinn will take your heart.' That's what her grandmother would have said. She could hear it clearly, as if the old lady were right beside her.

The djinn would take her heart.

Not just her body, but her whole bleeding heart with it. Because deep, deep within, in some miniscule, buried part of herself, she was a djinn too. And it was that part that Elijah had coaxed out, nourished, and tended to, until she had shed the layer that hid her spots. Hid her claws.

And she'd taken her hurt out on him because it had felt safer than taking it out on the one who'd hurt her in the first place.

August stared at her. 'You love him?'

A wind blew through the trees and clearing, ruffling Keira's skirt and causing her to shiver. As if it carried her scent over, August sniffed the air and a dawning realization fell over his features.

'You've – you've lain with him?' His lips twisted into a sneer.

'I have,' Keira breathed, stunned that he would know, wishing her reddening cheeks would not betray her so easily. He must have smelled Elijah on her, she realised; her skin once again sensitive to the remnants of him between her thighs. But how?

August spat at her feet. 'You're no better than a Nightlady.'

Keira sucked in a sharp breath. 'I'd rather be a Nightlady than marry without love.' It was not the Nightladies nor their actions that were the problem, she realised, but the people judging them and how they chose to live.

August shook his head and grabbed her wrist. 'Clearly he's messed with your head,' he said and began to walk again, pulling her after. 'But I'm a gentleman and I won't leave you here to become a feast for demons, though that is what I ought to do.'

Keira let out a cry of protest and dug her heels in, stumbling after when his force became stronger than her.

'I'll get you help,' he continued. 'We'll marry, and then I won't hear another word spoken about this. I'll find a way to forgive you once you're in a right state of mind.'

'No! August,' Keira shouted, scratching at his fingers. 'I mean it! Let go!'

A dagger whizzed past and lodged itself in the nearest tree, the handle still humming with the force with which it had been thrown. Both spun, Keira at first frightened that the emperor had come after them; August's eyes wide as they spotted the Woodland Witches stepping out from between trees and bushes.

'Keira. Is everything alright?' asked Makenna, her crossbow at the ready, an arrow nocked. Echo stood a little further back, twirling another dagger in her grasp, hostile amber eyes gleaming at August amidst painted black ink. His grip loosened around Keira's wrist as he stepped aside, keeping his hands so the witches could see them.

'Yes,' Keira said, gathering herself. 'I was just telling this *gentleman* that I didn't want to go.'

'Fine,' August said, shaking his head in disbelief, taking a few steps backwards. 'I give in. Stay, if that's what you want. Be a Nightlady, one of the wild people; I don't care—!'

Another dagger shot past, grazing his ear on its way. With a squeak, August turned on his heels and took off into the woods.

Keira could only glare after him, discovering, to her relief, that she did not feel at all sorry to see him go.

23
A WITCH'S RITUAL

'What are you doing here?' Keira asked the witches. Wading into the shallow end of the lake, she pulled up her skirt with one hand and shoved water onto her legs with the other, washing off remnants of the sticky substance that clung to her skin. Trying not to think of whether that would be the last time she'd have anything of Elijah on her.

'Isolde has been taken,' Makenna said, then paused. From shore, the Woodland Witches watched Keira carefully, Echo's nostrils pinching like August's had done when he smelled Elijah on her. The trees rustled with the breeze wafting around them.

'You've coupled with the Djinn of Lust,' she stated, not as a question, but as a fact. 'We hunt his brother.'

'They're in the ruins,' Keira murmured and returned to the witches' side, her thighs smarting from the cold water. She met Echo's gaze, penetrating through the black paint that framed her eyes, daring her to say something about her and Elijah, expecting her to say something critical. But the witch said nothing on the matter as a another came running up to them.

'Scouts reports the djinns moving through the woods towards the village.'

'Good, it will keep them occupied while we search the ruins.'

'But – the townspeople! We must help them!' Keira breathed.

Echo frowned. 'What have the townspeople ever done to deserve our protection?'

'Does anyone need to do anything to deserve help? Perhaps, even, Isolde is with them.'

With brows bunching further, Echo turned back to the other witch. 'Was she?' The witch shook her head, and Keira's stomach dropped. Why wouldn't the emperor have brought her with him? Was it because he wouldn't…or because he couldn't?

'Then she must be back at the castle,' Keira said, hoping against all odds that they'd still find her alive.

'Then that's where we'll go.' Echo's eyes hardened with resolution.

'What about the village? We can't let them fend for themselves.' The villagers were naïve and small-minded, to be sure, but she didn't think all of them deserved whatever violence the emperor was about to unleash upon them.

'Why don't you take the witches to the village, Echo?' Makenna said, coming up beside them, eyes rimmed in the same dark war paint as the other witches, blending like shadows against her pale skin. 'I'll go with Keira to get Isolde.'

Clenching her jaw, Echo seemed to consider it for a moment, before she nodded and kissed Makenna hard. Then she called upon all the witches to follow her.

Once the last of them disappeared between the foliage, Makenna turned to Keira. 'Let's go.'

Keira's pulse pounded as they ran through the forest, back towards the palace. Her thoughts racing a mile an hour.

Would they find Isolde alive? What had happened to Elijah when the emperor took over his body? Was he still in there?

Drawn in two directions, Keira's conscience lurched to run towards the palace and the village both. But she stayed the course, hoping to find Isolde. Hoping she would know how to stop the emperor. If only she'd still had her wish...

Without hesitating, Makenna ran inside, followed by Keira barking directions towards the ballroom. There, crumpled in a heap on the floor was Isolde, her face and arms marred with more cuts and bruises than when Keira had left.

'Quick!' Makenna breathed, gesturing for Keira to follow as she dived beside the Djinn of Gluttony, feeling Isolde's pulse and checking her breath. 'She's alive!'

'Isolde,' Keira pleaded with her friend as Makenna shook her gently until she groaned awake, then proceeded to prop her up into her lap, unhooking and uncorking a flask of water from her belt. 'How do we stop Aeros? Isolde, please. Tell me how we can get Elijah back!'

Water spilled over her face, washing blood out of the corner of her mouth, and Isolde's eyelids flickered and opened, her pupils struggling to settle on Keira. Her first words were mere incomprehensible hisses and Keira strained to hear them better. 'What?'

'Helena,' Isolde breathed, pointing at Keira.

'No, I'm Kiki. Iz, please, tell us how to stop him.'

'Get Helena...' Isolde's arm slumped, and she passed out in Makenna's lap, blood draining from the face of the latter.

'What did she mean, get Helena?' Keira gaped at Makenna. 'Helena is a saint.'

'She's also a spirit. A deity,' Makenna whispered. 'There's a ritual, one that can be used to call upon demons and gods alike. But it takes a whole coven to have them materialise in flesh and bone. I'm not strong enough to do it on my own.'

Keira thought long and hard. Looking around the space, gnawing at her lip, contemplating how useless of a power it was to be the one to make the palace open and nothing more. So much for being the heir of the emperor...

Something clicked.

'What if we use another body?' Keira asked.

'Only blood magic would be strong enough...' Makenna murmured, shifting a stray auburn lock of hair away from Isolde's forehead. 'We'd need someone of Helena's line to do it.'

'We have.'

Makenna looked at her with confusion before it seemed to dawn upon her what she meant. 'You? You would like us to offer her *your* body?'

'According to Iz, Helena is my ancestor.'

'Even if she is...' Makenna shook her head. 'Keira, there is no knowing what will happen to you if we do. She might take over your body completely and decide to stay in this realm.'

Keira swallowed. 'She is a saint. I guess I'll just have to trust that she'll act as one.'

24
PUPPET MASTERS

They carried Isolde between them down to the apothecary in the dungeon and laid her in the grand four-poster bed, wrapping the thick quilt of deep scarlet satin around her, before propping her up against the pillows.

It was no wonder, Keira realised as she looked around, that the place had reminded her of Isolde. As much as Elijah's chamber mirrored his persona, so did the apothecary mirror Isolde's.

Like an extension of her hut, bottles of wine filled racks along one wall, while shelves upon shelves filled with jars and herbs lined another. Dried plants and spices hung from the roof like slabs of meat, and an aroma filled the space, speaking of an era gone by. It had to have been the Djinn of Gluttony's chamber.

'I'll go gather the things we need,' Makenna said, shifting over to some shelves, gathering dried plants with one hand and candles with the other. Then she dumped it all on the worktop table and pushed it aside, revealing a summoning circle underneath, with a pentacle and other symbols and runes that Keira did not know painted inside it. Meticulously, Makenna traced the lines with onyx sand and chanted words under her breath. Then she placed the candles and herbs around the circle. As she lit a matchstick and lowered it towards the first candle, she turned her gaze back to Keira and nodded. 'Get ready.'

Drawing a deep breath, Keira let it out then steeled herself. 'What do I do?'

'Just step inside, stay still, and no matter what happens, don't leave the circle before I let you.'

She could do that. Fisting her skirt in her hands, Keira stepped into the middle of the circle and exhaled. Never had her corset and belt felt as tight as they did in that moment, her chest rising against the hard frames, her heart pounding.

What if Makenna was right? What if Helena did decide to overtake her body and stay in the realm? Wouldn't everyone take a second chance at life if they had one? Keira shuddered at the thought.

In quiet murmurs, Makenna moved around the circle, lighting the remaining candles. The scent of burning wake and smoke reached Keira with her hushed words. *'Saint Helena, upon thee we call. Saint Helena, protect us all. Show thy spirit through your blood. Unite with us against the enemy you fought. Lest your sacrifice be for nought.'*

When she stopped, the candlelight flickered a little, and Makenna and Keira both stood still, listening. Keira's heart raced.

When nothing more happened, Keira caught Makenna casting a glance towards Isolde, who lay unmoving, eyes closed and chest heaving.

'Spirit, spirit, hear our call; Spirit, spirit protect us all.'

Still nothing...until Keira could have sworn that she felt a pinch.

'Did you—' Keira started, but then Makenna inhaled sharply. Isolde groaned and twisted in her bed as a gust of wind rushed through the room and put out all the lights.

No sooner had they extinguished before a new light flared, coming from the circle itself, casting the room in a ghostly light.

Fear prickled along Keira's spine, and she gasped, nearly staggering out of her spot when something clenched at her heart, numbed her limbs, and pushed at her chest. Suddenly, her body was too tight, too vast at the same time.

'Don't move, Keira!' Makenna called, but it was of little use. Keira could not move, even if she had wanted to. Her body was unresponsive to the orders of her mind. Her panic increased.

'I smell your blood,' sang a woman's voice inside her head, hollow and distant, everywhere and nowhere at the same time. *'It is mine.'*

Startled, Keira felt the spirit of Helena stretch into every limb, attaching to every nerve. One minute, it was as if the possession stretched into an infinite amount of time; she could feel every agonising part of it, like an adolescent's growth spurt. The next, it seemed to move at high speed and it was over. So impossibly fast that Keira had a hard job gathering whether or not it had been her imagination and she was still the same as before.

But when her body cracked its neck, she knew it was not her who had asked it to, and when she spoke, it was not her voice that came out.

'Why have you called upon me?' Saint Helena asked Makenna through Keira's lips, her voice mythical, like lark song at sunrise.

'The Tyrant Emperor – he has returned,' Makenna said, her voice breathless and her cheeks drained of colour as she tentatively bowed her head, exposing the back of her neck in surrender.

'We called upon you through the blood of your heir,' said a feeble voice, and Keira – Helena – twirled towards it, sucked in a breath, and stared at Isolde gazing back at her from her bed. 'We need you to...put things right. To bring...Aeros to the Realm of the Dead with you...where he belongs.'

'Release me,' hissed the saint.

'Can we trust you?' wheezed Isolde.

'It is not I that should prove myself worthy of trust.'

If Keira could have controlled her body, she would have stiffened, remembering what Isolde had said. She had betrayed Helena. An image flashed before her, seen through the eyes of a woman resting in a plump bed in a gilded chamber, gazing at Isolde, looking much like she did now, with a baby in her arms. '*Trust me*,' she said, and the image disappeared.

As if she had been thinking of the same moment, the present Isolde turned her gaze to Makenna and nodded.

Without hesitating, Makenna stretched her leg across the markings on the floor, then broke the circle, pulling the onyx sand with her foot. Instantly, Helena moved outside, striding towards Isolde. Makenna shifted as if to step before her, but Isolde motioned for her to stay in her place.

Stopping before Isolde, Helena merely stared her down for the longest time without a word. Within, Keira could feel the ebb and flow of anger, hurt, more wrath, and a faint, faint trace of something warm. 'Where is he?'

'In the village,' Isolde said. 'Keira will guide you.'

Quiet. When Helena spoke again, it was without emotion, without wrath and without grief. 'Your day will come, Gale, Djinn of Gluttony.'

Isolde nodded. 'But that day is not today.'

They raced through the woods like Keira could only imagine the djinns and Woodland Witches had done before them. The further they went and the closer they came to E'Frion, the more Helena recalled old memories, all of them flashing before Keira's eyes. Some of Helena and the emperor. Some of Helena and Isolde. And some, to Keira's dread, of Helena and Elijah.

Mentally, Keira shut her eyes against the image of Helena and Elijah sharing a tender kiss beside his four-poster bed, and then another of the obvious desperation marring his face as he burst through the doors in Helena's last moments.

As Helena thought of him, that same warm feeling as before bubbled up inside Keira, yet even stronger, and for a moment, her own envy and jealousy rose to meet it.

What would Helena do if she realised Elijah was alive too? Would she take Keira's body to be with him? Would Elijah allow it? Would she spend the rest of her life, screaming against another woman's consciousness, only to remain voiceless, buried at the back of someone's mind?

Could Helena read *Keira's* mind even as she wondered these things?

Indignant ire and fear rose within her like bile, threatening to choke her, when she shook her senses and refocused her attention on the road ahead, realising they had reached E'Frion.

The village was in complete chaos.

All around, villagers were either fighting over something, fighting one another, or bawling their eyes out while seated on the ground, banging their fists against it. Some witches ran between them and pulled them into houses, as if that could protect them from the influence of the djinns perched on rooftops. Other witches tried to shoot the djinns down, nocking their arrows and taking aim, but the djinns merely dodged their attacks.

Two djinns moved their fingers like puppet masters, and as

their fingers moved, so did the villagers. The witches found themselves forced to avoid blows from villagers and disarm them instead, struggling not to harm them in the process.

From the corner of her eye, Keira could see the dark-skinned djinn strolling away from it all. A trail of men and ladies followed in his wake with slack and dreamy expressions of indolence.

They're affecting them, Keira thought as Helena walked their body into the village. Like Elijah had affected the Eleionomaes.

'Yes,' came Helena's voice in response, and Keira nearly jumped out of her skin.

Can you hear me?

'The Cardinal Seven each manipulate others with the vice that matches their individual natures. It is how they won wars and laid waste to courts. If you harbour their vice, they will latch onto it.' Her words hung heavy and full of meaning, and Keira realised then why her envy and wrath had felt so intense only a moment ago. 'And, yes,' her voice rang inside Keira's head, stoking her growing fire of discomfort. 'I know Elnatan is here. But I will not stay for him. I would not have then; I will not now. They are not meant to be loved, these djinns.'

This had Keira brighten and bristle at the same time, but before she could ask what Helena meant with her last words, there was a cry of war, and Helena spun just in time, skirt swinging, to avoid being skewed through with a staff by Miles.

He pulled it around and swung it again, violently and uncoordinatedly, his eyes unfocused as if he could neither see nor act within reason.

Biding her time, Helena grasped the wooden stick, pulled Miles off-balance, then knocked him over the head with the end of it. With a thump, he collapsed on the ground, his brown curls in disarray over his unconscious face.

A low chuckle sounded from the depths of an alley under the

shades of trees, and a young man stepped into the light, his green eyes lit with malice.

'So much envy in these human hearts of yours, it almost makes you all too easy to manipulate.'

'You're one to talk,' answered Helena, straightening Keira's back. 'As I recall, you were always seething with it, *Adrien*.'

The young man lost his countenance, but only for a second before his lips curled with a hiss. '*Helena*.'

'Have you no better things to do than play the trickster god in your brothers' shadow?'

He snarled, glaring at her from under a heavy fringe of black hair. Ink rays ran up his neck from his shoulder. 'Elnatan made sure I don't.' He stepped forward. 'Do you know? Do you know what he did to me? What he did to her?'

Helena didn't answer. The man's features darkened with bitter revenge staining his beautiful green eyes.

'He will know what it's like.' He made to move towards them, staring her down as if he could see beyond Helena, to the depths of Keira's soul within. But Helena held up her hand in warning.

'*She* still waits, Adrien.' This made him pause. 'If you want to be better than them, be better. Go see her. Leave the dark. Seek the light.'

'She...she lives?'

Helena nodded. 'She still waits. Don't let it be in vain.'

Keira did not know whom they spoke about. She had expected Adrien to be doubtful, to demand proof. Instead, his countenance was already slipping with surprise, desperation, and something else...

Hope. She saw hope in his eyes.

'If you lie,' the Djinn of Envy hissed, already retreating into the shadows, 'I will destroy this world and everything in it.'

'I don't,' Helena said, but Adrien was already gone.

What was that about?

'It's not my story to tell,' Helena answered, her voice low and contemplative. Sad. *'Come. We must find Aeros.'*

Someone groaned and Helena swirled, staring down at Miles taking to his head, his expression fazed and disoriented.

When his eyes cleared on Keira's face, he inhaled sharply and spluttered frantic incoherent words. 'Keira! I'm sorry – I couldn't – demons! It was like something had taken over my body!'

Bewildered, Keira watched him plead for her forgiveness, but before his panic could escalate, she was on her knees, imploring him to keep calm. To her surprise, it was her own voice that came out, and her own thoughts that controlled her muscles, as if Helena had simply handed her the reins. It eased something in her chest, and she realised how anxious she truly had been about Helena controlling her body. No doubt, Miles must have felt something of the same when a djinn controlled him.

'Miles,' Keira urged. 'Focus, please. Miles, did you see a tall, dark-haired man enter the village? Someone who didn't look like he belonged?'

Miles stilled and dipped his chin, staring wide-eyed at her. 'He was like a king of old, followed by his court. One minute everything was as it used to be, the road empty. The village quiet. The next they were there and then...chaos.'

'Did you see where he went?'

'To the Thornfells,' Miles breathed. 'To the manor.'

'I need to go,' Keira said, rising to her feet.

'I'm coming with you!'

Keira turned with a protest on her lips, but Miles beat her to it.

'He is *my* love too, Keira,' he said, mistaking her urgency for concern over August. 'And I might never be able to *touch* him, I won't ever be able to *marry* him like you or any other girl can, but at the very least I can be there for him.'

Keira looked at him, suddenly wondering if *this* was why Miles had always bullied her and been terrible to her. Not because they liked the same man, but because she, in this sleepy, small town they lived in, was the one who stood a chance at getting him in the end.

It did not excuse the things he had done, but she understood now why it might have been hard for him to make it easy for her. Why he might have wanted to push her into setting her eyes on someone else.

'Did you know?' Keira asked under her breath. 'Did you know what was put in my drink?' The bullying, she could move on from. For the bullying, she could be the bigger person, or try to be, at least. But the tampered drink?

Instantly, Miles shook his head. 'No. No, I didn't. I just wanted to poke a bit of fun at you, that's all. I didn't realise until I saw you. I tried to pull you out of the tavern, but you pushed me away and then there were so many others that gathered...then August came. And I hated it, hated that you were the one to leave with him, even then.' He looked down at his shoes, ears burning with shame.

She wanted to tell him that she no longer cared for August. That she deserved better. That *he* deserved better than to be pining for someone who would never be available to him. However little she truly knew August's heart, that much she knew. The emperor had said so himself, after reading his inner thoughts. August had gone hunting the stag to secure a *girl's* hand in marriage. If Miles was the one he secretly wanted, that would have been his chance. But Miles needed to discover that for himself, however...like she had.

'Fine,' Keira said. 'But if things turn dangerous, I'm not saving you.'

'And I'll leave you behind if it means protecting myself or August,' Miles said, meeting her roguish smirk with his own.

'That's a deal,' Keira replied, feeling relief at finally having found some common ground.

'*Let's go,*' ordered Helena's voice, laced with impatience.

'You're like a predator hunting after her prey, and yet you do not recognise that they have taken your claws and made you into their pet.'

— ELIJAH

25
DIVINE FIRE

Keira and Miles hurried through the village, passing villagers splitting into two groups and carrying weapons as they readied to attack one another.

Keira threw a glance to the rooftops where the djinns of Wrath and Greed still sat, smirking as they pulled the villagers' strings like marionettes. She was instantly reminded of her and Elijah's game of chess.

'Are they...using our people like pawns?' Miles panted as they ran, just as the Djinn of Greed threw his head back and laughed at one of the villagers running a hayfork into another. Wrath narrowed her eyes and had the baker's wife smash Greed's villager over the head with her rolling pin.

'It would seem so.' Keira frowned. With a shiver running down her spine, Keira turned her sight upon Thornfell Manor, resting upon the hilltop. The sooner they stopped the emperor, the sooner they would save E'Frion. Whatever was left of it.

The colourful landscape blurred as they rushed up the hill, and by the time they reached the top, both she and Miles were winded. Inside her head, Keira could hear Helena's voice complaining about the physique of her mortal body.

You're welcome to get another, Keira thought as they crept closer to the manor. A humid tinge lingered in the air from a fog barely lifted, as if the sky was about to open and empty its rain. Autumn had truly arrived, and briefly, Keira lost herself to the idea of spending the oncoming winter months lounging before the hearth, wrapped up in Elijah's arms. Her heart ached at the thought that she might never again.

'Let's get this over with,' came Helena's voice.

The manor was a stately home five times the size of her cottage, with blankets of foliage covering its walls. Fine beds with lavender, fox bells, and white wildflowers lay scattered around a winding pebbled path, leading them through the gardens and up to the terrace steps. Sneaking closer to the walls, Keira and Miles stole a few glances through the windows until they found what they were looking for.

Seated in an armchair in the living room, as if he were the master of the house, was the emperor, his poise still like a predator resting. On the carpet before him sat the Thornfells and the Merinos, with August's arms wrapped protectively around Gianna.

Miles stiffened beside Keira and she almost felt sorry for him, but not as sorry as she felt for Gianna. The petite blonde looked ready to faint from fear, trembling like a leaf in the wind against August's arms. Perhaps certain in her belief that he would protect her when it mattered.

Would he though? Even if he did, against the emperor it wouldn't be enough.

Keira startled as Aeros' voice drifted through the balcony door standing ajar.

'A union,' he drawled, his gaze falling upon the youths. August appeared to crumble underneath it. 'How lovely. Did you know that I once oversaw the union of your forefather? I sensed something familiar about you, but it's more poignant now in the presence of your mother...' He let out the word as if it was a slur. '*Fae.*'

Keira's mouth dropped open simultaneously as Miles' fingers grabbed her arm to steady himself. So that's why August could smell Elijah on her. He was of fae heritage.

'Did you know?' he whispered, but she shook her head. This was a secret the Thornfells would have been keen to keep, and judging by Mrs Thornfell's expression, the revelation wasn't taken as anything but an insult. Keira had to hand it to her: she was being kept a prisoner, and still she looked at the emperor as if he were mere dirt under her nose.

The emperor remained unaffected. 'Let me give you a gift.' He leaned forward and handed August a dagger. 'Better cut out her heart now, boy, before she gives it to someone else.'

The Merinos gasped and Gianna startled, shifting away from her fiancé. August dropped the dagger, fear and shock marring his face.

'Watch how she recoils from you,' the emperor hissed.

August turned towards Gianna, who was shaking her head, pleading with glistening eyes for him not to use the weapon. The distress in August's features smoothed with surprise, then hardened. He picked the dagger back up.

Before she knew what she was doing, or perhaps it was not even her doing it, Keira rose, walked over to the balcony door, and pushed it open, entering the living room. At her presence, the emperor shot up from his chair, his voice changing entirely, as if it came from someone else. 'Keira!'

Elijah! He's still in there.

'*Let me handle this,*' answered Helena's voice at the back of her mind.

We must save him.

'Trust me.'

When Keira opened her mouth to speak, it was Helena's voice that came through. 'Aeros, it is I.'

The emperor's forehead creased, then Elijah's voice sounded again, and the rasp in it cut through Keira's heart. 'Helena?'

'Let me speak to my husband.'

The emperor's expression darkened with his voice. 'What are you doing here?'

'I've returned to you. To take my place by your side once again.'

No! Keira thought, itching to flex her fingers, to block her lips with her hand. But she was not in control anymore. Helena was.

'I ordered your death,' Aeros said, his expression watchful. 'I killed you.'

'I betrayed you.'

He watched her as she trailed around the armchair, coming to stand before him, listening carefully to her every word.

'You thought you knew who I was, and then you found out I had lied. You acted in anger. You wounded me in return. I understand.'

Keira's conscience stung, remembering that she had done the same thing, made the same choice, when she'd discovered Elijah's hidden truth. How it had hurt her to learn of it, and how she had hurt and tricked him in return.

She supposed her pride did not fall too far from the tree.

The emperor's actions, however, had led to Helena's death. What if hers would eventually do to the same to Elijah?

They are not meant to be loved, these djinns. A sense of foreboding rose within her while recalling Helena's words, and suddenly, Keira felt the clammy hand of urgency grasping at her throat. *Helena...?* She tried, but the saint ignored her still. What was she planning to do to him? To them?

'I've returned to make things right,' Helena cooed, caressing the emperor's cheek. 'To make it as if my death never happened.'

From the corner of her eye, Keira could see Miles entering the living room and coaxing the Thornfells and Meronis out of the house. As he urged them on, they scrambled to their feet, stumbling over themselves to get out. The Meronis pushed their daughter before them while the Thornfells raced in front of them all, leaving August at the rear to be helped by Miles.

'It was my downfall,' Aeros whispered, and the tone of his voice pulled Keira's attention back to him. To where Helena kept his attention away from the people escaping behind him.

He stood, leaning into her touch, looking nothing like the menacing, powerful man that the legends were built around. Instead, his brows were tightly knit over such forlorn eyes that Keira almost took pity on him. *Almost.*

'Come, my love,' Helena purred, and took his hands in Keira's. All of Keira's insides squirmed at the sight. 'Let's go home. Let's take back what's ours.'

What? Keira thought. *Helena, what are you doing?*

But the deity did not answer. Instead, she pulled the emperor with her, out of the manor, racing so fast that Keira could only hope that Miles had already taken August and the others far away from there. *Helena, stop!*

'I'm sorry, little heir. I've waited too long to be reunited with him. Aeros is my love. I'm not letting him go now. I'm sure you understand.'

Images of Elijah smiling back at her flashed before Keira's eyes and her heart tugged in longing for him.

No... Keira thought. *You were sent to betray him. You were sent* to take the emperor down. You fought against his tyranny and brought his demise. For peace and freedom.

'Such a pretty little story, woven by petty little people. But they were wrong. About him. About us. We were meant to bring all of Equinox together again, but they got in the way. Now we shall make it right.'

'No!'

The sound escaped Keira's lips, and her body stopped, her hand pausing at her lips.

'My love?' Aeros asked, studying her face. 'Helena?'

'She fights,' Helena panted, taking his hand again.

Damn right, I am, Keira growled, panic rising at the thought of being stuck in her own body. Of both her and Elijah being mere presences in bodies that once had been theirs, cursed to forever watch as Helena and the emperor went on with their lives, ruling and making love.

Keira let out a raging scream at the thought, and Helena clamped her hands over her ears.

'*Helena!*' Aeros barked, grasping for Keira's body as she sank to her knees, gritting her teeth against the sound.

This body belongs to me, Keira snarled. *You will not take it. I will* never *let anyone take it without my permission ever again! I will destroy you both.*

'*You foolish girl,*' hissed Helena. '*There is nothing that can quench the shadow of a djinn but that of the light of a saint. You are powerless against us.*' She looked up, straight into Aeros' concerned gaze. And Keira wondered whether Elijah was in there still, looking back at her. Wondered whether she could take out the emperor without losing him in the process.

'The way you feel, that is how we feel. Our time together was taken from us. Let us have it.'

I'm sorry that they did, Keira replied in her mind. *But your time is over. And I'll not give you a single more minute of mine.*

Slowly, Keira felt tingles as her nails grew into physical claws, and she raised her hands before her face. Her facial muscles shifted and her mouth dropped open. Helena watched in stunned realisation as Keira slowly but surely took control back.

'Wait! We can trade places. I can make it so that you take my place as a saint.'

If you're what it means to be a saint, I'd rather be a sinner, Keira thought. Then she pulled her claws upon herself, clawing the sides of her waist. Over her shoulder.

Helena screamed, and Aeros screamed with her, shouting for her to tell him what to do. How to help.

'She's—' Helena started, but Keira slashed herself again, and Helena screamed anew.

Then the pressure in Keira's body loosened. She could feel every single nerve in her body. Could wiggle every single finger and toe.

Hunched over, her breathing hard and shallow, she could still hear the saint at the back of her mind, commanding her to let her go. Before her, Aeros pled for Helena to answer him.

'She's...managed,' Keira breathed, taking on the cadence of the saint, then looked up beneath her lashes to meet his gaze. His forehead remained furrowed, as if he didn't quite believe that Helena was out of danger. She needed to convince him, before he saw through her and used his powers on her.

Keira visualized the saint. The way she had seen her in Helena's memories. And slowly but surely, she felt her own appearance change. Her body altered, her light brown hair falling into golden locks that spilled over her shoulders.

'Helena,' the emperor breathed, lifting her chin, taking her hand as he helped her to her feet. 'I can't believe it is you.'

Keira rose, forcing a lover's smile on her lips.

'It is. It is I, and this is us, my love.' She cupped her hand against his cheek, bringing his face to hers. 'Together again,' she whispered, feeling Helena banging at the wall in the back of her mind as their lips met.

There is but one thing that can quench the shadow of a djinn... the light of a saint.

And as the heir of a saint, Keira let her light shine.

No sooner did their mouths meet, than light began to radiate from her pores and belt out from her skin. It grew by the minute, as the emperor began to try to pull away. But Keira held him firm, until her light became so bright she could barely keep her eyes open.

The emperor screamed, and so did Helena.

The sound ripped through Keira's mind until pins and needles travelled up and down her limbs. It was much the same sensation as when she was first possessed, only in reverse, the space within her body expanding, like a stone was being lifted from her chest. As if Helena was leaving it.

The light exploded out of her, ripping the emperor's features off the figure before her, until his dark hair turned light brown, and his shoulders slimmed. Until the eyes were warm and passionate instead of hard.

Elijah squinted through the light and called her name as he tried to reach for her. But she could not control it, could not stop the light. It overpowered her, wafted outwards, then left her crumpled on the ground.

'Keira! Keira!' called a voice. Numb and disoriented, Keira looked up as Miles came running to her side, lifting her by the shoulders. 'Keira, are you alright?' But she could not answer, for a chasm was already splitting her chest open as it dawned upon her what her eyes could not see.

The spot where the emperor had been stood empty, and she felt her body – felt the hollowness now present in Helena's absence – and she knew they were both gone... And so was Elijah.

26

AFTERMATH

Mr Burton picked up a piece of rubble and tossed it aside, his eyes squinting as he caught sight of the Thornfells, the Meronis, Miles, and Keira coming down the hill.

The villagers cried out and ran to the two families for comfort as they lamented and pointed to the wounded and dead. No one paid Miles or Keira any attention as they stood to the side, solemnly taking in the state of E'Frion.

According to the villagers, the djinns had caught sight of the light coming from Thornfell and simply rushed off, leaving destruction in their wake. Some villagers discussed whether or not they should chase after them, but Keira could not master the energy to care. Instead, she caught sight of the witches standing with the Nightladies and excused herself to Miles, heading to meet them.

'Keira!' Echo said and embraced her, taking in the state of her. 'Are you alright?'

'I'll be okay,' Keira mumbled, waving off her concern.

Echo frowned. 'Isolde? Makenna? Do you know where they are?'

'They...they were back at the palace when I...left.' With Helena sharing her body.

Keira's eyes fell back towards Thornfell hill, still expecting to see Elijah stroll down it, as if her mind refused to believe that he was gone. Gone to the Realm of the Dead or wherever the light of the saint had cast him to.

Would he have been there still if they had come up with another plan? If she had not so blindly trusted Helena, or if they had never let Helena and the emperor take their bodies? With every thought she could feel something inside her crack and shatter further, but there was no time to fall apart as Lord Thornfell's voice carried towards them, calling everyone's attention to him.

'People of E'Frion!' Lord Thornfell started, making Keira and Echo exchange glances but move closer, nevertheless. 'It is terrible what happened here, but we will rebuild and come together. We will return to life as we know it, unaltered. The people of E'Frion are resilient. We will recover. What we should not do, however, is forget. Let this be a reminder of the dangers of magic, and that magic does not have a place in a society such as ours. We have become too relaxed, too frivolous. We must tighten our customs and straighten our children, so that we do not invite it in.'

Keira blinked. Was he really taking this approach, knowing what blood ran through the veins of his son and wife? She exchanged a glance with Miles as loud murmurs of agreement rose amongst the villagers, and she felt the witches and Nightladies stiffen next to her.

'How did the djinns return in the first place?' called a villager.

'What brought them here?' called another.

'She did,' August said, pointing directly at Keira.

The crowd gasped and turned in her direction, eyes wide and angry at her.

Only Miles did not turn, his gaze unbelieving and his mouth open as he stared at August. Tentatively, he tried to pull at August's sleeve, whispering fervently in his ear. But August merely shook his head, lips pressed thin, his gaze hard and unforgiving on Keira.

And she realised that this had nothing to do with the siege of the Cardinal Seven.

This was all because of August's ego, and a bruised one at that.

Keira merely raised her chin as the heckling rose, calling for her to get out of town.

Carefully, Echo pulled at her elbow, and she left with the witches to the chorus of villagers cussing them out and away. Even after all the witches had done for them against the court of vices, they still didn't treat them better.

'You can come and live with us,' Echo murmured as they paused by her cottage, and Keira felt grateful that she did not throw an "I told you so" in her face for good measure. 'Isolde will probably insist on it.'

But Keira shook her head. 'No. This is my home. I've nowhere else to go.' And it was the first place Elijah would know to find her if he ever came back... 'Besides, their anger will recede. Eventually.' She met Echo's gaze, expecting to find pity in it. But it wasn't there.

'If you ever need us,' Echo said instead, 'you know where to find us.'

Keira watched them leave, holding at bay the emotions threatening to brim to the surface. It would be fine, she told herself. It would be fine.

Then she locked herself into the empty space of her cottage, cast one look at Elijah's empty mattress as the door closed heavily behind her – and slid down to the floor, crying.

27
REGRET

'Get out of the village, demon-lover; no one wants you here!'

'Yeah, move in with the witches!'

The heckling faded as Keira walked away, arms crossed tightly against her chest, trying not to listen while the wind ruffled her hair.

'Don't worry, hon, when they're away from their wives they all sound different,' a Nightlady crooned, giving her a wink. 'In fact, they'll probably pay good money just to have you.'

Keira huffed a joyless chuckle, her mouth attempting and failing at quirking at the corner before she kept on walking.

It'd been a couple weeks since the emperor attempted to lay siege to the village, but the people of E'Frion had not forgotten – would not forget – still living in fear that the vices would return. But she did not care. None of it mattered, but for the fact that Elijah was gone.

He was everywhere, yet nowhere at the same time. By the

peach stand, inside the ice cream parlour, strolling down the street, and, most frequently of all, by the fireplace. She never slept in her bed anymore; instead she spent her nights upon his mattress, absorbing his scent, staring at the flames flickering until she fell asleep, waking to ashes stretching like scars in the hearth. If she were to take the ash and paint her own scars, she would be covered.

Everywhere ached. Everywhere felt like she'd been cut through a hundred times over, even though her self-inflicted wounds from taking on Helena had healed. Although she knew how to change her skin now, she had kept them – changing the scars to match the floral ones from Faerie – like tiger stripes along her body. Occasionally she spent her nights imagining how Elijah would worship each and every one of them, her fingertips brushing against dried up rose petals on the floor.

She'd found her living room and bedroom covered in them and extinguished candles when she returned after that fateful day, the meaning of it leaving her in a state of utter despondency not even the Thornfells threats of shipping her off could shake her out of.

Keira rarely left her cottage if she could help it.

Most days were spent curled up in her chair, gazing out of her window, watching the villagers pass by. They'd pause to whisper and point before they hurried along, realising that she could see them.

The rainy days were her favourites. No one was around – not even Miles or Isolde, who had taken to checking up on her now and then – and the weather fitted her mood perfectly. She'd open the windows wide to stand in the spray, filling the whole cottage with the scent of Elijah. When the rain died down and a wind wafted by with the scent of petrichor, she inhaled deeply and closed her eyes, almost able to picture his breath on her skin, his lips drifting over the edge of her jaw and pausing at the beginning of her ear.

Then he was gone as quickly as he had come. And all she could think about was that it was her fault. That she had not appreciated him when he was there.

She sighed and let her eyes wander across the room, picturing him in every chair, standing by the mantelpiece, or winking at her from the kitchen.

She had wished to be mistress of a manor, and now she would have given anything to merely have her cottage and him. To spend every waking moment of the rest of her life secluded within these walls, embraced by his arms. To spend every sleeping moment before the hearth, the two of them sharing his mattress. To once again wake anew every morning to the feeling of him inside her – pounding, worshipping, devouring. Their limbs entwined with one another. She truly believed she could spend the rest of her life wrapped in him and still be as thirsty for more. Starving for his touch. His love.

She glanced up at the bookshelves, visualising the moment they came together in the palace library.

At first the memory would fill her with regret.

So deep, so overwhelming, that she thought she might drown in it.

She would wake, bathed in sweat, dreaming about the moment Elijah had let the emperor shift into his body and the things she had left unsaid.

That she loved him.

That she did not hate him for taking her body.

That she had wanted it, wanted him, for all their days to come.

Things she had been too proud, too wounded to say.

Eventually, her heart pieced her conscience together, soothing it with gentle words and silver linings. She had given her body to him out of spite, yes, but at least she would always have that. At least she had the knowledge of what it would mean to be with him.

It did not help the gaping hole in her chest threatening to swallow her whole, though.

She would do anything to have him back. If only she had another wish to make.

But she had wasted it. Oh, if she could go back to that day, she would have wished they'd never left the library.

She had tried to wish on multiple occasions as well. Sometimes sober, and sometimes drunk, staggering into the cottage after being chased out of the tavern.

She would take the lamp from the mantelpiece and rub its base, wishing – wishing with everything she had – that Elijah would rise from it again.

He never did.

Then one day, she screamed in blind rage and chucked it on the floor, shattering the glass. She stared at it, tears still streaming, and blinked until what she had done dawned upon her. She sank down to her knees and picked up the shards in her skirt.

She left the cottage and rushed through the woods towards the Woodland Witches' lair.

Her fists hammered on Isolde's door until it budged, Isolde's expression bewildered as she opened the door. 'Keira! What on earth is—'

'I broke it,' Keira sobbed, stumbling inside. 'I broke it, and you have to fix it. You have to fix it, or else he can't come back!'

Slowly, Isolde glanced down at the shattered pieces of the broken lamp and Keira's trembling hands.

'Why don't you come in for a moment?' she murmured, guiding Keira further inside, beckoning her to take a seat on her divan.

Makenna and Echo both appeared in the doorway of her bedroom, exchanging glances with their auburn-headed partner.

'Wine?' Makenna asked, but Isolde shook her head.

'Something stronger, I think.' She hunched down before Keira's shivering figure and took her hands in hers.

'Keira? I want you to listen to me,' she said. 'Elijah won't be able to return with the help of the lamp.'

'But he told me a master's wish is stronger than any magic. We just have to find him a new master. Someone who won't take advantage of him. Someone—' Keira paused as Isolde shook her head.

'I released him from the curse of the lamp a long time ago. Elijah has been his own master for years. I merely put him back in the lamp to stop him from searching for our siblings.'

'But...' Keira stopped herself. What about the promise he had kept, helping August? What about the wish he had obeyed when she asked him to free them from the library? And—Wait. Had he been searching for their *siblings*? Not for her like the emperor had said? Keira's head swam. If she got Elijah back, she would never touch another drink her whole life... 'I made a wish.'

'Whatever Elijah did under the pretence of fulfilling a wish, I'm sure he did it for you.'

Because he...loved her, she realised. Because she had made a wish in the ordinary sense of the word. A magical wish *might* have gotten them out, just as Elijah had said, but he had found the strength to heed her wishes and do it despite the emperor's magic.

Knowing as much did not help though. In fact, it made her heart ache harder.

'He...he is truly gone then?' Keira hiccupped, her gaze travelling aimlessly out the open door. Today, as it had consistently for the last several days, rain fell in a heavy pitter-patter outside, cloaking the leaves and grass in glistening wetness. She supposed it was fitting, really, that the rain had come to wash out the last heat of summer. It was well and truly fall now. And all around, life was dying. Had died.

'Not...necessarily,' Isolde said, and Keira thought she had misheard her at first.

'What?'

Isolde exchanged glances with Makenna and Echo.

Then Makenna stepped into the room and sat down next to Keira. 'Remember what I told you at the palace?'

Keira thought hard, struggling to connect her chaotic – and slightly inebriated – thoughts to one another. Then she recalled Makenna's words, about... 'The ritual,' she breathed, looking at the witch. 'The one that can be used to call upon demons and gods alike.'

Makenna nodded. 'It will require all of us to make a spirit materialise in flesh and bone.'

'Can we do it?' Keira asked Isolde, her spine straightening.

'Possibly. But...' The witches exchanged glances once again. 'But it'll require something more. Elnatan isn't just any djinn. And so bringing him back will not only require a demonstration of his vice, but also a treat, an offer, that his spirit can't possibly reject – an anchor stronger than the pull of the Underworld.'

Keira blinked. 'Another sacrifice? A body? *My* body?' She would do anything to get him back, and yet...the two of them sharing a body for the rest of their lives wasn't exactly how she had pictured their future together.

'In a way, yes. But also more than that,' Isolde said. 'It will require your souls, bound in Unholy Matrimony.'

28
RELEASE

Witches flurried ahead of her as their group made their way into the depths of the Woodland Woods. Their dresses were transparent and white, their cloaks and draped sleeves floating against the burnished trunks of trees and green leaves as they passed.

Ahead, Keira saw the flaming red top of Isolde's head, leading the witches forward. Behind her was Echo, her jaw set in hard determination, white lines of ritual paint painted between her eyes reflecting the fire of multiple torches dancing through the woods with them. The fire of her soul.

When Keira faced ahead again, she'd siphoned some of that fire, cradling it within her chest like a candle of courage. She inhaled deeply, and her breasts swelled against her laced bodice. It was the only solid piece of clothing she wore; the rest was a white tulle skirt fastened around her waist with a purity ribbon and bishop sleeves in the same material, billowing around her arms like puffs of smoke and cutting off before the shoulder. Her hair was braided at the crown and spilled down her back in a waterfall of her natural waves. Like the rest of the witches, white star flowers had been entwined between the spilling locks of her hair.

'Are we nearly there?'

'Very soon,' came Echo's voice from behind. 'Are you ready?'

Keira let out a long exhale. 'I believe so... it's just...'

'The witches will not judge,' said Echo, answering her unspoken trepidations. 'For us, this is not sin; for us, there is nothing purer than a witch letting herself go.'

'But I am not a witch.'

'You're one of us, and that makes you as good as one. We would not have aided you against the emperor if not.'

'My nan always said witches were married to the devil.'

'After tonight, you will be too.'

After tonight, Keira thought, as the clearing opened wide and the sturdy construction came into sight. A pergola. With legs wrapped in deep green climbing plants and faint pink roses, the construction carried a mattress nestled within a nest of branches and vines. Her marital bed.

The witches fanned out around it, encircling the object with their eyes upon her expectantly. Isolde gestured for the stairs. 'When you're ready, Kiki.'

Keira turned back to Echo once more, who dipped her head affirmingly. *We will not judge.*

She did not care, Keira realised, if they did. There was something else, entirely, that jostled her nerves awake. The fear that this would not work, or the trepidation at the prospect that it might.

Once again, Keira drew a breath before she scooped up the hem of her skirt and began climbing the ladder, the flames of the torches set around the construction warming her skin as she passed them by.

Chanting rose from the gathered witches, and Isolde took to the floor.

'I, Isolde, Djinn of Gluttony, Lady of Indulgence, Leader of the Woodland Clan, call upon thee, Lord Elnatan, great Djinn of Lust, Lord of Pleasure. We are gathered here today, as your humble servants, with a gift, a sacrifice, devoted to you.'

Isolde gestured for Keira to take her position, and she lay down upon the mattress, the witches and torches blending into a blur in her peripheral vision, her skirt fanning out beneath her. 'Come, Lord Elnatan, and claim your bride in the name of the One True Divinity. Bless us with your presence.' The witches' chanting grew louder, their faces shrouded in the darkness. All but Isolde's, who turned to Keira, nodding. 'Keira, it's up to you now.'

Keira closed her eyes and steadied her breathing, focusing on the wild thumping of her heart rather than the sound of the witches. Soon their chanting melded with the quiet of the night, becoming just another song of nature. 'Come, Elijah,' she whispered, and exhaled. 'Come back to me.'

Her hand travelled down to the inside of her leg, stroking the soft skin there the way he'd once told her to. She knew immediately that it was going to be a struggle, her fingers wrong and clumsy against drowsy nerves. The more the seconds ticked by, the more she tried to force it, until her eyelids shot open in frustration, staring at the tree crowns above. If she failed, Elijah wouldn't return. If she failed, they'd all have gathered for nothing.

Silver speckles shone down upon her from the sky, as if someone had taken a million star flowers and spread them across the vaulted midnight-blue ceiling of their world. Her fingers kept moving in circles, kept massaging and rubbing the soft, warm flesh between her thighs. Still, the only sensation she felt was the prickling of her skin, the wariness of all the witches' eyes upon her.

What would the villagers think if they came and saw her now? Would they think her gripped with insanity? Were they right? Had she truly gone mad? Was her brain befuddled by the devil? His demons? Panic struck her chest. A demon's wife. That's who she would be. The wife of a *djinn*.

A breeze swept across the torches, and she caught one of the flickering bulbs in her view. Within it, she saw Elijah. The fireplace of the cottage. *Their* cottage. Their world. And once again, she was there, before the hearth, with him resting beside her, his lean, sculpted body close to hers, the hush of his voice lulling her pulse into a deep sensual rhythm throbbing down through her body and pushing against the tips of her fingers.

Their movements increased more determinedly, more confidently, more intuitively towards her spot of pleasure, working it, letting the new craze that tore through her body build up.

Closing her eyes again, she could see him more clearly, and a jolt of excitement shot through her, causing her to gasp. Automatically, her hand began to rub harder, eliciting trickling moans and heavy breaths as she worked. With her mind's eye, she could picture him like she had done a thousand times in her dreams, leaning over her with his naked body, placing himself between her legs. She could imagine the heat in his gaze as he took her in and lowered his lips to her nipples, claiming them one by one with his tongue, his hands raking up and down her body like her own hand kneaded her sensitive spot.

Her hips were thrusting against her hand now, rolling and coiling against the limb she now pictured as his, trying to steer the building wave inside her towards release.

But something was lacking.

She needed him.

Needed the physical touch of his body entangled with hers. His heart beating with the frantic beats of drums like hers. Pleas evaporated like desperate prayers from her lips into the night as she grasped for a twig, for something to hold onto, and—

Suddenly, her hand caught around fingers.

Her palm clasped against another's palm. Her knees nudged against muscled thighs. And her hand, which now left the spot it had been working, moved to feel the steady beat of his heart through his chest.

'You came,' she breathed, looking into his eyes – beautiful seagreen eyes speckled with gold – hidden behind a fringe of darkened caramel.

'You marvellous creature,' he breathed, eyes devouring the curves of her body as if she were a full meal buffet, lingering at her breasts peaked towards the sky. 'As if I could be content with simply watching any longer.'

She groaned and spoke through bated breath. 'Won't you join me?'

His lips pulled at the corner, one brow arching. 'Oh, no. I'm not falling for this again. You will have to say it this time. Beg for it, actually.' His fingers started to circle her inner thigh, and she shivered, feeling jolts of electricity as he moved closer, toying with the tips of his fingers along her mound, brushing them against her opening.

'Elijah,' she whimpered, sliding her fingers where his would not go and arching her back. 'Please.'

'Say it,' he growled, settling in between her legs. The witches around them were forgotten; their presence blended with the trees. There was but her and Elijah in the world now. Them and fire. 'Do you wish me to break my promise?' he asked, his breath caressing her earlobe, a bite scratching at her neck.

She exhaled a shivering breath and nodded.

'Say it.' Two fingers slid into her, his thumb stroking her button.

She cried out. 'Yes! Take my body. Take it now!'

He entered, covering her gasp with his mouth, catching her in his embrace. Then he rolled his hips and pulled out again, slowly, before sliding back in, stoking at that fire she had cradled, teasing it into a blazing inferno. Their bodies moved against one another, her hands clasped in his grip, his tongue – his tongue claiming all of her upper body like his hardness claimed her below. Masterfully, deliciously.

It rose now, the wave, belting against the roof of her centre of pleasure. She clenched her teeth and locked eyes with him, watching the same pleasure consume him like it consumed her, driving him over the edge, the last stroke of his hardness bringing her with him. Toppling their souls over the universe and beyond.

They were left with their mortal bodies, panting and pressed up against one another. His eyes never let go of hers while his lips left small kisses upon the bridge of her nose.

It was done. Their marriage consummated; their spirits bonded. Entwined with her body – his head resting upon her chest – lay her husband. The Djinn of Lust, Lord of Pleasure.

'Devoted, huh?' Elijah murmured after they'd managed to catch their breath, alluding to Isolde's speech. His thumb caressed the bottom pillow of her lip, eyes rapt upon it when she let her tongue taste the salt of it. 'In what way, Peaches?'

Her hand reached down to cup his base, brushing a finger over the smooth patch of skin behind it, eliciting a shiver and a gasp from him. 'In every way you desire, my lord.' Her purr drowned in the guttural growl arising from the back of his throat, making her toes curl. And before they could be claimed by his, her lips coiled with sweet, wicked delight.

EPILOGUE

'Isolde! You're here already,' Keira said, coming down the winding library staircase to the pool area below and adjusting her skirt, making sure it appeared somewhat less rumpled. Isolde raised a brow and gave her a look as if to say *don't even bother*.

'Where were you?' She set a book back in its place and stepped back to take in the room, its walls lined with bookshelves and potted plants, its floors covered in chequered tiles framing the pool filled with lush, clear water. Between Elijah and Isolde, the two djinns had restored the palace to its former glory using their magic.

'Oh, we were simply'—Keira cleared her throat—'enjoying some of the rooms. You know, testing the beds, getting lost in the hallways—'

'Feasting by the dinner table,' Elijah said, appearing in the doorway, peach in hand, before taking a bite. Keira's cheeks heated as he licked the juice off his lips and gave them a half-grin, eyes twinkling.

'And that,' Keira murmured under her breath, the flesh between her legs still tender and warm from Elijah's so-called *meal*.

'Bookshelves are quite sturdy too, sister. You should try them out.'

'Been there, done that,' Isolde said, and the two djinns winked at one another. The Lady of Indulgence and Lord of Pleasure; two sides of the same coin. Then Isolde turned back to Keira, taking her hands in hers. 'You sure you want to leave all this behind?' She lowered her voice. 'We could make them forget, you know. The people of E'Frion wouldn't bother you here. They'd readily believe you're their King and Queen even, if you want them to.

Keira smiled. 'Thank you, but there are too many places to see in the world, too many cottages to—' She cleared her throat, suppressing a giggle at Isolde's raised brow. 'Sleep in.'

Isolde made a sound at the back of her throat that assured her she'd caught what she meant.

'Besides, this has always been your home more than mine. I think it is time you tried your hand at reigning, *clan leader*.

'We'll see. I'll have my work cut out for me hunting down our siblings again.' Isolde glanced at Elijah. 'Speaking of which, where will you go?'

'Out to see new worlds, then perhaps one day back to Faerie,' Elijah said, stepping closer and wrapping an arm around Keira's shoulder. 'Can't avoid it forever.' A flash of a shadow passed over his eyes.

'Perhaps we'll ask the Spring Queen about my real parents as well,' Keira chimed in. 'Maybe we'll find out more about them on our travels.' *Eventually.* She wasn't in a hurry. Things were finally good, and she was ready to leave the past in the past to enjoy her future and honeymoon with a certain Lord of Pleasure.

Elijah smiled at her as if reading her mind, the need of her body, but then exchanged a glance with Isolde, both of their expressions speaking words Keira couldn't read. She was about to ask why when Isolde broke eye contact first and forced a smile of her own. 'Splendid. Will you excuse me for a moment? I need to go grab something from my chambers.'

Keira waited until she had left before she pulled Elijah around. 'What was that about?'

'Hm? What?'

'That look, between you and Isolde?'

'I assure you'—Elijah chuckled and leaned down; his kiss almost toe-curling enough to distract her. *Almost*—'I have no idea what you're talking about.'

He smiled as innocently as the devil. Scowling at him at first, Keira then cracked a sly smile of her own, trailing her fingers under his shirt, over the muscles of his back until heat pooled in his gaze. So, he was hiding something from her again. She did not worry. She knew now how to make him talk...and she could already think of a few ways she would like to try.

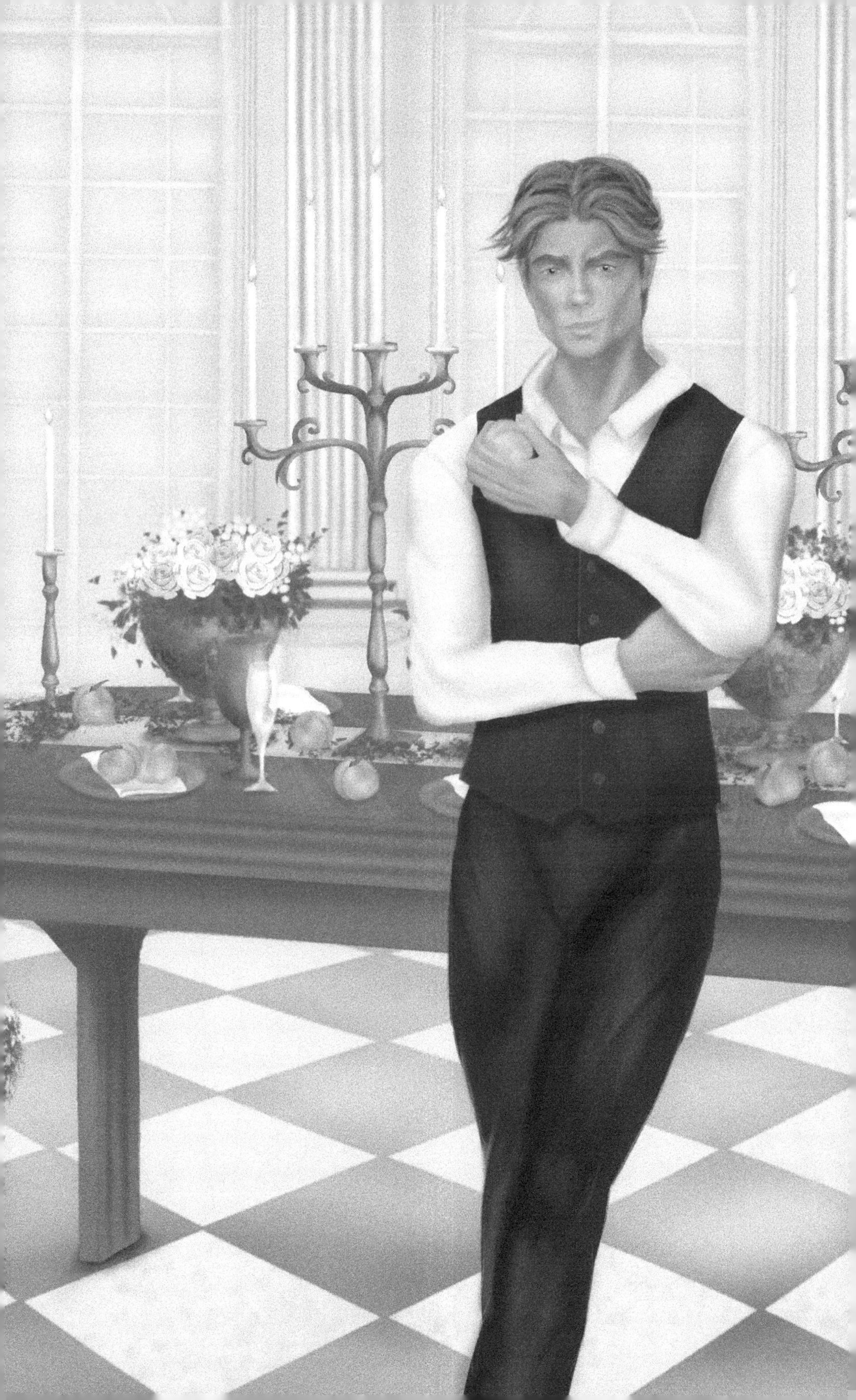

Curious about questions left unanswered? Find clues and answers in past and future books!

To learn more about Equinox's history in book 2 of *Fallen Sins,* pre-order

STORY OF HELEN

featuring the full story of Saint Helena and the Tyrant Emperor

Not ready to leave Keira and Elijah yet? Flip through the backmatter for a short bonus scene!

DEAR READER

Why did I write this book? Well, the easy answer is because I was inspired to. But, as you dived into the story of Elijah and Keira, you might have found that there's a sub element or a running theme of liberating yourself as a woman, reclaiming what you want sexually without shame.

And I think a lot of that was bound up in my own experience with sexuality as well. I became curious about sex quite early, even before my nan accidentally bought me my very first book with smut (I think I was ten at the time, possibly) – which happened to be titled "The Dream Prince" or something like that (so we'll have to forgive her the misunderstanding). She probably thought it was a fairy tale of sorts, and I learned pretty quickly that it was not. That said – side-note – it's still, probably, one of the best spicy books I've read as far as my memory is concerned. Anyway, I digress.

I actually wrote stories with sex early on. Many of my first pieces of writing were lust-filled, containing descriptions of yearning and want (let's hope these never see the light of day, hah!). Yet somewhere along the line – just like with writing romance in general – I felt ashamed about it. I don't remember if someone made me feel like this or if it just happened, but I know that simultaneously, I grew up learning, thinking – or being conditioned to think – that sex was something for the boys. It was something for them to want and do, and for us girls to be done to. If they had sex, they were heroes. If we had sex, we were—well, I think you know the word.

It's only been in the recent years that I rediscovered my love for spicy books, through open-door romantasy books such as Jennifer L. Armentrout's *From Blood and Ash* series and Scarlett St. Clair's *A Touch of Darkness* series. And there was something so empowering about these female main characters learning, figuring out, discovering what they liked and wanted, and finding these amazing men – these book boyfriends of ours – that made it okay. And it just threw me back to so many years – things that had been said, things that had been done – that made me feel so small, so scared, to even consider what I needed. Instead, it was always about what they needed. And that, if they left, then that was because of me or something I'd done wrong.

And so, I wrote and dedicated this book (and Elijah) to women who were made to feel small so that men would feel big, but it is also just as much a homage and love letter to authors such as those mentioned above, paving the way for readers to discover what they want and yearn for everywhere. Elijah is the effect these books had on me personified, and I'm beyond proud to join the ranks of open-door spice authors, with this book as my *first* contribution.

There is a revolution happening. One of sexual liberation where women in particular are discovering what they truly want and need through books, as well as they are finding their voices to demand it.

It is no wonder that some men may cower.

But the good ones? The Elijahs of the world?

Darlings, if a man's worth your time, he'll relish the challenge.

Enjoyed Heir of Sin? Be a peach and leave a review to let other readers know!

BONUS SCENE: HONEYMOON

She was spent.
Every muscle in her body ached after they had decided to check into an inn, although it had nothing to do with the journey itself – and more to do with Elijah taking it upon himself to show her what he had truly meant by there being other ways of making her scream.

What he hadn't done with his tongue, fingers, or the rest of his body, he'd done with his magic. And her mind still swirled with the feel of a particular kind that had made the air vibrate around her sensitive spot until she came and came again.

Even then he hadn't been done with her, making her come twice more as day turned to night, barely pausing except to get her a glass of water – before he promptly continued showing her all the erogenous zones she did not even know existed.

Yet she needed more. Craved more, always teetering on the edge as if each orgasm had merely been a steppingstone, a build-up, towards a grander, bigger release.

It came as she was sitting on his face. As she was rolling her hips with his tongue working inside her, and the sight of him beneath her was more than she could bear.

She was so close. So close that she feared her cry would shatter the windows if she let it out.

Sensing her distress, he growled. 'I want to hear you.'

'What if the other guests hear?' she whimpered, because surely, this time they would, Elijah's magic walls or not.

'Then let them wallow with envy,' he said, before proceeding to drag the tip of his tongue – his torturously slow tongue – over her sensitive spot. So slowly, it felt like there was an invisible claw raking down her spine, building a moan within her so deep and guttural it forced itself out.

She shattered. Went rigid and dissolved, all over him, grasping the headboard with all her might.

Beneath her, Elijah's eyes shone with triumph and smug glee, and she would have smart-mouthed back at him if she'd had any breath left.

Shifting, Elijah sat up so that he was propped up against the pillows. At her back, she could still feel his erection, and closed her eyes from the need it brought forth. She dug her nails into his chest.

'I stand by what I've said before. As far as punishments goes, I don't think this'll have the effect you intend it to,' she crooned, raising a brow at him. 'I'm rather tempted to run off just so you'd do it all over again.'

His smile dimmed, causing her own to dwindle in turn.

'Where you run, I run,' Elijah said, solemnly, his hands gripping her thighs harder, as if he was scared that she would run that very same moment.

She swallowed, her heart clenching. 'Even after what I did?' Her voice was barely a whisper. 'Even after I...tricked and used you?' She'd been scared that he would feel trapped in this marriage of theirs, knowing that he did not ask for Keira and the witches to perform the ritual. Had he even forgiven her for what happened in the palace library? 'If you're still angry with me, I'd understand.'

He flashed her a cocky grin and pulled her close. 'I was angry with myself, not you. I'm not the kind of guy to be upset about sex, Peaches. You may use me as much as you like, as long as you need me.'

Once again, she felt his fingers at her entrance, and she closed her eyes, arching against the ripples of pleasure and yearning already building anew inside her. She did not think there would ever be a day where she did not need him.

'Insatiable,' he murmured and met her gaze. Then he slipped a finger inside and curved it delicately.

Whimpering, Keira eased into his touch and the thought of the release soon to come.

Insatiable. That she was. But only for him. Completely and utterly insatiable.

Visit www.chaselouiseqvam.com, sign up for my newsletter, and get access to an exclusive bonus chapter from Elijah's POV!

ACKNOWLEDGEMENT

A big, hearty thank you goes out to those who have been with me for the creation of this book.

From the very beginning, this includes editor Tayler Bailey McLendon, Julia (a.k.a. @entirelybonkerz), and Nastasia Bishop-McHugh who all provided feedback and thoughts during the early stages of getting the story down.

Following up with my early readers Rai, Kristine, Stephanie, Hope, Kat, Stacy, Becca, Vanessa, Maddi and Diksha, whose excitement and input has been invaluable in the process. Extra peaches must be handed out to Stephanie, Rai, Becca, Kat, Diksha and Maddi for reading multiple alternative structures and scenes when I was stuck. I *hope* you'll find the final result juicy enough that it was worth it.

Thank you to my proofreader, Rachel L. Schade, and cover designer Maria Spada for making this book shine, and finally

ACKNOWLEDGEMENT

thank you to my other half for helping me with *cough* research. I love your peachy behind.

Last but not least, thank you to every single reader, peach and sinner who have read the book, loved it, spread the word about it and generally helped other readers discover it in every single way. Thank you for loving Elijah and Keira's story as much as I do. Hopefully, it won't be long till we see them again. *winks*

PS: A special mention must also be made to @entirelybonkerz and Chiara Karys for inspiring a chess and cookie scene, and Kat for naming Mr Burton. Elijah sends kisses to you all.

ABOUT THE AUTHOR

C. L. Qvam has been lost and found on more than one occasion, and now it seems she has been found again by you!

Growing up loving books with magical dimensions, natural deities and chosen ones; Chase has always been a bit of a dreamer, certain that stories is our portals to worlds where magic can be lived and experienced.

Neurodivergent and with a taste for a bit of everything, Chase's projects ranges from upper YA fantasy stories filled with mythology/lore, mystery, and dashes of sizzling romance, to romantasies with more explicit adult content.

Check out published and planned books to come, as well as recommended reading orders on www.chaselouiseqvam.com

instagram.com/chaselouiseqvam
tiktok.com/@chaselouiseqvam

Looking for something to read while you wait for book 2? Curious about Keira's parentage?

Check out my debut trilogy taking place before *Heir of Sin*, and see if you can spot clues and cameos to HoS in *Spindle of Life*.

An ancient war between the three Fates and their heirs caught in between

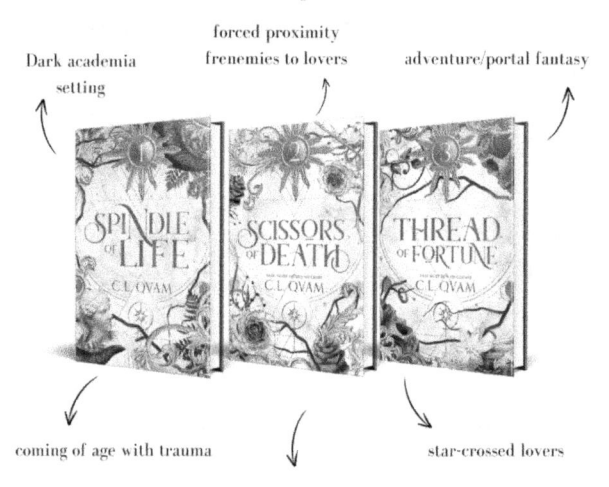

forced proximity
frenemies to lovers

Dark academia setting

adventure/portal fantasy

SPINDLE OF LIFE
C. L. QVAM

SCISSORS OF DEATH
C. L. QVAM

THREAD OF FORTUNE
C. L. QVAM

coming of age with trauma

star-crossed lovers

multi-cultural mythology and folklore

This is a YA fantasy series featuring an ancient war between the three Fates, their heirs caught in between, and intricate worldbuilding. It has closed-door romantic tension throughout book 2 and 3, but the first book is the darkest with only a romantic side-plot. If spice and romance is your preference, book 1 is recommended as a palate cleanser.

Milton Keynes UK
Ingram Content Group UK Ltd.
UKHW041923171124
2894UKWH00003B/10/J